AFTER

THE

FALL

KATE HART

FARRAR STRAUS GIROUX · NEW YORK

Farrar Straus Giroux Books for Young Readers
An imprint of Macmillan Publishing Group, LLC
175 Fifth Avenue, New York 10010

Text copyright © 2017 by Kate Hart
All rights reserved
Printed in the United States of America
Designed by Elizabeth H. Clark
First edition, 2017

1 3 5 7 9 10 8 6 4 2

fiercereads.com

Library of Congress Control Number: 2016028790

ISBN 978-0-374-30269-6

Our books may be purchased in bulk for promotional, educational, or business use. Please
contact your local bookseller or the Macmillan Corporate and Premium Sales Department
at (800) 221-7945 ext. 5442 or by e-mail at MacmillanSpecialMarkets@macmillan.com.

For Catherine,
first and favorite raisin girl

PART I

BEFORE THE FALL

"We yearned for the future. How did we learn it, that talent for insatiability?"

—The Handmaid's Tale *by Margaret Atwood*

RAYCHEL

It's entirely possible Matt can see up my shorts.

I don't really care—my best friend has never shown any interest whatsoever in my underwear—but the only ones clean this morning were black and lacy. Not ideal for rock climbing, and not ideal for a photo shoot, especially one for his school assignment. I shift my position on the cliff face, trying to cover up.

"You okay?" Matt asks, lowering the camera.

"Just trying not to flash you."

"Don't worry." The clicking resumes. "I'm surprised you're not more hungover today," he says a minute later.

"I didn't drink that much."

He snorts. I only had two beers last night, but arguing will make him ask why I threw up, and that's not a conversation I want to have right now. Luckily Matt won't ask about the rest of the evening. He never does. "I'm ready to come down," I say instead.

"Hang on . . ." He steps sideways and tilts the camera. "This angle looks badass."

If that's a pun, it's not worth acknowledging. "My arms hurt. I'm going to fall."

"You're only a few feet up." But he moves out of the way so I can jump down. My foot hits a rock when I land and pain shoots up my leg, making me yelp. The rest of me hits the ground with a thud that snaps my jaw closed.

Matt's beside me in half a second. "Are you okay?"

"I'm fine," I lie, struggling to my feet.

"Let me—"

I bat his hand away and take a cautious step. It hurts like a mad bastard and I can't keep from wincing.

"Are you crying?" he asks.

"No!" I rub my eye. Black smears the back of my hand. I knew I shouldn't have worn mascara.

"Sit down," he says, gesturing at a moss-covered rock. "Let me check it."

"Having a doctor for a daddy doesn't make you one." He stares pointedly at me until I sit, then pokes and prods, trying to rotate my foot. "Ow! Damnit!"

"Sprained, I bet." He stands to retrieve his backpack. "We'll have to tape it."

"You don't even—"

"They taught us this summer." His explanation is muffled, his head already half-buried in his enormous backpack. I teased him about it this morning and called him a Boy Scout when he mumbled something about "being prepared." Going to Outward Bound was supposed to make him more comfortable in the woods. Instead he came home with a million worst-case scenarios and their solutions loaded on his back.

But I can't make fun now. "Should I take my shoe off?"

He pulls out an ACE bandage. "It'll swell too much. You won't be able to hike out." The thought of four miles back makes me groan. "I could carry you," he says, voice flat, and I smack his arm in answer. "Okay then." He starts to hand me two ibuprofen, but stops to pour water on my palms first, rinsing away the dirt. "That's what I like about you, Raych. You're not afraid to get dirty, like most girls."

I stick my tongue out before swallowing the pills.

. . . . .

The return hike takes three times longer than usual. Whenever I stop to rest in clearings along the trail, Matt paces, his shadow long and looming. The sun's already dipped behind the treetops and we're not even out of earshot of the Twin Falls yet. He keeps glancing at the sky, like I don't know we're burning daylight. "I'm going as fast as I can," I snap as he checks the time.

"I know." He runs a hand through his hair. "I'm not worried."

Liar. Matt's always worried.

MATT

By the time I get Raychel back to my house, my hands are cramped from clutching the steering wheel on the curvy Ozark back roads. The drive to the Twin Falls trailhead is dangerous enough in daylight; at night, all it takes is one deer to kill your car, and you, for that matter. There was no conversation to distract me, at least, but Raychel's choice of music and the fact that she's probably pissed just made my hands clench even tighter. "I'm sorry," I say, as we reach the front door.

"For what?"

"For making you climb just so I could take pictures. I could have—"

"Matthew," she cuts me off. "I like climbing. And you didn't tell me to jump down or put a rock in my way. But you *did* tape my ankle and get me home. So chill."

I nod.

"And thanks." She gives me a hug, more awkward than normal with her balance messed up. My hand accidentally brushes her boob, but she doesn't notice, or doesn't care.

"Ready to face the Inquisition?" I ask. I help her inside to the living room, where my parents are watching a preseason football game.

"Raychel!" Mom gasps, hitting MUTE. "What happened?"

"Just twisted my ankle," Raychel says, shrugging.

But Dad's already standing up. "Better let me take a look at it."

Raych rolls her eyes at me as she follows him to his office, and I return it, even though this was the whole point of bringing her to my house: seeing Dad will save her the co-pay at the ER.

They emerge a few minutes later, Raychel clomping down the hall on crutches like a three-legged horse.

"You were right—it's sprained," Dad says with an approving nod at me, "but not too bad. Just remember to RICE it," he adds to her.

Raychel sighs. Rest, ice, compression, elevation. I recognize the prescription from years of soccer injuries. "How long do I have to use these things?" she asks, tapping a crutch against her good foot.

"A week or so. And no hiking for a while." He glances at me again.

She snorts. "Matt's not my keeper."

"No, but I know how you two are," he says.

I am hardly the bad influence here, but I nod dutifully. Raychel just thanks him and turns to Mom. "I meant to return your book," she says. "It's in the car."

Mom smiles. "Did you like it?"

"It was so good! The ending made me cry like—"

Blah blah blah. They can talk books all day long, so I tune them out and watch the game until Raychel whacks me in the calf with a crutch to let me know they're done. She's basically the daughter my parents never had, and I'm pretty sure they'd trade me for her in a heartbeat. "You ready?" she asks.

"If you're done with your BFF." I make a face at Mom.

"Hit him again for me," Mom says, and Raychel obliges.

. . . . .

In the morning, my brother stumbles into the kitchen, hair sticking out in every direction. "Morning," Dad says. Andrew grunts and takes a coffee mug from Mom, who's holding it out like a bone to an unfriendly dog.

"Are you dressed?" I ask. I'm not being a dick, I really can't tell, but he scowls and doesn't answer, too busy spilling Fruity Pebbles all over the counter. At least he's not wearing any of my clothes. "Be in the car at 7:15 or I'm leaving you here."

He waves off my empty threat. Every time he screws up, my parents take his car away, which means I'm the one who really suffers the consequences. Making me play chauffeur is easier than bothering with chores and grades. For him, anyway.

At 7:25, Andrew finally makes it to the car, slamming the door behind him and immediately glaring at my stereo. "What is this emo pansy bullshit?"

"Raych had it on yesterday," I lie, and back out of the driveway.

He scrolls through my collection. "Your music sucks."

"So I hear. Every freaking time you're in my car."

Andrew finds something that meets his standards and sits back with his eyes closed while I drive to Raychel's. I usually give her a ride, since the bus sucks and her mom can barely afford food and rent, much less a second car. When we reach the duplex, she's trying to balance on the crutches while fighting to open the screen door. I hop out to help, but I don't offer, again, to fix it, because I know she'll refuse. Even though we both know no one else is going to do it.

I lock up as she hobbles to the car and points Andrew to the backseat. "I already called shotgun!" he protests, as if he doesn't lose this argument every time he rides with us.

"Ladies first," Raychel says. "Or up front. Whatever."

He grumbles but does what she wants, just like always.

RAYCHEL

Andrew keeps kicking my seat. I should have given him shotgun—he's too big to sit in the back, two or three inches taller than his big brother. They have the same dark hair and eyes, and almost the same birthday, one year apart. But Matt's a little skinnier and nerdier. Andrew does what he can to accentuate their other differences: longer hair, grungier clothes, stupider behavior. Matt wants to save the world; Andrew's pretty sure he's its center. He went to Outward Bound too, but came home convinced he's invincible.

"Quit!" I say, twisting in my seat and slapping at his leg. When I face front, he kicks again, so I turn up the volume instead. "At least you found something halfway decent to listen to this morning."

He laughs. We've always double-teamed Matt on music because he basically has the same taste as his dad. We also share majority rule on pizza toppings, weekend plans, and movie selections. Andrew and I could probably be closer friends, but he's never serious about anything—not school, not rules, and definitely not girls. Good-natured and fun, but not reliable.

Unless you need weed. Then he's your man.

"Did you finish your history paper?" Matt asks me, not taking his eyes off the road.

"Yes, Mother." I know he means well, but it's early and my ankle hurts. I spent most of last night trying not to worry about the day that awaits me. My injury is just going to draw more attention when I'd rather have none at all.

At the parking lot, Andrew snags my backpack and jogs ahead, ignoring my protests that it's not even heavy. I hobble along with Matt and try to avoid the fake horseshoe prints embedded in the sidewalk. We're the Big Springs Cowboys. So stupid. No cowboys ever herded cattle through the Ozarks; the mountains were just big enough to make them detour west around Arkansas. But I guess our appropriate mascot options were slim. The "BS High School Hillbillies" doesn't really strike fear into the hearts of your rivals.

As we reach the front doors, our hands reflexively stretch out to pat the statue of Cowboy Chester. Touching his bronze boot is supposed to bring you luck, like a redneck version of Saint Peter. Only seniors are "allowed," but Andrew steals some luck anyway.

Inside the lobby, the late August temperature rises fifteen degrees. The space is mostly glassed in, which sounds cool, but in reality smells like a sauna full of wet dogs. We've almost made our way across the room when I hear Mindy Merrithew calling. "Oh yikes!" she says to me, her friendly tone not quite a match for her expression. "What happened?"

"Pole dancing injury," Andrew says. Her eyes flicker between us as I whack his arm. "It was awful," he adds. "Tassels everywh—"

"Rock climbing," I interrupt. "I fell."

"Ouch." Her momentary frown flips right side up. "Can I borrow Matt for a sec?" she asks. "For Student Council stuff?"

I shrug. Mindy's the quintessential good girl: Student Council, cheer squad, Bible study twice a week, and a kind word for everyone, whether she means it or not. Bless her heart. I know she thinks Matt and I are sleeping together on the sly, but we're like a very chaste arranged marriage. We wear each other as habits.

And Matt remains clueless about the massive crush she has on him. "I should probably stay with Raych," he says. "I told my dad—"

"We're headed to the same hall," Andrew says. "I'll call 911 if she starts seizing or anything."

"You should keep your foot up during class," Matt says. "And we can get some ice at lunch."

I restrain myself from saying "Yes, Mother" again and give him a fake salute.

"Hope you feel better!" Mindy calls after us. Her cheerfulness is obscene this early in the morning.

Andrew puts my pack on his chest, walking beside me as I crutch up the wheelchair ramp. "How long you stuck with those sticks?" he asks.

"A few days. Are we dicks for leaving Matt with her?"

"Nah," Andrew says, snickering. "That kid needs to get laid."

I snort. "Which one?"

"Both. Maybe he'll meet someone on campus this year."

"Doubtful." In Big Springs, "campus" always means the local university, which is so close to our building that we call it BS High School Thirteenth Grade. They start recruiting us early—both the admissions office and the fraternities and sororities. We can also take classes there for dual credit, so this semester Matt is taking Cal 3. But I'm betting his female classmates are smart enough not to date seventeen-year-olds.

College courses are too expensive for me, but at least we have a big selection of AP classes. The university professors want their kids to have plenty of opportunities to overachieve while they're here. But they rarely want their kids to *stay* here for college, which is part of why the Richardsons are always on Andrew's ass—they can afford better schools and want to send him to one. I mean, this one is a decent university, so far as state schools go, but if you're from here, it's just same shit, different day, bigger toilet.

And there's plenty of shit to avoid. Like the cluster of guys blocking our way in the hall.

"Richardson!" a guy shouts. Andrew stops to talk and I wait impatiently. I try not to look at the pack of boys in white baseball caps with matching red brands, bills dirtied and bent to identical perfection. Maybe that's why we're the Cowboys. Maybe Chester was famous for rounding up herds of wannabe frat rats.

A booming laugh tells me the one I dread seeing is with them. I can't decide if I'd rather Carson Tipton ignore or acknowledge me, but when he turns and ticks his square chin up in greeting, I realize the former would be better. "Hey," I say to Andrew, gesturing at my bag. "We're going to be late."

He turns back to me, holding the pack just out of reach. "Wait, is it true?"

"What?" I clomp closer.

Andrew head-tilts toward Carson. "Did you two hook up this weekend?" He pretends to be shocked, putting his hand to his throat. "Did Raychel really break her 'no high school boys' rule?"

Unexpected rage floods me. "Could you be a bigger dick?" I demand, too loudly. I thought I was prepared for this crap, but not from Andrew. His hand lowers in surprise, so I jerk my bag away and make the most dignified retreat that crutches will allow.

"Raych, wait!" he calls after me.

I ignore him. This is why I have that "no high school boys" rule. And why I shouldn't have broken it.

MATT

Outdoor Club is canceled Monday afternoon, so Raychel comes home with me to hang out. Andrew gets a ride with some friends, probably to go smoke out, but at least he won't be hanging around like he did all summer, making fun of me and trying to get Raychel on his side for everything. Going back to school sucks, especially since most of our friends graduated last year, but at least I get Raych to myself.

She won't let me help her in or out of the car, or down the step into the sunken playroom. She doesn't need my help to win at pool, which is embarrassing, but as consolation, I get to watch her shoot. I have great admiration for my best friend's pool skills, as well as her ass, and I am smart enough not to admit to either.

"You break," she says, hanging the triangle on the wall. "Stripes or solids?"

"Solids." I line up my shot and watch the cue ball drop. "Damn."

Raychel plucks the ball from the corner pocket and appraises the table, but her shot goes wild when she tries to stand on her injured foot. The eight ball drops into the pocket beside me.

I poke her with my cue. "You don't have to take it easy on me."

She scoffs and waits for me to rack a new game. "Hey, can you give me a ride to work this evening?"

"Sure. You need one home?"

"Nah." She usually takes the campus transit service home from Pharm-Co, which I hate, though she claims it's perfectly safe.

I break instead of arguing with her, not noticing Andrew's arrival until he stealth-slaps the back of my head. "Hey," he says, dodging the chalk I throw at him and walking around to Raychel. "Can I talk to you for a minute?"

Her expression makes me laugh. "What'd you do?" I ask.

"I'm sorry," he says, ignoring me, and rubs the back of his neck. I lean against the table and wait for her to explode.

To my disappointment, she sighs instead. "I'll be back in a sec," she tells me.

I twirl the end of my cue against the floor as they step into the kitchen. I can hear Andrew apologize again, but not what Raychel mumbles in reply. "I know," he says. "And it's none of my business if you did."

Ah. So that's the issue. Rumors about Raychel were every-where today, claiming she screwed Carson Tipton in his truck Saturday night. I'm not sure exactly what happened, but *some-thing* did, a fact that makes no sense because Raych quit giving high school guys the time of day when we were sophomores. She had a boyfriend at the time who got mad about how much time she spent at work, so he told everyone she was cheating on him with a much older co-worker. She's had a reputation ever since.

I honestly don't know how much of it she deserves. College guys are still fair game and I know she's hooked up with plenty of them at campus parties. But she appears to have made a high school exception, and I have no idea why it was for Carson, of all people. He's a nice guy and never has a problem getting chicks, but he's dumber than a box of rocks. She must have been really drunk, because Raychel doesn't suffer fools.

Except for fools like my brother, apparently. He comes back into the room alone, his expression contrite. "Are your balls still intact?" I ask.

He grabs his crotch. "They're a damn sight bigger than yours will ever be."

"Tough talk from the dude who's scared of spiders," I say.

"Says the one who puked at Silver Dollar City."

I flip him off as Raychel snorts from the kitchen. She's heard all about last spring's ill-fated roller coaster ride. "At least I didn't blow chunks all over Spencer's dorm room," I call to her.

I get no answer, and Andrew grins as I put down my cue. My turn to face her.

RAYCHEL

I listen to the boys argue, rolling my eyes and taking a few deep breaths before I have to deal with them again. Andrew's comment this morning was just the first in a day full of "knowing" glances and whispered comments and dirty gestures.

And it's my own fault. I brought this on myself.

I expect a few high school kids to show up at frat parties, but Saturday's party was at our friend Spencer's dorm. It should have just been me and Matt, plus Spencer and his girlfriend,

16

Asha, who both stayed here to go to college together. There weren't nearly enough folks to drain the keg some optimistic freshman paid for, but Carson turned up with a few of his crew. When we ended up chatting at the end of the hall, he was surprised how much I knew about football. I was surprised he was having a conversation with me at all. Not that he's ever been mean or anything. He just never seemed to notice me much.

So when he needed a smoke and asked if I wanted to come with, I said, "Yeah, sure," and shouted down the hall to Matt so he wouldn't worry.

Everyone saw us go.

Everyone saw me come back an hour later, hair wild and eyes wide.

Everyone saw me grab a beer, chug it, and proceed to throw it up in Spencer's room.

Matt comes into the kitchen and I open the fridge so he can't see my expression. "Are you okay?" he asks.

"Yeah." The cool air feels clean on my face. "I'm fine."

· · · · ·

The rest of the week doesn't improve much. On Tuesday, a group of sophomore girls corner me in the hallway to ask how big Carson's junk is. Wednesday, I'm tagged online in a few pictures from the party, and a shot of Asha holding my hair over Spencer's sink draws a lot of comments about my virtue and lack thereof. Thursday, someone coughs "Slut!" as I walk down a crowded staircase.

But I've dealt with gossip before. What I haven't dealt with is Carson. If he would just ignore me, this would blow over, but instead he insists on smiling, waving, winking—everything short of actually striking up a conversation. And yet a stupid part of me is insulted that he hasn't talked to me.

Maybe if he did, I could laugh it off. Put it behind me.

Stop thinking about it.

The last thing I want to do Friday night is go out, but I promised Asha I'd go with her to a frat party, and I kind of owe her for last weekend. However, she'll ditch me the minute Spencer appears, and I'm not going to brave it alone. "How the hell are you going to wear a toga with crutches?" Matt asks.

"I'll figure something out," I say, shifting the phone. It'll be easier than wearing the usual heels, skirt, and barely-there-top combo anyway. "Please come." Matt doesn't answer. "Bring Andrew too."

"He's got plans."

Bummer. Andrew would make things more fun. "We can leave early," I say, changing tacks. "Please?"

"Fine," he says grudgingly. "But we really can't stay late. I have StuCo in the morning."

"Deal," I say, not even gloating. "We'll meet you there."

· · · · ·

I wait forever at the bus stop and finally manage to take the transit over to Asha's. She lives in the worst dorm, on the farthest edge of campus. The parking sucks, the food's gross, the bathrooms are disgusting, and I am so freaking jealous I can barely stand it. One more year. Just one more year and I can have my own crappy dorm room on a campus far away.

She's already several drinks ahead when I get there. "You gotta catch up," she says, handing me a watered-down tequila mixture that's supposed to be a margarita. "Have a Drink on Me" blares from the speakers. I sip when AC/DC commands and Asha tries not to jab me with safety pins as she arranges my bedsheet into a toga. She looks pretty, draped in one of her mom's saris.

"Does your mom know you're wearing that?"

"Ha," Asha says. "No, and don't spill anything on it or she'll kill me."

My sheet literally pales in comparison—it used to be floral, many bleachings ago, but now it's mottled and ugly. "Where's your roommate?"

"She's never here," Asha says, taking the pins out of her mouth. "I don't think she likes Spencer."

"What? Why?" Everyone likes Spencer. He is the definition of nice. Polite, kind, quiet, and completely in love with Asha.

"I don't know. I think she's a racist."

I snort. "Maybe she just doesn't like the nonstop sexfest."

Asha pokes me on purpose. Everyone knows she and Spencer screw like rabbits—except her parents, who are pretty traditional. Her mom wants Asha married as soon as possible, and her dad . . . well, her dad is the answer to "who doesn't like Spencer?" Mr. Chavan got over the fact that Asha dated Spencer in secret for their entire sophomore year, and he claims to be over the fact that Spencer is black instead of Indian. But now that Asha stayed in Big Springs to be with him for college, Spencer is back on Mr. Chavan's shit list.

Asha claims she's here for the well-respected social work department, but that doesn't make her dad any happier. Her older siblings are an oncologist and an engineer, and Asha, as the baby of the family, is supposed to complete the trifecta of success. Preferably as a surgeon. Lawyer, like her dad, is also acceptable. But what she really wants is to start a nonprofit and save the world, like Matt.

I'm just going to save myself and major in business. "Did you drop that statistics class?"

She steps back to examine her handiwork. "Yeah, but I'll have to make it up at some point."

"Ugh." The chorus comes around again and I gulp from my mug.

"You ready?" Asha asks, looking for her keys.

"I think." I tug experimentally at my toga and its hundred thousand safety pins. That sucker is going nowhere. "I hope this party blows less than the last one."

Asha laughs, a little higher and sillier than when she's sober. "You're not looking for another round with Carson Tipton?"

My pulse spikes, sending lukewarm margarita straight to my head.

She fake punches my arm. "The dude has a Confederate flag license plate, Raychel. What were you thinking?"

"Good question," I say, and drain my mug.

MATT

I told Raychel that Andrew had plans, but he cancels them when he hears about the toga party. He takes forever to find a sheet, finally wrapping himself in an old one with Sesame Street characters, and by the time we find a parking spot, then walk all the way from the parking deck to the frat house, I'm sure we'll be late.

But we still beat the girls to the party and have to stand on the lawn waiting for them, watching a crowd of costumed kids walk, or stagger, inside. Finally Spencer the Friendly Drunk shows up and we go inside to escape the heat. He offers his flask to everyone in sight, but I turn him down. When the girls finally show up, they're already stumbling, and the smell of tequila washes over me as Asha rests her forehead against mine. "Hiiii, Maaaattt."

Well, this should be fun.

Raychel hugs Andrew. "Nice toga," she says, looking him up and down, then turns to me. "Where's yours?"

"He's a modern Greek," Andrew says. "Banker type."

"I said I'd show," I say, "not that I'd dress up. Where're your crutches?"

She points toward the door, where they're leaning against the wall. Andrew passes her Spencer's flask and before I can argue, she takes a swig, shuddering. "Oh, that's disgusting."

Great, we're mixing liquors tonight too. "You're not drinking on painkillers, are you?"

She rolls her eyes and takes another swig before handing it back. "Thanks, Spence."

"No problem." He puts it in his pocket, just in time for Asha to make an attempt at swallowing his entire face, glasses and all.

Wonderful. "Don't you have to work tomorrow?" I ask Raychel.

"Not until noo-oon," she says, poking my arm. I bite back an angry reply. All week, she's been furious that her hookup with Carson is the topic of conversation, but it's not stopping her from another weekend of public debauchery.

A girl in a toga made of plastic wrap comes over to Andrew. "You want to dance?"

He looks at us, grinning, and Raychel waves him away. When he's lost in the crowd, she leans over to talk into my ear, and gestures at Spencer and Asha. "Let's give them some privacy," she says, vowels long and slow.

The ridiculous hormonal part of my brain wishes she'd bite my earlobe.

Instead I half carry her to a corner, where she slumps on a sticky couch. Her laurel wreath crown, which looks suspiciously like it's made from the holly bushes outside Asha's dorm, slips and catches in a tangle of brown waves that change color with the DJ booth's flashing lights. Red, yellow, green, back to red, flashing like a strobe. She stares at it without blinking.

"Tequila, huh?"

Her heads lolls toward me. "How'd you guess?"

"Asha had margarita breath."

That strikes her as funny and I have to wrap an arm around her waist to keep her from laughing herself off the couch. Raychel has this problem when she drinks: she starts to slide off whatever seat she's in. We call it the puddle effect, and it's funny when she's not nursing an injury. My fingers line up with her ribs, skin warm through the sheet.

"That tickles!" She squirms away from my hand, closer to my lap, her head resting on my shoulder. I could kiss the top of it if I wanted to.

The idiot hormonal part of my brain wants to kiss her mouth instead.

The urge to kiss a pretty girl shouldn't be surprising, even if it's Raychel. It's not that I don't want to, because god knows I do, but this *is* Raychel, so I shouldn't.

She doesn't smell like tequila. She smells like limes. Tart.

But we're friends. And not the kind with benefits.

I make myself turn away.

· · · · ·

We watch people migrate to the makeshift dance floor until Asha and Spencer find us again. They have drinks for us as apologies, but I decline, since everyone else is obviously past the point of no return, and someone has to get Raychel home.

That lucky someone is me, but what else is new.

"Hey," I say, shouting over the bass. "Are you guys staying? I think we're heading out."

Asha looks at Raychel the Puddle and giggles. "I was going to see if she wanted to dance, but uh, guess not."

"Yeah, pretty sure she's done." I wade into the crowd to get my brother, but he's found some other friends and wants to stay. For once, I'm irritated that he's ditching us, because I could use some help getting Raychel out of here. Back at the couch, I pull her to her feet and she groans in protest. "Ready for the hike to the car?"

"Can't you bring the car here?" she asks.

"It's all the way over by the stadium."

She pouts. "Then can we get ice cream on the way home?"

"We'll see," I say, trying to move her toward the door. "Ice cream and alcohol don't sound like a great combination."

"But you dumped me!"

I snort and leave Spencer to hold her up while I go get her crutches. I'll never live it down: We dated for four days in the seventh grade, until Mindy Merrithew smiled at me in the hallway. Then I dumped Raychel, Mindy immediately started acting like I had leprosy, and Rach has used it as her trump card ever since. I want the last cookie? "But you dumped me!" I want to hike at Eagle Point and she wants to go to Roger's

Hollow? "But you dumped me!" I want to sleep and Raychel wants to have a two-hour conversation? "But you broke my heart!"

Maybe next time I'll say, "Let me make it up to you. Let's go out again."

Right after I magically grow a pair.

Instead I hand her the crutches and we make our way through the crowd. "Ugh," Raychel says as we step outside. It's muggy and still, the kind of night where leaving the AC is like walking into a wet spiderweb. But her gaze is on an approaching pack of guys from school, with Carson jogging ahead of them.

"Sanders!" he says to Raychel, and nods at me. It feels more like a dismissal than a greeting. "Y'all leaving already?"

Raychel mumbles something. She suddenly seems a lot drunker than before, and she's holding on to the crutches like she needs them again. I glance to make sure her toga's still up. "Somebody pre-gamed a little too hard," I say.

Carson laughs. He's a redneck, but he's all right. His mom was our Cub Scout leader, but my brother knows him better than me since they played baseball together until Andrew quit this year to "focus on basketball." As if Andrew can focus on anything. "Where's Hana?" he asks.

"Hana Mori?" I ask, confused, and he nods. "We broke up a long time ago." She stayed here for college, but I haven't seen her since graduation.

"Oh. Right." He nods at Raychel. "You dating this one now?"

Ah. Now I get it. "We're best friends," I say, and Raychel squeezes my arm.

"Well, in that case . . ." he says, and grins at her. "You sure you don't want to stick around?"

I wait for Raychel to respond. I don't want her to say yes, obviously, but she clearly has something going with this guy, and I know from past experience that if I answer for her, I'll hear about it later. The way she's holding herself rigid makes me think she might be about to barf, though. "Raych?" I prompt. "You want to stay?"

She leans against me. "Tired."

Carson's friends are starting to crowd us. "Aw, come on," he says, lifting and resetting his baseball cap, but she shakes her head.

"She started drinking tequila at six," I say, trying to help him save face so we can leave. "She's going to pass out any second."

"That's what he's hoping," one of the other guys says.

I pretend not to hear, since I'm way outnumbered. Carson adjusts his hat again. "Well," he says. "See y'all later then."

Raychel sighs and pulls my arm against her like a teddy bear as he walks away. "I'm your best friend now?"

"You've always been my best friend," I say. Pressing inside my chest is a wish that I was more like Carson: not afraid to make a move, though with a few more morals about when to do it. Although maybe my morals aren't so much better, considering that I was thinking about kissing her when she wasn't any soberer. I try to pull away. "And you're also really drunk."

26

"I *am*?" She laughs, squeezing me harder before she lets go. "I love you."

"I love you too," I say, and I mean it. Lately I mean it more than I want to.

RAYCHEL

Stripes of sunlight stab through the blinds, past my eyeballs, and into my brain.

So does a god-awful thumping noise. And my mother's voice. "Raychel!"

Every blow on the door reverberates in my head like bass through a crappy subwoofer. I lurch out of bed and stumble across the room to open the door. "What?"

She frowns. "It's eleven."

"It's Saturday." I blink. "Isn't it?"

"Doesn't mean you should sleep the whole day away."

I try to shift my weight. My ankle doesn't hurt, but it's a little stiff. "I don't feel very well."

She raises her eyebrows, forehead wrinkles disappearing behind her uneven bangs. She's had the same haircut since I was ten. "Weren't you sick last weekend too?"

"I just had a few drinks," I admit, not bothering to lie since I smell like a bar sink. "And Matt drove me home."

"Is he driving you to work today too?"

I glance at the clock, reality waking me all at once. "Oh—crap . . . Mom!" She's already walking down the hall. "Can you give me a ride?"

"I'll be late to work if I do." She taps her wrist over her head. "You do the crime, you do the time."

· · · · ·

Unfortunately, the time is "five." As in, I have been late to work five times since my current boss, Roland, started at Pharm-Co a few months ago. It's only ten minutes, but he scowls at my frantic apologies, his patchy mustache twitching when I try to blame the crutches. "The transit stop is right outside," he points out. "See me at the end of your shift."

I take my place behind the cash register, making sure to exaggerate my limp. The real problem is my stomach. Leftover tequila, aspirin, coffee, and a cold Pop-Tart make a horrible mix, churning as I try to sort through last night's fuzzy memories.

I remember that Matt was perfectly willing to let me stay there with Carson. I used to think Matt had never noticed that I'm a girl, but the truth is, I'm just not the kind of girl he wants for himself. That's embarrassing in its own way, but not as bad as him thinking I would actually want to stay with Carson Tipton.

Or as bad as Carson thinking the same thing.

· · · · ·

The afternoon drags. Working at a pharmacy sucks, but it could be worse—I could have Mom's job. She's on the university custodial staff, cleaning up after brats like Asha and Spencer at the dorms during the week and special events on the weekend. It was a step down from her old position as an assistant manager, but the restaurant chain went bankrupt and she lost her job. By the time the janitor gig came along, it was a welcome opportunity.

The pay's not great, but the benefits are good. The employee scholarship program will pay my tuition if I want to stay here for college. I don't, but it's a nice security net. I have the test scores and the GPA to go to some fancier schools, but those require a lot of cash, and even here I'd still have to pay for room and board.

So for now, I put in my hours and save my money, pretending not to notice who's buying hemorrhoid cream and who needs yeast infection medicine and who has to pay in loose change. I am reassuringly blasé to the embarrassed preteen buying tampons and the guy buying extra-small condoms.

I wish I could ignore customers completely when two of Andrew's ex–baseball teammates come in—Shane Martin, who's a complete dick, and Benjamin Cruz, who's nicer and goes by his last name for some reason. My stomach roils at the sight of the potato chips and Red Bull they're buying. Or maybe it's because they were with Carson last night. "Hey Sanders," Cruz says. "You make it home all right?"

I nod, reaching for the rolling papers he indicates.

Shane leans on the counter. "You busy tonight?"

"That'll be five twelve," I tell Cruz.

Shane's not deterred. "My folks are out of town, so . . ." When I don't answer, he straightens up. "Gimme a pack of Marlboros."

"You're not eighteen." I push Cruz's change across the counter.

"How do you know?"

"Your birthday's in January, like mine." Our names were always together on the birthday cake poster in elementary school, but he obviously thinks I remember out of interest. So I smile back with fake sweetness. "You're not getting anything else, either."

Cruz cracks up, but Shane's jaw works. "Too bad," he says. "I was hoping . . ." He pretends to suck on something.

My stomach gives another lurch.

"Come on, you asshole." Cruz tips a pretend hat at me. "See you later, Sanders."

I manage to wait until they're out the door before rushing to the bathroom. Puking makes me feel a little better, but the urge returns when I find Roland standing at my register. Next to my crutches. *Damnit.* "Go ahead and cash out," he says.

I finish up and shuffle to his office, dreading the speech I'm about to get. I wish I could get a better job, but what's available after school is essentially all the same—cashier gigs with college-dropout bosses on power trips. Better to deal with the dickhead you know than the one that could be worse.

Roland stays at his desk when I enter, and he doesn't ask me to sit. "Raychel . . ." he starts, then leans back, putting his hands behind his head. "You know I have to let you go."

My stomach threatens a second round. "No," I say weakly, "I did not know that."

MATT

Saturday morning Student Council meetings should be illegal, much less at 9 a.m., but since StuCo isn't a class period and all the members have a billion other commitments, we have to schedule meetings at weird times. It's a lot of work just to get some extra points on college admissions. I should at least get to add "wrangled drunks until the wee hours of the night and still arrived on time for early-morning commitments" to my applications. That seems like a more accurate representation of what surviving college will require anyway.

"Matt!" Mindy waves me up to the front of the room. She stopped acting like I had leprosy early in high school, about the time I grew a foot taller and started dating. This morning she's the one who looks different, and it takes me a minute to realize it's because she's not wearing makeup. It's disconcerting to realize I haven't seen her actual face in years. "Hey, Rosa's home sick today," she says. "Can you be secretary?"

"Sure," I say, shrugging, and take Rosa's spot at the head table. "What's she got?"

"Stomach bug," Mindy says, with air quotes and a glance at Mrs. Nguyen, the math teacher who serves as our sponsor. "Are you going to the Grove tonight?"

"Maybe." A clearing in the National Forest outside of town is an unofficial gathering spot, and two out of every three parties there get busted, but we keep going back because no one has to face angry parents and a wrecked house afterward.

Mindy frowns. "You should go!"

"I might. But we're going to Music on the Mulberry tomorrow, so—"

"Oh," she says. "You and Raychel."

"And my brother." I don't know why I need to add that. Last year I would have invited Mindy to come along, but the big crew of friends that used to go with us is gone to college now, and it would be weird with just the four of us.

Luckily we're interrupted as Trenton Alexander Montgomery the Third takes his seat beside her. In elementary school, Trenton Alexander Montgomery the Third insisted that everyone, especially teachers, call him by his full name, and it stuck, much to his junior high chagrin. On the plus side, he had the longest campaign posters in the hallway, which probably helped him get elected vice president this year. "Richardson," he says, pulling his chair out. "What are you doing up here?"

"I asked him to be secretary," Mindy answers. "Rosa's sick."

He grins at me. "Ah, why don't you fetch me some coffee then, Madam Secretary?"

"I'll get right on that," I say dryly.

"You know what you ought to get on?" he asks, and Mindy clears her throat to start the meeting.

. . . . .

Two hours later, we've planned the basics of two fund-raisers, an anti–drunk driving campaign, a staff appreciation week, and a blood drive. My proposal to protest the use of pesticides in the building is rejected, but somehow, I have gotten roped into a committee for half the other projects, and somehow, Mindy is on the same ones. A few years ago, StuCo discovered that offering really good food at the blood drive increased participation, so our first task is to solicit donations from local restaurants. As we walk to the parking lot, she gives me a megawatt smile, pulling her dark blond hair up into a twist. "Are you busy today?"

"Um, I have some homework." She gives me a disbelieving look. "Because of the festival," I explain. "I have to do it today."

"Oh, right." Her smile slides back into place. "Can you spare like, an hour or two? I thought we could get a head start on talking to restaurants?"

I check my phone. "It's only eleven," I say out loud, so she won't think I was looking for texts. "Yeah, I could probably do that."

She lets me drive, and I let her do the talking, both in and out of the car. She asks how a hybrid works (I don't know) and if I'm going to play soccer again this year (yes) and if I'm still in choir (no). "I've never been to Music on the Mulberry," she says, after she's sweet-talked a Mexican place into donating chips and dip. "Is it all day?"

I start the ignition, almost whacking her with my hand when I turn to reverse. Mindy always looks like she swallowed a broom handle, with her chest well out in front of her, and my gaze flits for a millisecond to her V-neck shirt before I snap my eyes away. I'm not complaining, but I am aware that we're alone in my car, and I don't want to creep her out or anything. "Yeah, it starts at eleven," I tell her. "Bands play until two in the morning sometimes."

"It sounds really fun." She lets me pull on to the main road undistracted, then clears her throat. "Who's playing?"

"I don't even know," I admit. "It's just a tradition, so we go."

"Have you ever seen Suddenly, Spiders? They play all-ages shows downtown a lot."

I try not to make a face. "Yeah, but once was enough." Realizing how jerky that sounded, I add, "They're not as bad as those sophomores that played at the talent show last year, though."

"Nothing could be that bad," she says. "Except . . ." She laughs and puts her hand over her mouth.

"You can't not tell me," I say, stopping at a red light. "Come on."

"Trent." She lets a giggle escape. "He has a band."

"Trenton Alexander Montgomery the Third?" I can't imagine Trent in a band. He's even taller and skinnier than me, with a long neck and a chin that juts forward. Combined with his slicked-back hair, he looks like he's constantly walking into a stiff wind. "What does he play?"

"The drums."

"He must look like a Muppet on stage."

She giggles again. "He does look a lot like Animal."

I grin. "Please tell me they're The Electric Mayhem."

"No," she says, play-slapping my arm. "They're TAM3."

"That's even worse than 'Suddenly, Spiders.'"

"Still not as bad as his music though." It's the meanest thing I've ever heard her say. She reaches into her giant purse and pulls out her phone. "He sent me one of their 'tracks' last year to like, audition for prom." Her eyes roll up, as if God will share her disbelief. "You want to hear it?"

"I'm not sure."

She scrolls through. "Oh, this thing's nearly dead anyway."

"My charger's in the glove box." She opens it and Raychel's emergency supplies tumble out onto the floor. "Crap, sorry, I should have warned you."

Mindy picks a brochure off the top of the pile. "Thinking about Duke?"

"My dad is." He's bound and determined that I'll attend his alma mater. I try to intercept any promotional mail he might use as an excuse to lecture me.

"What's all this?" she asks, trying to put the other junk away.

Toilet paper, sunglasses, tampons, sunscreen, hair ties . . . a condom, which was funny at the time. "It's for hiking and stuff.

We always get way out in the boonies and then Raychel realizes she forgot something."

"Oh," Mindy says, and closes the glove box without retrieving the charger. "Of course."

I decide not to point out the tampon still lying beside her foot.

RAYCHEL

For once, Matt doesn't say "I told you so." "Fired?" *he repeats* incredulously when I call Sunday morning to tell him I can't go to Music on the Mulberry. "Because you were late?"

"Yeah."

"You should still come," he tells me. "It's only fifteen bucks. I'll spot you."

"I have the cash," I argue. "But I should save it. And I need to apply for new jobs ASAP."

"Come on," Matt says. "It's Sunday. Andrew's going to meet us there with his friends." When I don't answer, he sighs. "I went to the toga party for you."

"Fine," I say grudgingly. "I'll go."

· · · · ·

Mom gives me a ride to the Richardsons'. "Thanks," I say, hopping out of our rust bucket of a car.

"Call me when you head home—I have plans this evening."
I duck back through the window. "With the boyfriend?"

Mom smiles, but doesn't offer more information. I don't press. I'm sure I'll meet him soon. I met the few others that lasted this long.

Inside, Dr. R. examines my ankle and gives me permission to leave the crutches behind. Matt and I spend the long drive to the Mulberry brainstorming jobs I might apply for. It's nice that Matt wants to help, but he doesn't know anything about working. He can afford to spend his time volunteering instead. I try to tell myself that working and volunteering count the same on college applications, but I doubt that "ran a cash register" and "helped the homeless" carry the same weight.

At the festival, Matt pays for parking and insists on getting our tickets while I unload our stuff, so I sneak the cash for my share into his glove box when I lock up. "Sucks," he says when he rejoins me, pointing at the overcast sky.

"Yeah, bummer." I'm actually glad. Last year I got so sunburned I couldn't lift my arms for two days. It was worth it, though.

Matt and I take our traditional spot along the river, but without our usual crew, our spread of blankets and lawn chairs is pathetically small. He must be thinking the same thing. "I don't know how to do concerts without The Nuge for inspiration," he says. We call our friend Randy "The Nuge" because he looks just like a young Ted Nugent—seventies rock star Nugent, not scary racist libertarian Nugent. He's skinny but cut, with bushy auburn hair, and he plays a mean air guitar.

"I know," I say. "And no flailing." Daniel Fischer is an enthusiastic, if less than skilled, dancer. But Bree and Stanton and Asha are awesome, and even Matt and Andrew are pretty good ("for a couple of white boys," Spencer says). And Nathan is great when his girlfriend Eliza will let him have fun, but that's rare. I hope she's lightened up since they went to college together in Texas.

Asha and Spencer are the only ones at a school close enough to make the trip, and they both bailed because they have papers due tomorrow. I haven't talked to anyone besides them since school started, unless you count a few mass emails Matt added me to. I mean, I know everyone is busy. I didn't expect fountain pen letters on stationery or anything. It's just that I've always felt like they're more Matt's friends than mine, and having that as proof gives me a slow sinking feeling.

But as we head toward the stage, the music lifts me back up. Sometimes dancing is hard for me—everyone else moves to the drums and my hips move to the bass. But the amps whine, and the beat thuds in my chest, and I stop caring who might be watching. Sweat rolls down my back. The music pulses under my skin, like my soul is swelling. I can't *not* dance.

When The Underground Township takes the stage, the crowd doubles in size. I lose track of Matt in the sea of camouflage and crop tops, white hats and white-boy dreadlocks, Tevas and Timberlands. Finally, I spot him with some girl and a bunch of Andrew's friends—including Cruz and, unfortunately, Shane.

I don't see Andrew, though, so I squeeze through the cracks in the walls of people and find him sitting by our stuff. He turns my water bottle upside down when I reach for it. "Empty. Sorry, kid."

"Damnit, Andrew. You should have brought your own stuff."

"I did!" He flicks two fingers in my direction, smoke trailing from the joint between them. "I'll even share."

"You have any beer?" I haven't smoked weed in ages. It makes my head fuzzy and it's not predictable like alcohol—you never know how strong it'll be.

"Cruz's brother was supposed to get us a case, but he forgot." Andrew pinches the roach and takes a hit, the end glowing orange as he inhales. "You up?" he rasps.

The scent pulls me over. I could use some fuzzy-headed time, and we're not going to score any alcohol. Even if we could find someone who's twenty-one, this county is dry on Sundays.

Not that you could afford it anyway. Because you got fired.

I take the joint and promptly burn my fingers. The first hit goes okay, but the second makes me cough so hard I think I'm going to die. "I suck at smoking," I choke.

Andrew laughs. "You know what they say—if you don't cough, you don't get off."

"I'm going to the bathroom." I head for the concessions area. I'm dying of thirst, but there's no free water on-site because they want to charge you three bucks a bottle. My stomach growls at the smell of corn dogs, Indian tacos, funnel cakes, cotton candy . . . All these people buying all this stuff, and my only cash is locked in Matt's glove box. I'm not going to cut in while he's dancing with another girl and ask for his keys. Or his money, for that matter.

"Hey girl!"

I turn around. An older man gestures to me from a cluster of tents by the tree line. His tie-dyed shirt barely covers the stomach that flops over a sizable belt buckle. "Come here." He's smiling under his full beard. When I get there he asks, "You got anything to smoke?"

"Me?" I glance around, like someone might have materialized beside me.

"Yeah, you. You look pretty fried."

Right. Raychel the lightweight. My eyes probably look like hell. "Oh, no, it's a friend's. I think he's out," I lie.

"Aw, that's a shame. We got this case of beer to trade for something good."

My throat is killing me. "I don't suppose you'd be willing to part with one of those, would you?"

He laughs. "Can't break up the set, darlin'."

"Oh." Dickhead. I start to leave, but his friend calls me back.

"Hey! We might be willing to give you one, for a peek!"

The older man frowns at him. The younger one has a goatee and green tattoos run like mold all the way up his skinny arms into a sleeveless Lynyrd Skynyrd shirt. "A peek?" I repeat.

"Titties!" He pretends to grab his own chest.

"Jack," his friend warns.

I stare at them, wondering if they know I'm underage, or just don't care. "You'd give me a beer to see my boobs?"

Jack snickers. "Honey, I'll give you the whole case for a feel."

"She ain't gonna do that!" the older man protests.

Now it's a dare. Seeing me waver, Jack snorts. "They're just boobs."

They're just boobs. Maybe that's the secret to life. Body parts are just parts—you use them or they use you. Hell, a guy grabbed my ass while I was dancing and he didn't even ask first, much less pay me.

I look around, then yank my shirt up. Tattoo guy squeezes with both hands and yells, "Honk!"

"Jack," the other guy says, disgusted.

It's fast and ridiculous, like a secret handshake, and Jack and I are laughing for very different reasons. So what if he thinks I'm trashy. Sometimes trash is a force to be reckoned with. Landfills rise into mountains and pollute entire waterways.

Okay, maybe I'm a little stoned. But I still feel victorious, hugging a case of beer to my meaningless chest. Andrew's face glows with pride when he sees what I've brought. "Leave it to you to find beer on Sunday," he says, and raises the can I give him. "A toast. To Raychel and her incomparable skills."

"And my boobs," I say.

"And your boobs," he agrees, tipping his can toward them. "One of your greater assets, I'll admit."

We clink cans. Andrew chugs but I take small sips, to make it last.

MATT

It starts to drizzle near the end of the Township's set. I've been dancing with an older girl who laughs as I spin her, long skirt swirling around her legs, but when the rain starts to pick up, she wanders off with her friends. I go to find Raychel, stopping on the way to buy some Cokes and a giant soft pretzel to share.

She's sitting, half-baked, beside my brother, surrounded by empty cans and a few of Andrew's friends. She thanks me and takes a bite of the pretzel. "Where'd you get the beer?" I ask.

"Our girl Raych is handy," Andrew says, slinging his arm around her shoulders.

She laughs and blinks bloodshot eyes. "It's raining."

"I noticed." Andrew smiles placidly, tossing a Hacky Sack up and down with his other hand, while Cruz holds out a small pipe. "I have to drive," I tell him. It's true, but it's also true I'm an uptight nerd who doesn't smoke, and I'm pissed off to see Raychel partaking. "You want to leave?" I ask her.

"No!" She sits up straight. "We've barely danced at all!"

"Then let's go!" Andrew motions to his friends and jumps to his feet. Raychel grabs both our hands, dragging me along instead of letting me sit and stew, like I'd prefer. We kick off our shoes because the dancing area is quickly turning into a mud pit, and Raychel starts to sway, arms slowly working their way into motion with the beat, rivulets of rain running down her bare shoulders. Andrew's more interested in starting a mud fight, but I shake my head when he eyes me, so he rushes Cruz, tackling him into the slop. Raychel giggles and keeps dancing.

"Where'd you get the beer?" I ask again, but she doesn't hear me over the music, so I give up. Occasionally I take her hand or put mine on her waist, more to keep her upright than to touch her. Mostly. When the band goes into a jam, she goes into a trance, her feet barely moving but hips in constant motion. It's sort of hypnotic. I move closer and she backs up against me.

This never used to be a big deal. I've danced with Raychel a thousand times.

But that same weird feeling, the one that made me almost kiss her Friday night, makes me move back. Her eyes open to slits, then close again as she dances farther away. I watch her. I try not to be obvious.

I'm not sure if I want her to come back or stay away.

· · · · ·

It's hard to convince Raychel we have to go home, but it's already ten and we have school in the morning. I'd gladly leave my brother, but his friends went home, so I have to drag his sorry ass to the parking lot too. I toss him a towel. "Don't get mud all over my car, you tool."

Andrew flips me off. "Why do you only listen to dead white guys?" Raychel asks from the backseat. She gives up on my music and leans forward to turn on the radio. But the joke's on her, because the classic rock station is the only one with decent reception this far out in the sticks, and by the time we get on the road, she's lying down, singing at the top of her lungs. Andrew joins in without missing a note.

It's annoying, but damn, Raychel can sing. I thought our choir director was going to cry when she didn't try out this year, and I wanted to tell him it was because the new uniforms were too expensive. But Raych would have killed me if she found out. She nearly killed me anyway when I told her I had quit too, though that wasn't out of solidarity. I only joined in the first place so she wouldn't wuss out of her own audition. I didn't expect to get in, and once I did, I was stuck, cummerbunds and bow ties and all.

Now I realize I haven't heard Raych sing in forever. Her alto expands through the car, with Andrew's gravelly bass grounding it here and there. An old song by The Band comes on and Raychel's head appears in my rearview. "Turn it up!"

Andrew obeys, launching into the first verse with her. What the hell. At the chorus, I add tenor to their harmony. "And . . . and . . . and. . . . she put the load right on me!"

We keep the classic rock going until we reach the house. I

make Andrew strip down to his boxers in the garage while Raychel stands there, humming to herself, holding her shoes. She's mostly clean, but still damp from the rain. "Do you want some clothes?" I ask. She nods.

"I'll get 'em," Andrew says. He returns, redressed, with the pajama pants Raych keeps here and one of his old Grateful Dead T-shirts.

While she changes, Andrew raids the kitchen and plows through a munchies spread of cold cuts, cheese, and chips. Raychel comes in and makes herself a sandwich that's bigger than her face. She's tied one side of his borrowed shirt in a knot and it rides up, letting a sliver of smooth stomach peek out. I make myself look away and notice she has mayo on her cheek.

That stupid hormonal part of my brain wants to lick it off. I remind it we hate mayonnaise.

RAYCHEL

"Why don't you come home?" Mom asks when I call.

She's not worried because I'm sleeping over with boys—I've been crashing at the Richardsons' since seventh grade, when she had to work nights occasionally. I think she's just jealous. She worries that Mrs. R. will replace her. "It's late and we're really tired."

"You're going to wear out your welcome over there."

"It's fine. They don't mind."

When she finally gives in, I hang up and flop next to Andrew on the leather couch. He kicks my ass at *Mario Kart* while Matt throws our dirty clothes in the washer. "Can I wear this shirt to school tomorrow?" I ask.

"Sure." Andrew's smile turns into a grimace as my car careens off the screen. "Look," he says, trying to take my controller. "If you'll press this and then—"

I wrestle it away. "I don't need you to mansplain this, Andrew."

He puts a hand to his chest in mock offense as the game restarts. "Raychel Sanders, I'm shocked you would use such a sexist term! Lumping all men together like that." He *tsks*.

"Yeah," I say, rolling my eyes. "Good thing guys never 'bitch' about it or we'd have to change our entire vocabulary."

Matt laughs from the doorway but Andrew just says "Aha!" and runs me off the Rainbow Road.

· · · · ·

We get ready for bed together, as usual. Andrew splashes water all over the counter and gets toothpaste on the mirror. Matt scowls at the mess as he sits on the edge of the tub to floss. When it's my turn at the sink, Andrew shakes his head. "I still can't believe he lets you use his face wash."

I've never asked, but I always use Matt's fancy organic stuff—it's a lot nicer than my Walmart generic. "It's because I don't squeeze out half the bottle every time like *some* people."

Andrew musses my hair, not waiting for me to dry my face. "Night."

"Rematch!" I call after him, leaning out the door. "*Mario Kart*! Tomorrow!"

He walks backward long enough to smirk and blow me a kiss. I pretend to swoon and duck back into the bathroom. If he'd done that at school, I'd be getting the stink eye from twenty different girls right now.

"Tomorrow's going to be rough," Matt says, yawning.

"We'll need extra coffee rations." I lean close to the mirror and pick at a spot on my forehead. Must. Not. Squeeze . . .

"What did you think of The Flying Buttresses?"

"They were okay," I say. Matt's hanging a towel over the shower rod, so I take a chance and lean closer. Can't resist. Must—*eeeew*. Gross. I wipe the goo off the mirror before he can see it. "Two Ton Pickup killed it."

"Yeah, they were good." He follows me out to the guest room and stands in the doorway. "You need anything?"

"Nah. See you in the morning."

He shuts the door. I turn the light off and climb into bed, trying to get settled. Trying to tell myself that I'll find another job easily, and that it's a good sign Shane and Cruz didn't say a single word about Carson today. Maybe some new scandal from this weekend will replace me tomorrow.

Maybe Carson will go back to ignoring me and I can pretend nothing ever happened.

I stare at the ceiling, watching tree shadows dance overhead.

That night in his Blazer wasn't fun, but I have to be overreacting. If it was really as bad as I remember, he would be avoiding me like the plague.

I put a pillow over my head. He made me feel . . . I can admit it. Unworthy. Worthless.

Used.

I've never felt that way before. I like knowing that my occasional college-boy hookups are temporary. That I'm in charge. That I can walk away at any time.

But I can't walk away from Carson. He's everywhere.

I toss and turn for what feels like hours, trying to find a calm spot for my brain to rest. Finally, I fling back the covers, and my bare feet cross the plush rug to the hallway's hardwood floor. I hold my breath passing Andrew's door and tap lightly on Matt's as it cracks open. "Matt?"

Yawning, he sits up and blinks. "Bad dream?"

I nod.

He pulls back the blanket. "Come on."

MATT

My brother got a ride with Cruz this morning, so I don't have to deal with his cranky ass, but Raychel isn't much better after our late night. "Why are you wearing Andrew's shirt?" I ask. It's his best one, a souvenir Dad passed down from the band's last tour, right before Jerry Garcia died and a few years before we were born. No way would I let anyone else wear mine.

"I like The Dead," she says.

"Uh-huh." I turn the radio down as she sips coffee from her travel mug. "Name three songs."

"Um . . . 'Truckin',' 'Sugar Magnolia,' and . . ." Raych glances out the window. I laugh. "Shut up!" she says. "I'm thinking!"

I don't really care, but I give her a few obvious ones anyway. " 'Casey Jones'? 'Friend of the Devil'?" Dad's collection of Dead bootlegs is a wall of cassettes in his office. We weren't allowed to touch them when we were little, and now no one touches them because we don't own a tape player. " 'Touch of Gray'?"

"That one doesn't count," she says. "It sucks."

I concede the point. I'm in a great mood, having woken up with her wrapped around me. When we were younger she had nightmares all the time, and sneaking into my room to sleep was the only thing that seemed to help. At first we figured that if my parents caught us, they'd understand; as we got older, we realized they'd probably kill us, but the nightmares got less frequent anyway, so it's been a long time since she needed me. I'm not happy that her bad dreams are back, but I'm not unhappy to help either.

Because I don't know what those nights mean to her, but last night made me realize they mean a lot to me . . . and make me hope we manage to pick colleges near one another, when the "no high school boys" rule won't apply to me anymore.

RAYCHEL

The gossip Monday morning still involves me, but only in a roundabout way: Shane got a DUI after Music on the Mulberry, thanks to the beer I procured. I'm glad he didn't narc on me, but I still choose to think of it as cosmic justice for his behavior at the pharmacy, enacted via my boobs. His daddy's a bigwig at Walmart corporate so he'll just end up with a slap on the wrist anyway.

But I feel bad for waking Matt up in the middle of the night like a little kid. Maybe cosmic justice is punishing me for that, because I walk into fourth-period calculus to find Carson sitting at the desk in front of mine. "Sanders," he says, turning around in his chair.

"Hey," I say slowly, trying to muster the slightest bit of cool. "What are you doing here?"

"I dropped Spanish and my schedule got moved around." When I don't ask more, he clears his throat. "Y'all have fun Friday night?"

I glance up. The question sounds innocent, but his smirk makes me think he's implying that Matt and I went home for a different kind of fun. "It was fine," I say, pretending to search my purse for something. "Did you have a good time?"

He shrugs. "It was all right. I didn't stay long, since you left."

I stare into the depths of my bag, hoping an escape will appear there. "I had to work the next morning," I say. Ugh, why am I making excuses?

"Me too," he says, and I look up in surprise. "I mow lawns on weekends."

He waits for me to talk about my job, but thankfully Mrs. Nguyen calls class to order. Carson raps his knuckles once on my desk and turns around.

I try to hold my breath for the rest of the hour, but still end up with a headache from his cologne.

. . . . .

After school, Matt has an Outdoor Club meeting, so I catch the transit and try to find a job. Our little downtown has lots of good possibilities near home, but no one has openings— they've already hired college students. I even brave the patchouli smell of the natural foods store to apply there. "Can you work mornings?" the guy asks.

I shake my head. "I have class."

"It's cool, we can work with your schedule."

"It's not really flexible," I say, disappointed. "I'm still in high school."

He takes my application, but doesn't leave me with much hope. Neither do the people at the bead shop, the used bookstore, the two banks, or the performing arts center. I walk down the hill to the abandoned railroad station that houses our favorite coffee shop, Coffee Depot. "Where's your guy friend?" the barista asks, twisting her nose ring.

"Oh, I'm actually here to apply for a job." She's cute—I'll have to tell Matt she asked about him.

"Right on. You know how to make a cappuccino?" she asks. I admit I don't. "Well, no biggie—we're not hiring right now anyway, but I'll put your name down and let you know if something comes up. Hey, here," she adds, holding out a to-go cup as I turn away. "On the house." I try to argue, but she insists. "You look like you need it."

She's not wrong. With no car, not much experience, and a firing behind me, I'm not much of a prospect. I visit the boutiques on the historic square and even stop at a few restaurants, though I've never waited tables before. But nothing seems promising.

"Just apply at the mall," Matt says Tuesday morning in the car.

I sigh. I've already explained this. "The transit schedule is weird on the weekends. It'd be hard to get out there."

"The university?"

"They have work-study, they don't need high schoolers."

"Hmm." He taps a finger on the steering wheel. "Let me think about it."

I do nothing but think about it. A resale shop calls Wednesday, but they say never mind when I can't make their early-morning interview.

Otherwise, it's crickets.

Which leaves me with the realization that without a job, I also have no life. My mom is spending every free minute with her new boyfriend, and when Matt's not at some kind of meeting, he's at the gym, getting ready for a soccer season that's months away. Asha and Spencer are still adjusting to their college schedules, and Andrew's always hanging out with guys I don't like.

I'm lonely, I realize. And it sucks.

．　．　．　．　．

Thursday in calculus, Carson greets me with his standard "Hey Sanders," turning to straddle his chair. His continued friendliness has dulled my reaction to his presence from humiliated panic to embarrassed caution. "Nice shirt," he says.

I look down. My V-neck looked fine in the mirror, but it leaves little to the imagination from his perspective. "Thanks," I say, yanking it up.

He laughs. "Sorry. I just meant the color."

His apology throws me. "It's Asha's," I blurt.

"Oh yeah. Spencer's girl. I remember her."

I snort. "You just saw her two weeks ago."

"I was distracted by someone else," he says, resting his massive forearms on my desk. Crap. He's been chatting me up every day since his schedule changed, and so far I've managed to avoid this conversation. But now I'm stuck. Mrs. Nguyen isn't even in the room yet. All I can do is blush.

But miraculously, he moves on. "You gonna be at Cruz's party tomorrow? After the game?"

"Um . . ." Andrew has been trying to talk us into going, but Matt doesn't want to. "Maybe."

Carson grins. "Well, maybe I'll see you there."

I almost smile back, but stop myself, annoyed by the impulse. "Maybe you will and maybe you won't."

MATT

At the end of the week, Raychel and I meet as the entire school bottlenecks at the gym doors. I'd rather go to seventh period than a pep rally, but school spirit is compulsory. When most of us are crammed into the stands, the cheerleaders start a disjointed routine. "Did they practice at all?" I ask.

"They're junior varsity," Raychel scolds me. "They're still learning."

She claps for them when they finish, giving me a pointed look until I follow suit. At least the next group's picked some decent music. I'm halfway enjoying the James Brown tune when something flicks my ear. "Damnit!"

"What's shakin', kids?" Andrew leans in from the next bleacher up and points at the girls on the floor. "Besides Mindy Merrithew, I mean. Scoot over," he says, shoving in between us.

Raychel leans over and inhales. "Someone's been busy."

"Cruz and I skipped lunch for some herbal refreshment," he says, winking. "Are y'all coming to his house tonight?"

I roll my eyes at his "y'all." Much to my Chicago-born parents' dismay, my brother and I have picked up some of the local accent, but I think he makes his worse on purpose just to annoy them. "We're not going," I tell him right as Raychel says, "Maybe."

I turn toward her. "I thought we were hanging out with Asha and Spencer?"

Her response is lost in a swell of voices shouting "Cowboys!" The cheerleaders point across the basketball court, where the other side yells, "Big Springs!" When it's our turn again, Andrew jumps up. "Cowboys!" he yells, doing a little jig on the bleacher.

Raychel yanks him down by the hem of his shirt. "You're going to bust your ass. Or get your ass busted."

"Nah," he says, but he sits down and watches the next routine. "Oh shit," he says admiringly. "Keri Sturgis got hot."

"Who?" Raychel asks.

He points to a short Asian girl in the back row who I'm pretty sure he dated last year. "Eh," I say, "she's all right. Not really my type."

Raych rolls her eyes at me. "Your type? She could be a body double for Hana." I start to protest that she looks nothing like my ex when Raych adds, "I wouldn't kick either one out of bed."

Luckily I don't have long to think about that because Trenton Alexander Montgomery the Third grabs the mic. "Give it up for our spirit squads!" he says, raising his arms like he's directing a gospel choir. The crowd more or less obliges. "Now, some other fine ladies would like to show the football team some support. Let's hear it for the Big Springs High School Diamond Dolls!"

Seven baseball players come out in drag and start dancing. Carson Tipton is in the middle, his usual hat perched atop a blond wig, his hairy tree-trunk legs sticking out of a cheerleading skirt. At the end, he flips up the back to reveal red shorts with "Big" emblazoned on the ass. The other asses line up to spell out "Springs."

"That takes some balls," I say.

"Or not," Andrew replies.

I notice Raychel doesn't weigh in.

· · · · ·

After we escape the gym, Andrew spots Eddie, one of the school janitors. "Y'all go on," he says, slowing down. "I lost a hoodie and I want to ask Eddie to keep an eye out."

"Good idea," I admit. Eddie's a good dude who'll try to find it. One time he dug through every trash can in the cafeteria to rescue a girl's retainer.

Raychel doesn't reply. She's been moody all week and I keep asking what's wrong, but she keeps blaming it on getting fired, which I'm pretty sure means "Figure out what's really wrong so I don't have to tell you."

She slows as someone calls her last name across the lobby. Carson, thankfully back in his own clothes, bypasses me to catch her sleeve. "Hey, you dropped this," he says, holding out a piece of paper. He gives me a quick nod. "Richardson."

I twitch my chin in response and wait for Raychel to cram the paper into her backpack.

"So where you headed?" he asks her.

"Home." She's half turned toward the door already, which gives me some petty satisfaction.

He smiles anyway. I have to admire his dedication, at least. "About that party tonight—"

"Matt!"

I turn around, bracing myself. Mindy's hair bow flops on top of her head like a broken red propeller. "Hey!" she says. "Apple-bee's called and they are totally in for cheese sticks."

"Oh." I can't eavesdrop and answer her at the same time. "Um. Great! That's awesome. Nice work."

She beams. "Did you—"

We both look over as someone hoots across the room. Carson flips the guy off and turns back to Raych. "Well, maybe I'll give you a call?"

She gives him a shrug and he leaves, seemingly undiscouraged. Her eyes find me, cut to Mindy, then back to me. "Ummm . . ." I say, trying to remember what Mindy asked.

"The bakery," she says, taking pity. "Did you ask them about cookies?"

"Oh." I shake my head, trying to focus. "I did, yeah—the manager is supposed to call me back."

"Well, let me know when you hear. Are you going to Cruz's party?"

"Are you?" I ask, surprised. Mindy's not really a party girl.

She smiles. "I might."

"Oh. Um . . ." I glance at Raychel, who's pretending to

read a poster on the wall. "I'm actually busy already." Mindy's smile slips just enough to make me feel bad. "Have fun, though."

"Yeah, you too," she says. "Bye, Raychel!"

Raych waves back limply, not saying a word until we get in the car. Then she gives a huge sigh.

"Problems?" I ask.

"Huh?" She buckles up. "No. I'm just tired."

I try not to grin. Maybe she's jealous that Mindy tried to make plans with me. She did just shut down Carson. "Well, at least we have a chill night ahead of us."

"Yeah," she says, gazing out the window at Carson climbing into his ugly Blazer. It's bright red, with KC lights on the bumper *and* the roof, and a horn that plays "Dixie." Anyone with tires that big is compensating for something.

I start to ask Raychel if that's true, but she turns on some obnoxious music of Andrew's full blast, so I decide against it.

RAYCHEL

Carson asked me out.

Not a date, exactly, but close enough.

While Matt was distracted by Mindy, Carson offered to take me to Cruz's—to pick me up and walk in together as a couple. Not in so many words, of course, but that's what it means: an unofficial declaration of togetherness.

Carson's willing to make an honest woman out of me. After making it clear, on the night we hooked up, that he had no interest in such a thing.

And honestly, I'm so confused that I almost said yes.

I settle back into the passenger seat, wishing I could cover my face and scream. The gossip last week sucked, but the truth is that I don't really care if people think I'm a slut. They don't know what I do and don't do with college guys, and I don't care what they assume.

Because the reputation comes with a funny kind of power. "No high school boys" gives me the upper hand—both with boys, who see me as a challenge, and with girls, who would never dare say no to the guys I've turned down. I learned early in life that things that are hard to get are always worth more.

But by hooking up with Carson, I'm back on the same playing field as those other girls—with far less game, in their opinion. Showing up at Cruz's with Carson would turn my scarlet *A* into an ace.

I've got half a mind to say yes. But saying yes is what got me into this mess.

"Hey," Matt says, startling me out of my thoughts. "I'll see you at seven?" he asks. "Dad's making dinner."

"Yeah," I say, climbing out of the car. "I'll be there."

· · · · ·

Inside, it's dark and stuffy. We don't run the AC when no one's here. I leave the blinds closed and lie down on the couch with a cold washcloth over my eyes. But Mom comes through the door before I can get any rest. "Hi, honey! I'm—what's wrong?"

I sit up. "Just a headache. It's going away."

She drops her purse, keeping the mail in one hand. "Do you want something to drink?"

"Yes, please." I accept the can of Dr. Thunder she brings me, but I dream of the day we can afford real Dr Pepper. "How was your day?"

"The usual. Martha and I were five minutes late from lunch and Gary about had a heart attack. The man don't have the sense God gave a wooden goose. How was yours?" she asks, opening an envelope.

"Fine. We had a pep rally."

"Oh?" She starts to ask more, but instead reads the mail and says in a different voice, "Oh."

"What?"

She tries to smile. "Nothing. Tell me about the pep rally."

But I can see her lip trembling. "Mom," I say, holding out my hand for the letter. "Come on." She doesn't offer it. "You're a terrible liar. I'm just going to think it's something horrible unless you tell me."

"Don't worry," she says, handing it over. "But your dad's check bounced."

"Goddamnit." My dad's signature is the most I've seen of him since he split when I was in kindergarten. "It's just one month," I say. "Right?"

Mom shakes her head. "This is the sixth one in a row."

"What? Why didn't you tell me?" The checks have bounced before, but never so many all at once. If we had a computer or Mom had a fancy phone, we could at least find out before getting hit with overdraft fees.

She sits down and smooths my hair. "I didn't want to worry you."

I snort. I should offer part of my paycheck, but my last Pharm-Co check is only going to be half as much as usual and I don't want to explain why.

"We'll just have to tighten up a little," she says. "I asked for some overtime."

"Maybe I can get some too," I lie.

"You don't need to do that, baby."

I don't answer. I'm not sure how she plans to "tighten up" when our budget is so squeezed already. Mom makes just enough that we don't qualify for government assistance anymore, and we can't go after my dad in court because it takes money and time off of work that we don't have. And what's the point, when he doesn't have the money either?

Sometimes I find it comforting that he sends the check regardless. Proof he remembers I exist, at least once a month.

But today is not one of those times. Today is one of those times when I remember it's just me and Mom against the world, and the world is winning.

MATT

When Raychel comes over later, her mood has not improved, so I take her to my room to see the pictures from our hiking trip. She looks beautiful in them, fierce, with leg muscles as hard as the rocks she climbed, and I want them to cheer her up. But she points to the one I knew she'd focus on. "Oh my god, what's wrong with my face?"

"You were yelling at me to hurry."

She frowns.

See, this is what I don't get about girls, or what I don't get about Raychel Sanders specifically. She'll take "ladies first," but she gets mad when I try to help her. She can blame hormones, but I cannot. She lets me pay, but pays me back in secret. She wears makeup and black lacy panties on hiking trips.

I'm not complaining about that last one. I'm just saying.

But I'm glad I got rid of the photos where her underwear was showing.

She sits down on the bed and stares into space. I wave my hand in front of her face. "Hey. You okay?" I ask for the millionth time this week.

"I'm fine."

"Yeah, you seem fine." I sit and put an arm around her. "Do you want to go to the party tonight?" I offer, in a fit of self-sacrifice. "Would that cheer you up?"

When she doesn't answer, I pull away and realize she's crying.

Crap.

RAYCHEL

My brain is a blender, spinning from one worry to another, mixing them up until I can't separate them at all.

We're broke. My mom didn't tell me. My dad's the worst. The whole school thinks I screwed Carson and even my best friend believes I'm interested in the guy. But why wouldn't he? I can't tell him what really happened. The only people who know the truth are me and Carson, and apparently we remember two different things.

I've known Carson since kindergarten. So when we got to the parking lot outside Spencer's dorm, and he popped the tailgate and told me to have a seat, I didn't think anything of it. I was too busy thinking about how great it was to have a chill in the air in August and hoping the cold front would stick around for my hike with Matt later that weekend. I hopped up beside Carson and tried not to breathe in his sissy Camel Lights. Turned down the one he offered me. Mom still smokes, and we can't afford it, but she says she can't afford not to. It's one of the many ways in which she doesn't want me to be like her.

When Carson stubbed out his cigarette, he chewed a piece of gum. It was spearmint, which I know because he kissed me unexpectedly. Turns out Carson is a fantastic kisser, though I was surprised as hell that he tried. My policy is pretty widely known, so I was a little impressed that he made the attempt.

But besides that, I like kissing. I like making out with boys.

And summer had been a long dry spell, with all the college students gone. So when Carson whispered, "We should get in the truck," I decided it couldn't hurt to have a little fun.

He put the seats down and closed the back, then laid me down and kissed me silly. Kissed me stupid. One hand crept under my shirt. I let it go, because his hand was as talented as his mouth. But when he tried to move south, I stopped him.

"What?"

"No," I repeated, trying to sit up. "Sorry." I wasn't even trying to be coy. I was just on the rag.

"It's okay," he said. "Don't worry about it." And we made out some more.

But he tried again.

"No," I said, and tried to sit up. With his knees on either side of my hips, it was difficult. He rubbed himself against me and I thought he'd gotten the hint and moved on to other pastimes. It felt good, but after a minute, the seam of my jeans digging in was too painful. I told him it hurt, so he moved.

Behind him, a streetlight flickered. I heard his zipper at the same time. Then he blocked my view. He grabbed my hair. Held me half-sitting up. It wasn't violent—it was almost gentle—but I couldn't get away. I didn't know what else to do.

So I closed my eyes. And before I could say anything, he opened my mouth.

When he was done and rezipped, he tugged on my ponytail

and wiggled his fingers at me. "You sure you don't want a turn?"
I shook my head. "We should do this again sometime," he said.
I made a noncommittal noise. "I mean, like . . . you know." He
coughed. "For fun. Not like, a girlfriend thing."

"Yeah," I managed. "Yeah, no. Whatever."

He gave me a quick peck on the lips. He walked me back to
the dorm. And then he rejoined his boys and got a drink and
some high fives.

I found Matt and a second beer. Tried to wash away the salt
and sweat.

It didn't take me long to puke.

· · · · ·

Here's the thing: I've given blow jobs before.

It really shouldn't be that big a deal. I know that's what people
would say, if I told them what happened. Either that, or they'd
ask why I didn't fight. Why I didn't scream or bite him.

I just didn't know what to do. It happened fast.

And I don't know what to do now, when he's acting like it
was no big deal. Maybe it isn't.

But I know what I shouldn't do, and that's sob in front of
Matt.

Yet here I am.

Matt kneels beside me, one hand on my knee, and I want
him to leave me alone. Or put me on his lap and wrap me up
like a kid. Something—anything is better than this splintering

inside me, sharp edges puncturing the soft organs around it, small blood balloons leaking into my bones and making them weak. Seeing myself in those pictures—seeing myself through Matt's eyes . . . What he sees is something better than me. Something he wants me to be.

Something I'm not.

"Raych," Matt says quietly. "Just tell me."

But I can't. We joke about sex, talk about other people's sex lives, but personal details are off-limits. Awkward. Verboten. If I break that rule, he'll lecture me about being careful. Or he'll try to kick Carson's ass. Or he'll badger me into telling a parent—if not mine, then his. Matt will try to fix it, and he'll only make it worse.

So I lie. Or rather, I tell him the little bit of truth that's safe. "My dad's checks have been bouncing for the last six months." He sits and puts his arm around me. "If I can't find a job, and Mom keeps getting deeper in debt . . ."

Matt hugs me tighter. "I know," he says. "But it'll be okay."

"You don't know," I tell him. "Your family's perfect." The Richardsons are rich and that's ironic and hilarious, ha ha ha. "My folks are just poor white trash from the Delta. That's never going to change."

"You're not them," he says, rubbing my arm. "You can do anything, Raych."

And I want to believe him. But it's hard. Matt was born with a silver spoon. I was born with a plastic straw. He can't possibly know how much that sucks.

MATT

Raychel is quiet during dinner while the rest of us argue about football and TV shows and whether the weather forecast is right. There's an awkward moment when Andrew asks why her eyes are so red, and another when Dad wants to know if Andrew's signed up for the next ACT and gives him a lecture on responsibility. But Mom starts telling us about the excuses her law students give for missing class ("He said he had a guild raid on *World of Warcraft!*"), and by the end, even Raychel's laughing.

And then, over dessert, Dad says, "So, Raychel, I've been thinking. Did you hear my office assistant quit?"

She shakes her head. "I'm sorry."

"Oh, it's fine," he says. "She was terrible anyway. But I was thinking—would you like to work for me? Just part-time, very flexible so you don't have to worry about school, nothing too strenuous. You'd mostly be doing data entry. I can't let you take things home, of course, but you're here all the time—"

"That'd be great," she interrupts, her face lighting up. "I don't have a computer anyway."

"Great, great," Dad says. "We can hammer out the details later, but if you want the job . . . ?" He leaves it hanging like a question.

"Did you put him up to this?" she asks me.

"Definitely not," I say, my mouth full of cake. I may have

mentioned she got fired, but I thought Dad might have leads. I didn't expect him to give her a job himself.

"Okay," she says, with a real smile. "That would be fantastic, actually. Thank you."

"Oh no, thank you!" He grins. "Wait until you see the pile of work I have for you."

"I can't wait." She sounds like she means it.

· · · · ·

After dinner, we take turns playing pool. "Are you going hiking tomorrow?" Andrew asks.

"We were going to do Roger's Hollow, now that Raych's ankle is back to normal," I say, "but it's supposed to rain."

"You want to come?" Raychel asks him. It annoys me, but then again, we just said the trip's unlikely anyway.

"Yeah, if you end up going." He lines up a shot and misses. "You should come to Cruz's party tonight," he says, stepping aside so Raych can shoot. "It's at his parents' lake cabin, so there's no way it'll get busted."

"Can't," Raychel says, and sinks a ball. "Asha and Spencer are coming over."

"Good luck with that," he says, punching me in the arm. Asha is nice, but she talks. A lot. They arrive right as he's leaving, and we try to watch a movie, but Asha chats through most of it, telling Raychel about her eighty-seven cousins and how her sister's refusal to have a traditional wedding is making the entire family argue. I wonder if Spencer has developed some kind of superpower that lets him tune her out, because he stares at the television the entire time, laughing at the funny parts. At least they look funny.

But after they leave, it's just Raychel and me. She beats me at pool, I beat her at some video games, and we both beat our personal records for how much cookie dough we can fit in our mouths. We laugh so much that Mom has to get out of bed to tell us it's 2 a.m. and time to shut up, so we leave the mess for morning cleanup and tromp up the stairs out of earshot.

It's just like old times: a couple of hours to ourselves after hanging out with our friends. That's probably why we've been bickering so much lately. Our only buffer these days is Andrew, who does nothing but annoy me, and combined with all my weird feelings for Raych that weren't there before . . .

It's just nice to remember why we ended up best friends in the first place.

·　·　·　·　·

The next day is not so idyllic.

After we finally go to bed, Raychel stays in the guest room all night. I try not to be annoyed that I've woken up alone, since it means she managed to sleep well on her own, and she needed it after her little meltdown.

But it seems to set the tone for my entire Saturday. Andrew's hungover, snapping at everyone until Mom sends him out to clean the garage as punishment. This morning's rain has petered out, so I suggest we hike Twin Falls instead, but Raych shoots that idea down.

"We could float," I say, waiting for her to make the next move in a thrilling game of Scrabble. "The Mulberry will be flowing and Dad said we can take the canoe."

She wrinkles her nose, staring down at her tiles. "Let's just hang here."

"If Nathan was around, he'd go with me," I say, teasing.

But it pisses her off instead. "Well you're stuck with me, so suck it up." She leans over the table, bra strap peeking out of the old T-shirt she borrowed from me this morning. "Triple word score."

· · · · ·

The rain returns as thunderstorms, which makes the argument moot. After she beats me at board games, we go upstairs to read, and she curls into the papasan chair by my window. "What do you want to listen to?" I ask.

She shrugs. "Something mellow."

I hit shuffle on my rainy-day playlist and stretch out on the bed. We're both working on projects for the senior seminar we're taking. It's kind of an independent study, kind of not. We're all assigned a bunch of reading, and we have weekly class discussions that the teacher, Ms. Moses, leads, but we also pick our favorite book and create a presentation about it for the final. Mine's *Crime and Punishment*. Raychel's changed hers so many times I can't keep track.

Over the top of my book, the curtains frame her, rain

streaming down the glass behind. She's tucked her knees inside my T-shirt, and I bite my tongue because she's stretching it out. She glances up. "What?"

I shake my head. "Nothing." But she knows, giving an exasperated sigh as she pulls her legs out and sits cross-legged. "What are you reading?" I ask to distract her from the fact that I'm a picky pain in the ass.

"The Handmaid's Tale." She shows me the cover.

"Oh." I sit up and settle against the headboard. "I couldn't get into that."

"But the imagery is so amazing!" She lays the book on one leg. "When she's talking about the sound the rim of a wet glass makes and says something like, 'That's what I feel like, the word *shatter*'? Or the women using butter as lotion because they have nothing else, like they're just . . . food or something?" Her wide eyes wait for me to take it back.

I probably should, but I don't. "No, yeah, I mean . . . I guess the writing is good—"

"You *guess*?"

"It's so . . . flowery." I rush on as her eyes narrow. "But I mean—okay, writing aside, the story itself is sort of boring."

"Boring?" she repeats incredulously. "The United States is taken over by religious extremists who basically enslave women and it's *boring*?"

"Yeah, that's the problem." I put my own book down. "We don't see any of that. We just follow the main character around the house all day."

"Okay, first of all, that's not even true, and secondly, those parts are like, half the point!" Raychel pushes her hair out of her face. "She *can't* leave—"

"Yeah, but she barely even tries."

Raychel stares at me. "Because she'll *die*," she says slowly, like she's translating.

"Wouldn't that be better?"

"Seriously?"

"Okay, maybe not," I backtrack, recognizing the look in Raychel's eye. It is the *I would happily put your balls in a vise right now* look. "I mean, it's just not believable if we never even learn how they got into that situation in the first place."

"Because it's what already happens!" She sees my involuntary eyebrow raise. "Women have been treated like that for thousands of years and we just accept it with no explanation—"

"Well it's not very convincing in *this* book," I interrupt, trying to end the argument. "To me, anyway."

She crosses her arms and huffs. "This from the guy who's read *Lord of the Rings* ten times. Where, I might add, women are treated—"

"That's different," I say. "That's fantasy, not misguided commentary on society."

I expect more argument, but her mouth closes, and her whole body seems to shut me out. "It's just my opinion," I add. "I didn't mean to hurt your feelings."

She glares. "Yes, my delicate feelings are definitely the problem here."

She's pissed that I apologized? "I didn't—"

"Oh, I know." She shakes her head and picks up her book, face disappearing between the dark blue cover and dark gray window. A female figure in red in the corner is the only blot of color. I didn't finish the book yet, but from what I've read, I'm guessing she got herself stuck there, and though I hate to admit it, it's easy to see why Raych likes the story so much. I feel bad that things are so hard for her right now, and her parents are obviously terrible, but she's the one who got so drunk that she was late to work. She's the one who decided to hook up with Carson. She's the one who continues to get trashed at parties but never wants to face the consequences.

Everything is always everyone else's fault. Nothing is ever hers.

RAYCHEL

I go home Saturday night instead of staying over because Matt is being such a bitch. I was so happy, getting a job offer and some time with Asha *and* a fun night with Matt—and then he had to ruin it. He acts like I'm hormonal, but I swear he has his own *men*-strual cycle. Funny how unfunny the joke is when it's about him.

I stay up late and try to finish that "misguided commentary" he "couldn't get into." He wants it spelled out for him, how a world like that could happen, but won't even let me finish a sentence to explain. Must be nice, not being able to fathom a world where you're the bottom rung, being so sure of your opinion that you judge a book by what you wanted in it instead of what's actually there.

I'm restless most of the night, and I fall asleep so late that I don't wake up until eleven on Sunday. Mom is still crashed. Not surprising, since I heard her come in at one. I make lunch and then put my frustration into doing chores. I don't mind cleaning. Mom spends all her time picking up after other people's kids. She shouldn't have to pick up after me.

For a minute, I consider talking to her about Matt, or even Carson. But I know she'll be smug about Matt, who she thinks is a stuck-up rich boy. And I don't want her to guilt-trip herself for letting me go to parties and stuff. Mom trusts me to be responsible because she thinks she's the best example of what can go wrong.

Which means me. She ended up with me. I'm what can go wrong.

So I'm left to either mentally rehash my argument with Matt, or else replay that night with Carson, trying to find something I missed. Some way he and I misunderstood each other. Because the truth is, I want to be wrong. I don't necessarily want to give him a second chance, but I do want to believe that I just didn't make myself clear. He thought we were on the same page. He thinks he did nothing wrong.

Or maybe he thinks his mistake was not admitting he actually likes me.

I swipe a rag over the bathroom mirror, not looking at my reflection. If that's the case, I don't want to lead him on. And surely if I keep turning him down, he'll get the message eventually.

I hope.

. . . . .

Mom doesn't emerge from her bed until I'm cleaning the living room. "You're still here," she says, yawning.

"Sorry, I tried to be quiet."

"You didn't wake me." She shuffles into the kitchen.

"I made mac and cheese," I call after her. It's gross because we're out of butter, but she'll figure that out soon enough. She bangs around and returns with a bowl of toxic-orange noodles. "Ew, cold?"

"Doesn't taste any better warm," she says, her mouth full. "You have fun at Matt's?"

"It was fine. We did a lot of homework."

I can't tell if her expression is disbelief or pity. "Well, at least you'll have fun with Asha tonight."

"Nope," I say, more rudely than I intended. "She bailed." We were supposed to hang out, but apparently even Sunday night is party night in college—and apparently I'm not invited. Not that I was in the mood anyway. "Oh hey, I got a new job though."

Mom swallows another mouthful of pasta. "Why?"

"Um . . ." I decide to keep it simple. "Dr. Richardson offered me a better-paying position, so I took it."

"Oh." She taps her spoon against the bowl lightly. "Don't you think you spend enough time there already?"

I shrug. "Now I'll be earning my keep."

"I just think you rely on them too much."

I swivel around to face her. "It's not an allowance. I'll be *working.*"

"Okay," she says, taking another bite. "If that's what you want to call it."

"What I want is for you to get over your problem with the Richardsons." I dump my cleaning supplies in the middle of the coffee table. Trust Mom to shit on the one thing that's going right in my life at the moment. "We need the money, remember?"

It's a low blow, but it shuts her up until she knocks on my door an hour later, telling me she's heading out. I don't even ask where she's going. "I'll be late," she calls.

Good, I think, but don't bother to answer.

. . . . .

I finish my math homework. I paint my toenails. I watch Dallas beat the Giants, and the Packers lose to the Seahawks, and I make myself a sandwich for dinner, but neither Mom nor Matt calls to apologize.

Mom's no surprise, but I thought Matt would at least check

to see if I still want a ride tomorrow. I don't, and the fact that my reliance on him proves Mom right makes me so angry that I decide to just call him and prove them both wrong.

But a strange voice picks up his phone. "Yo."

"Matt?" I demand.

"Better."

All my indignation deflates with a whoosh. It's Andrew. "Why are you answering your brother's phone?"

"He went to a movie with Mom and left it here. Is this a booty call?"

I snort. "Not so much. I was just . . ." Pissed. Sad. Lonely. "Bored."

"You want some company?"

"Here?" Matt comes over occasionally, but I've never had Andrew over by himself.

"Yeah," Andrew says. "I got a B on my chemistry test, so I got my car back."

"I'm okay."

"I don't mind." He switches to a teasing tone. "I'd be happy to come kick your butt at *Mario Kart*."

"I don't have it," I admit.

"That explains why you suck so much."

· · · · ·

While I wait, I look around for embarrassing things to put away. "Boobs" do not occur to me until I open the door and cold air rushes in, reminding me I never put on a bra.

"Uh . . ." Andrew's been rendered speechless by my nipples.

"Hi," I say loudly. He blinks and holds out a shopping bag. "What's that?"

"*Mario Kart*. And provisions."

"Provisions" turns out to be chocolate, weed, chips, games, and real Dr Pepper. We sit on the back porch with the light off and smoke from his red glass pipe, which he says will make me cough less. He's right. Our neighbors are grad students, so at least I don't have to worry about them telling Mom. She'll kill me if she finds out I'm "doing drugs," even if pot's legal all over the place now. Sometimes she hints that my dad was into the real stuff. But god forbid she ever tell me the whole story.

Back inside, Andrew holds out some choices. "You want to play a real game?" he asks.

I shake my head. "I hate that shooting shit."

"Racing it is." We sit on opposite ends of the couch and play track after track. I'm even worse stoned. After my *Donkey Kong* character crashes into yet another wall, Andrew takes a bathroom break, and when he returns, he moves closer to me. "So Raych," he says, while forcing me to sit through the entirety of another cartoon trophy ceremony. "What's the deal with you and Carson?"

I pretend the fireworks over Bowser's castle are fascinating. "Nothing. Why."

"He was just saying some stuff, asking me about you."

My grip tightens on the controller. "Well, tell him to screw off," I say, a little too aggressively.

Andrew laughs. "That's more or less what I said."

I try not to show how surprised I am that Andrew defended me. "I thought y'all were friends."

"He's always been kind of an asshole. That's part of why I quit baseball—most of the team's that way." He changes his character to Luigi, which reminds me of the year that was his Halloween costume and Matt was Mario. "I'm glad you two aren't . . . you know."

"Yeah. No. We're definitely not."

Discussing Carson should make me tense, but knowing that Andrew dislikes him actually makes me relax. We goof off and joke as usual, play-fighting over races until we're sitting so close that our legs touch. I pretend not to notice, but it's nice. Unexpectedly comfortable.

And maybe it's just the weed, but the conversation gets more personal too. "I actually want to go to Duke," he admits. "But I bombed my first try at the ACT."

"You can always take it again," I argue. "Do a test-prep class or something."

"Yeah, I guess." He picks Kalimari Desert for our next bout. "I thought Dad would be psyched, but it seems like he's put all his hopes into Matt."

"He'll figure it out," I say, frowning at the screen. "Matt'll end up at a little liberal arts school and you can carry on the legacy."

Andrew's already listened to my many conversations with Matt about college, so he changes the subject. "When do you start your new job?"

"Tomorrow," I say with relief. "You're going to get sick of me being around all the time."

"Doubt it." He bumps my shoulder.

"Good thing, because I need the money." I fill him in on my current situation, but Andrew doesn't offer a single suggestion.

He just squeezes my knee. "I'm sorry, dude. That sucks." And then he hits me with a turtle shell and cackles. I can't help but laugh too.

. . . . .

We wrap up our night at ten, when my mom texts to say she'll be home in an hour. Andrew looks at his phone too. "It's getting kind of late," he says, slipping it back in his pocket. "And you've got a big day tomorrow." We stand at the same time, staying closer than necessary. "Workin' girl."

I don't know what else to say, but I don't really want to move away. "Oh, you know what? I still have your Dead shirt."

"You keep it."

"Are you sure?"

Andrew touches my arm. There's no spark, no jolt, no surge between us, but his hand drags down to mine and pulls me closer. "Oh, I'm sure."

It feels like my bones aren't connected to one another. Like my muscles have gone on strike. "Raych . . ." he says, like it's a warning.

I don't answer, just look at him, trying to discern the question so I can figure out the answer. I force some words over my lips. "Thanks for coming over."

"You sounded sad." When I nod, he reaches for my face. I've never seen Andrew act like this. "I like you. I don't like when you're sad."

It's such a simple statement but, *god*. There are tears in my eyes. What the hell is happening? Andrew lowers his head toward mine and my brain turns to sponge. Our lips touch. Then we're kissing harder and he's stepping backward, knees buckling when he runs into the couch. I climb on top, straddling his lap, and kiss him. And kiss him. And kiss him.

But when his hand drags up my ribs, I pull away, to see if he will too.

And he does. "Sorry," he says, breathing hard. "Is this okay?"

"I'm just a little ticklish," I lie.

He presses his forehead against mine. "I've wanted to kiss you for a long, long time," he admits.

I can't say the same, but I can tell him something true. "I'm really glad you did."

MATT

I tear my room apart looking for my phone, but it doesn't materialize until Andrew tosses it on my bed before school Monday morning. "You missed a call."

"You stole my phone?" I throw a pillow at him.

He dodges. "No, dumbass, you left it on the kitchen counter. I grabbed it for you." No missed calls show up, but Raychel is on the recent list. "I answered it for you too," he says.

"Goddamnit, Andrew." He's going to make me ask. "And? What did she want?"

"I dunno," he says, holding his hands up when I grab another pillow. "But she was bored so I went over there to hang out."

Of course he invited himself over. "That poor girl. What did you do?"

"We played video games, mostly." He turns to leave, slapping the top of my doorframe as he goes. "Oh hey—she said she doesn't need a ride this morning."

Her mom must be headed that way. A minute later, I hear the garage door opening, and glance at the clock to make sure I'm not late. But it's still early.

I make a mental note to check hell for ice.

· · · · ·

I wait for Raychel at her locker. A red rose is sticking out of the vent, and when she and Andrew walk up, she looks at me suspiciously. "Is this an apology?" she asks.

My forehead furrows. "Uh, no." I don't even know what I'm supposed to be sorry for.

She twirls the stem between her fingers. "Oh. Weird."

I glance at my brother, suspicious of his early-morning rush. "Don't look at me," he says. "I'm not that slick."

She laughs. "I'm impressed enough that you got us here on time."

Asshole. *He's* why she didn't need a ride. I think over our weekend, looking for a reason I'm in the doghouse. "Are you still mad about the book thing?" I ask, then rush ahead when she glares. "I mean, sorry. About the book thing." It's hard to apologize when you're not really sorry.

She rolls her eyes. "Thanks so much. How was the movie?"

Andrew watches with a grin I'd like to smush into the floor. It should be a rule that little brothers have to stay littler in size forever. "It was okay. Kind of boring," I tell her. I'm definitely not going to complain about what a chick flick it was.

"Oh hey," Raychel says to Andrew, digging in her backpack. "You left this." She hands him his pipe, keeping it hidden between their palms.

"I guess *you* two had fun last night," I say rudely. Raychel's life is hard enough without Andrew getting her suspended for possession.

"Oh yeah, we . . ." Andrew glances at her, and something in their expressions turns my anger into dread. It hadn't occurred to me that they'd smoke, and now I'm wondering what else they did. "She still sucks really bad at *Mario Kart*."

But my trepidation disappears as she puts the flower behind her ear. "Matt's right. You're an asshole."

He shrugs, grinning at me. "It's genetic."

RAYCHEL

Awkward.

I figured Matt would be a little weird about me hanging out with Andrew on my own, but he's acting like someone took his favorite toy. It doesn't encourage me to fill him in on any other details. Not that it's any of his business, or that there's much to tell. I'm not deluding myself into thinking that a little kissing with Andrew means anything. He's a notorious manwhore and I'm . . . well, whatever I am, he's not expecting a white picket fence and 2.5 kids.

But we did have fun. I actually slept well for the first time in a while, and I woke up excited to start my new job—like maybe things are going to turn around. I even made up with Mom over breakfast.

And then I get to calculus. "Pretty," Carson says, grinning.

"What?" He points at the rose behind my ear and my shock subsides. "Oh, yeah. Someone left it in my locker."

"Did they?" He looks amused . . . or maybe smug.

"Please take your seat, Ms. Sanders," Mrs. Nguyen calls.

I sit, letting the disappointment sink in. It hadn't crossed my mind that the flower might be from him, and I don't want to give him the satisfaction of knowing I liked it. I lay it on the corner of my desk and leave it there when the bell rings.

· · · · ·

My new job doesn't disappoint, however. Andrew drives me to his house, where Dr. R. is waiting to show me the ropes. "Basically, we've had these sitting around forever," he explains, showing me the stack of files in his home office. "It's all old financial stuff, nothing patient-related, but no one at the clinic has had time to weed through it. We just need you to organize things and get them in the computer."

"Sounds easy enough. Do you want me to work certain hours?" Dr. R. has a busy schedule—some days he has appointments, some days he's on call at the hospital, and it's rarely the same week to week.

He shakes his head. "Whenever's convenient." We figure out a few details, and he promises that when this project is over, he'll find something else for me to do. Then his phone goes off. "Damn," he says, looking at the screen. "I'm sorry, I have to go in. But I really appreciate your help, Raychel."

"It's no problem. I . . . Thanks, Dr. R."

He smiles and heads for the hospital. I get to my own work. He wasn't kidding—some of these files are ancient. The first box is printed on that paper with hole-punched perforated edges. I get through about an hour before the dust is more than I can handle, then head for the kitchen to get a drink.

Andrew has his head in the fridge. "You want a Dr Pepper?" he asks.

"Yup." I boost myself onto the counter and take the can from his hand. "What are you doing?"

"Just went for a run. Thought I'd see how your first day on the new job was going." He wedges himself between my knees.

Okay then. Round two. "It's going pretty well." I open my can and take a sip.

He steps closer, playing with the hem of my shirt. "Look, about last night—" I start to respond and he pretends to pinch my lips shut. "I was thinking. I know you have your 'rule' and all . . ."

I look down. I'm weirdly bummed out by this rejection, even though I wasn't expecting anything more.

"Hey," he says, and I meet his eyes. "I'm just saying—I'm up for whatever. But maybe if we keep it quiet, you could . . ."

His hands on my thighs are very distracting. "What?" I ask.

"Reconsider your rule. Plus then my parents won't be breathing down our necks."

Relief bubbles up as laughter. "Maybe I could."

"It's something to think about." But before I can think, he leans in and kisses me. I wrap my legs around his calves to pull him closer.

The garage door slams and we break apart, laughing nervously under our breath. I assume it's Matt coming home, but instead Mrs. R. calls, "You kids want pizza?"

"Does the pope shit in the woods?" Andrew calls back.

"Andrew. Richardson."

"Sorry." He winks at me.

I wink back. The perks of my new job are awesome.

MATT

When I get home Monday evening, Andrew's already taken Raychel home. He's also eaten all the veggie pizza, which I know he doesn't even like, he's left my favorite vinyl album out of its cover, and he's dropped a wet towel on top of my laundry. We don't talk until bedtime, when I need something from the bathroom while he's brushing his teeth. I can't keep myself from asking, "So what'd you guys really do last night?"

He exhales loudly and spittle sprays the glass. It reminds me of Raychel stealth-popping a zit: something pretty high on the list of things that should gross me out, and yet it's okay when she does it, probably because I know she'd never do it in front of anyone else. "We just enjoyed each other's company," Andrew says, widening his eyes innocently.

"Just . . . tell me you're not screwing her, okay?" Even using that phrase feels wrong, but I can't admit that I care who Raychel might or might not be sleeping with, especially if that person might be him.

"No," he says, and laughs at my visible relief. "I am not going to screw her." And he walks out of the room, leaving me wondering if we're using the same definition of the word.

· · · · ·

In the morning, his alarm wakes me up. Sometimes I bang on the wall, but today I let him sleep through it. He stumbles into the kitchen thirty minutes later, yawning as usual, and accidentally puts salt in his coffee.

I don't even laugh. I just jangle my keys in his direction and say, "See you at school." He knows I'm driving Raychel, and if he doesn't, he'll figure it out soon enough.

And that's all it takes to reestablish our morning routine. But the afternoons change, for obvious reasons: since she's going to work at our house, it makes sense for her to catch a ride with him when I have after-school stuff. I can't complain, but it makes me look forward to basketball season, when he'll be staying after school as much as me.

I still have Raychel all to myself at lunch, though, and it's amazing how much her mood improves with a few days of work. I don't find my own responsibilities nearly as fulfilling, and I wonder if it's because I don't get paid. Homework feels like a full-time job, plus there's Outdoor Club, Key Club, extra time in the darkroom for photography, staying in shape for soccer season coming up . . .

By the time Friday rolls around, I'm exhausted, and I still have to meet up with Mindy for StuCo responsibilities. We're already behind, and it's my fault: I'm busy, but also I'm trying not to give Mindy the wrong idea. She's pretty and smart and friendly and ambitious, and if *I* were smart, I would probably ask her out on a date.

But I'm not smart. I'm stupidly hung up on my best friend, whose indecipherable love life and mood swings are slowly driving me insane.

I meet Mindy in the parking lot, and she insists on driving this time because she has to be back at school by six to cheer at the game. "Where are we headed?" I ask. StuCo wants to give the teachers gift baskets with little . . . somethings in them.

"I thought we could go to Pharm-Co?" She makes the slowest left-hand turn I've ever seen. "They have those bulk bins of nail polish and stuff—" She laughs at my confused expression. "They do. I promise."

"If you say so." It's not like I have any better ideas. Mindy chatters about how Rosa doesn't want StuCo to sponsor a talent show this year because she wants to have a winter dance instead. It's not a subtle segue. "Do you have a date for Homecoming?" she asks.

"Nah. I'm not going." I was actually going to ask Raychel, but last night she and Andrew were talking a lot of trash about the dance, so I don't think she wants to go. "But you're going with Trenton, right?" I ask, trying to keep the conversation light.

Mindy laughs. "No. I might ask Alan Li."

"You guys will have fun," I say.

"Yeah." Then she's quiet, and I realize that was my cue to ask her out. But I don't want to, and now I don't know what to say. I don't want to hurt her feelings, but I can't seem to avoid it, so I stay quiet too.

RAYCHEL

So far, Andrew's been good about letting me get actual work done in the afternoons, but Friday he cannot be deterred. "So Raych," he says, kicking back in his dad's office chair. "You really don't want to go to Homecoming?"

It's all I can do not to flop onto the floor in mental exhaustion. The truth is that I'd like to go with Andrew, but that would kind of ruin the whole secrecy thing. And anyway, Carson already asked me. Sort of. Thursday, he walked into calculus and handed me a cup from Coffee Depot with a big smile. "What's this?" I asked.

"It's for you."

"Okay . . ." I took the lid off to make sure it wasn't some kind of joke. "Um . . . thanks?"

"I knew you liked that place because I've seen you there when I cut their grass," he said, and pointed. "Two sugars, whole milk."

"How did you know my order?"

"I asked Chloe, the barista. I warmed it up in the cafeteria," he added as the first sip burned my mouth.

"Right. Well. Thanks."

"Sure." He smiled. "Listen, is Matt taking you to Homecoming?"

I almost choked on the coffee. "Um . . . no. Sort of," I sputtered, trying to cut off his next question. "We're not going. But we have . . . plans."

Carson frowned, but he was nice about it. Andrew, on the other hand, had a field day when I confessed the embarrassing scene to him on the way to his house yesterday. "You shot down Carson Tipton?" he asked, laughing, and high-fived me across the car. He also made me do a victory lap when we got out. And then he made Homecoming jokes all night, much to Matt's confusion.

I'll admit, I partly told Andrew just to see if he'd be jealous. And I can't tell where his current question is leading. So I laugh. "No," I say. "Last year was boring." Matt took Hana, and I went stag with Bree and a few single guys. We had dinner at the Waffle House and left the dance early to go bowling.

Andrew puts his legs on his dad's desk. "Dances suck."

"True." I push his feet aside to rescue the file beneath them. "So why'd you ask?"

"I thought we could do something else instead."

I don't know if he's suggesting a date or what, but it doesn't really matter. "What about Matt?" I ask.

He makes a face.

MATT

After shopping, I go work out, which puts me home after dinner. "Man, what are y'all planning for StuCo?" Raychel asks. "World domination?"

"I got stuck doing some errands with Mindy before I hit the gym."

"Oooh," Andrew sings. "Miiiiindyyyyy . . ."

Raychel laughs, but she moves on. "Get some food," she tells me. "We're having movie night."

I want to complain that they made the decision without me, but at least we're not going out. In the game room, all three of us flop together on the L-shaped couch like a pile of puppies. It used to be a bigger pile, when all our friends were here, and Raychel points to the armchair. "Doesn't it seem weird that Nathan and the Ice Queen aren't sitting together over there?"

Andrew laughs but I shrug, fiddling with the remote control. "They'll be home for fall break in a few weeks."

"It doesn't bug you, how MIA everyone's been?" she asks.

"I get texts from them all the time." I guess the real truth is that I hear from Nathan once or twice a week and the other guys sporadically, but the conversation moves on before I can elaborate.

"Well, I don't," Andrew says, feigning insult. "Except from Eliza. She wants me to defrost her."

"She's just . . . reserved," I insist.

Raychel snorts, leaning against me with her legs across Andrew's lap. "She's never reserved her opinion about me."

"She likes you fine." We've been having this argument since freshman year, when Eliza was my girlfriend and got fed up with Raychel being around all the time. We're cool now, but the girls never really worked things out.

"Yeah, no," Raych says, still laughing, and Andrew joins in. "That is false. Eliza hates my guts."

Eliza can be cold, but to be fair, so can Raychel. "She has a lot going on."

"Being a band geek is so time-consuming." Andrew steals the clicker so he can get the movie started.

"It is, actually, but you know she worries a lot about her sister," I say.

"Why?" Andrew asks.

"She has cystic fibrosis."

"So?"

"So that can be fatal," I snap. "So be cool." The opening credits come on and I realize we're watching a vampire movie. Worse, it's the first in a series. "I cannot believe you guys are making me watch this."

"Um, some of us are actually looking forward to it," Raychel says.

I glance at Andrew, who shrugs, but more in a *you lose* way than commiserating. And I have to admit, the movie does turn out to be pretty funny, just not always on purpose. "Whoa!" Andrew yells during a scene halfway through. "He bit her!" He falls off the couch, writhing on the floor to imitate the screaming actress.

I play along, dropping to my knees to take his hand. "It'll be okay!" I say, attempting to mimic the actor's horrible accent.

"Don't you kiss me, you bastard." Andrew jumps to his feet

and we square off like bears. He falls but manages to grab my legs and take me down too.

Raych pulls her feet up onto the couch and steals the popcorn. "Oh shit, that girl vampire pulled his head off."

"Really?" Andrew lets go of me and leans against the couch, reaching up for a handful of popcorn, and I follow suit, leaning against Raych's knee. The scene changes from a funeral pyre to another character scattering ashes over a field. "That's what I'd want," Andrew says.

"To die in a fire?" Raych says.

"No, I mean after I die. No coffin. I'd rather be cremated."

"Definitely," I agree. "Throw me off Eagle Point or something." They both nod. The conversation is kind of disconcerting, but less for the topic than for how open Andrew is being. I'm not used to this sincere little brother of mine, especially not in front of Raychel. It's kind of a nice change.

Then another vampire gets staked through the heart, blood and gore spattering the camera lens. "Holy shit!" Andrew yells, and we're laughing again.

RAYCHEL

Saturday morning, Matt's gone before the rest of us wake up. "Do we have to do this?" Andrew complains, pouring milk into his Fruity Pebbles.

"Yes." I pop some bread into the toaster. "Be a good brother. At least he didn't rope us into helping, like that thing for Key Club." The Outdoor Club is having a fund-raiser at the Farmers' Market, so I told Matt we'd come buy a couple of the reusable water bottles they're selling. It beats the afternoon Andrew spent in a dunking booth last year while I collected money and another sunburn.

"Okay, but we don't have to stay long, right?"

I pat him on the head. "We'll do a lap around the square, say hi to Matt, and then we can leave."

We drive downtown, singing along to the soundtrack from last night's movie, which is considerably better than the film itself. Andrew finds us a parking spot a few blocks from the square, and opens my door while I'm looking for my sunglasses. "M'lady," he says, offering his hand. I take it, but he doesn't let go right away. Instead he pulls me closer.

I laugh and pull away. Last night I lay awake, wondering if I could sneak into Andrew's room. Thinking how awful it would be to get caught. Dr. R. just gave me a job, and Mrs. R. has been taking care of me for years. And it's not how I want Matt to find out. He's going to get suspicious sooner or later, and I'd rather the news come in a kinder way than him walking in on me and his brother together.

Andrew bumps my shoulder as we walk up the hill toward the crowded square, but doesn't take my hand again. I pretend it doesn't feel a little empty.

MATT

Autumn never really hits Big Springs until October, but I always forget and assume September mornings will be cool. By ten, I'm sweating through my T-shirt and wishing I'd worn shorts, not to mention a hat or something. Cruz mans the booth with me, calling out to passersby like a circus barker, so all I have to do is make change and friendly small talk.

Until my brother walks up with my best friend. I'm jealous, but they're bound to hang out more when I'm constantly doing school stuff. At least they seem to be just friends. If they had a thing going on, they would touch more, like Asha and Spencer, or make weird inside jokes like Nathan and Eliza. Raychel and Andrew just tease each other and make fun of me, like always.

"Matthew," he says, gesturing grandly at the table. "Give us two of your finest water bottles." I roll my eyes in disbelief when Raychel laughs. He ignores me and fist-bumps Cruz. "What's up, dude."

"Not much," Cruz says. "You busy later? Got a delivery from a friend over in Newton County."

A lot of the weed in this area comes from Mexico, but the rural areas east of us make their homegrown contributions. "I got plans," Andrew says. "How long y'all stuck here?"

"All day," I say. He already knows this. "Are you coming over for dinner?" I ask Raych.

She frowns. "I told my mom I'd eat with her tonight."

Frustrated, I drop the change I'm making for my brother. She kneels down to help me pick it up. "We could hike tomorrow?" she suggests.

"I can't. That Cal 3 class is kicking my ass and I've got to catch up."

"I'll come over and do homework with you," she says.

That's not what I want. I want to do fun things with her, and goof off. But it's better than nothing. "Okay," I say, standing up and handing her the rest of the change. "That'd be good."

She gives me a hug, but it doesn't make it any easier to watch her walk away with Andrew.

RAYCHEL

I assume we're going home after the market, but Andrew suggests we go to the park and climb on the castle.

I'm glad Matt can't hike tomorrow. It's too hot to even walk the mile trail around the park, but the castle is surrounded by shade trees. The base is made of stacked sandstone, perfect for climbing. Short plaster towers stretch up into fanciful shapes, some covered in tile mosaics, others adorned with gargoyle faces. The creek that bisects the park runs under a decorative concrete bridge, pooling into a half moat full of lily pads. It's not a majestic or awe-inspiring structure, but it's funky and weird and one of the things I like about our town. "You know," I tell Andrew, dipping my feet in the pond, "if I hadn't grown up here, Big Springs would be a great place for college."

"It's not *that* bad." He sits beside me on the bridge, our legs brushing. "I mean, it feels small sometimes, but it's really not."

"I guess." Our area has the same population as Albuquerque or Tucson, a fact I know thanks to all the university recruiting stuff. "It's not the size that bothers me," I tell him. "It's the people." The university's influence keeps Big Springs from being a Southern stereotype. But Dr. and Mrs. R. are always talking about the constant tensions between the academics, the hippies that moved in during the "back to the land" movement in the sixties and seventies, the yuppies that move here from the coasts to work for Walmart corporate, and the church conservative good 'ole boys who are more like the rest of the state. "I don't have the money or the connections to matter here, and I'm neither redneck nor crunchy enough to fit in otherwise."

"You've thought about this way too much." He splashes a little water on my thigh. "Come on, it's not that bad. We have awesome hiking, good local music, decent museums, sports teams that win every once in a while . . ." I laugh, because we almost never win, and he goes on. "I want to go to Duke, but if I have to stay here, it's not the end of the world." When I don't agree, he bumps our feet together. "Living on campus would be way different from living at home."

I don't point out that paying for room and board here might

still prove a challenge. "I guess it's not the place I want to escape," I say. "It's my place in this place."

He laughs.

"Seriously!" I say, splashing him back. "I could become president and this town would still think of me as 'that girl whose mom's a janitor.'" *That* slutty *girl whose mom's a janitor,* I add mentally.

"Hey, screw what they think," he says. His payback splash starts a war and we both end up in the pond.

· · · · ·

Later, I get Andrew to stop by the grocery store on our way to my house. Mom has been apologizing in her own way for not telling me about our financial situation—braiding my hair, packing my lunch, offering me lots of rides. I want to make an effort, so I decide to use my last Pharm-Co paycheck on groceries and surprise her with dinner. Or at least side dishes. I'm not above turning my effort into a ploy to get her to make me chicken fried steak.

But when Andrew drops me off, I find her crying on the couch. "Mom? Are you okay?" I drop the grocery bags, rush over, and put an arm around her. "What happened?" My mind races through the possibilities: She's sick. She's been fired. Her boyfriend dumped her.

Not on the list is, "We might get evicted."

I start to drop my arm, but she's crying so hard that I can't let go.

"I've used up my emergency money," she says.

"All of it?" I croak.

She nods her head miserably.

I drop my hands to my lap. I know what this means. She needs my college money. And if I pay the rent on the duplex, I'm resigning myself to at least another year in it—even the cheapest dorm in Big Springs is six thousand dollars a year, and meal plans are another four. For somewhere like Vanderbilt or Northwestern, it's closer to fifteen. Fifteen thousand dollars. Per year. I can barely make half of that in twelve months. Unless I quit school and work full time, which kind of defeats the purpose.

Defeated. Before I even start.

But there's no choice. "It's okay," I force myself to say. "Just use what's in my account." Standing up, I point to the groceries. "And put that food away," I tell her. "It'll go bad."

I walk to my room and go straight to bed.

MATT

As it turns out, I don't even get boring homework time with Raychel.

I call Sunday, but she doesn't answer, texting back later to say she's not feeling well. Andrew tries too, but she tells him the same thing.

I try not to gloat.

Monday morning, she still seems off, but assures me it's just a cold or something. She's not coughing or sneezing, but her eyes are red, which makes me think it's probably allergies. She doesn't seem to get better as the week goes on, but she doesn't get any worse either, so I quit pestering her to tell my dad. She'll get over it when the weather changes, and in the fall in Arkansas, that happens every other day.

Meanwhile, the school is in a pre-Homecoming craze. I don't see why we have to decorate a building that's already designed in our school colors, but I still end up helping Mindy and the rest of StuCo make the place impossibly more red and white. There are cardboard cowboys and cactuses and cow skulls as far as the eye can see.

Tuesday, we have an assembly to announce the Homecoming Court. When the last name called is Rosa's instead of Mindy's, Mindy's shoulders droop, but she still claps and cheers as they attach a giant corsage to Rosa's shirt. I pat her on the arm, wondering how she can care so much about this place and its opinions when we're so close to escaping it.

Raychel, on the other hand, doesn't even know who won. "Did you skip?" I ask at lunch, incredulous. Raych likes to pretend that she has a bad-girl reputation, but she never really breaks the rules. She works too hard, both at school and at work, to let something stupid like bad behavior mess up her college chances.

But she shrugs. "I just sat with Andrew and his friends on the back steps by the tennis court."

"You're lucky you didn't get caught."

"It was fine, Mother." She stands up, crumpling her paper bag. It's weird that her mom is making her lunches again. "Ms. Moses did almost catch us, but Eddie the janitor told her we were helping him look for some lost keys."

"At least someone around here is thinking," I mutter, and she gives me a dirty look.

RAYCHEL

My mom keeps apologizing, but it just makes me feel worse. I adjust my schedule so I see her as little as possible, only texting her the essentials when it's unavoidable.

It's unexpectedly easy to convince Matt I'm just sick. I started to tell him the truth, but part of me is holding out hope for a miracle. Most of me, however, is too depressed to even bring it up. He'll just lecture me about scholarships and not giving up, and while I appreciate his positive attitude, I'm positive I would rather not hear it at the moment.

But he doesn't really seem to notice anything's wrong.

Andrew, on the other hand, had the truth out of me by the time we got to his house Monday afternoon. He didn't give me advice. He just gave me a hug and let me get to work.

At least I didn't blow any cash on a Homecoming dress. The event buzz at school is nothing but background noise to me, and Carson is like an annoying bee. Every day, he gives me some kind of compliment—something I can't ignore, but can't bring myself to appreciate either. On Wednesday, he brings me a doughnut, and accepting it makes me wonder if I'm somehow being unfaithful to Andrew. I want to slap the question out of my head the minute it appears.

"It sucks that you're missing the dance," Carson says. "But you should meet me at the after-party, at Trenton the Third's house."

"What will your date think about that?" I ask.

He shrugs. "I'm only taking Haley because her parents will freak if she goes with her girlfriend."

I pause. "That is . . . weirdly nice of you."

"Weirdly?" He tilts his head. "I'm a nice guy."

"Yeah." My fingers toy with the lid on my coffee cup. "I guess you are." What's weird is that I almost mean it.

· · · · ·

Asha calls Thursday with an invitation for Saturday night. "Hey," I say. "Long time no see."

She huffs. "It hasn't been that long. What are you up to?"

"You know. The usual." I consider telling her about Andrew, but Asha tends to confuse secrets and public knowledge when she drinks.

"Well, Spencer said Matt told him that y'all are being your usual boring selves and skipping Homecoming, so I think you should come with us to a party at Liam's frat instead."

Liam is a kid who graduated with Asha and Spencer last year, but I don't know him very well. "Didn't he rush—"

"I know," she interrupts. "His frat is super weak. That's actually part of why he wants y'all to come—he's hoping Andrew will be a recruit. They're going to lose their house if they don't get more members in the next year or two."

My feelings are a little hurt that Asha's not the one who wants to see us. "I don't think Andrew is staying here for school."

She snorts. "Please, Andrew is going to smoke his way to a 2.0 and party his way through college. He's staying here."

I can't argue she's wrong without giving myself away, but it makes me feel bad for the times I would have laughed and agreed. "If you say so," I say instead. "I'll talk to the boys and see what they want to do."

MATT

Friday afternoons are usually the least crowded time to be in the weight room, and I'm looking forward to burning off some frustration. It's been another long week, with Mindy hounding me about StuCo responsibilities, Cal 3 being basically incomprehensible, and even my parents complaining that I dropped the ball on some chores.

But after I've been there about fifteen minutes, Carson and some of the baseball team stroll in. "You gettin' ready for soccer?" he asks.

"Yeah." I wipe my forehead. "Baseball's a ways off, though, isn't it?"

He shrugs. "Can't start too soon."

I nod and wait for him to step away, but he stays. "You need a spot?"

"Yeah," he says. "I can wait though."

"Nah, it's cool." The faster I get it over with, the faster I can get back to my own workout. I'm pretty strong from rock climbing, and taller than Carson, but he outweighs me by at least fifty pounds, and he's pressing two of me. He does several reps, letting the bar bounce off his chest for help, but I'm not about to critique his form when he could wrap me around the bench.

On the last rep I'm scared he's going to blow the tendons out of his arms, but he manages to get the bar back into place. "Shit," he says, breathing hard. "You need one?"

"I'm good, thanks."

"Cool." He goes about his business and I go about mine, but he comes back while I'm doing pull-ups. I crank out twenty more, just to prove I can. "So," he says, when I drop to the floor. "You and Sanders. Y'all sure hang out a lot."

Damnit. I towel my hair, hiding my face for a moment. "Well," I say, dropping the towel to my shoulders, "she's my best friend, so that's bound to happen."

"Cool." I take a gulp of water right as he says, "She gives good head."

Choking, I dry off the front of my shirt. "Uh . . ." It doesn't seem like he's bragging or trying to piss me off, just stating a fact. The mental picture makes me want to bleach my brain. "I . . . wouldn't know," I say finally.

"Bummer." He stretches, giant muscles popping under his skin. "What's she doing tomorrow?"

I'm not her goddamn pimp, I want to say, but I shake my head. "We have plans." *But they won't include you.* Not if I have anything to do with it.

RAYCHEL

Predictably, Andrew wants to go to the frat party. Matt does not.

"I thought we were having movie night," he says, absently shuffling through the files I've just put in alphabetical order. It's the first time he's made it home from school early enough to see that I'm doing real work.

"We had movie night last weekend," I point out. It feels like a million years ago. I've spent as much time as possible over here working. I had hoped I'd also spend a lot of time kissing Andrew, but he hasn't been around—he keeps saying he has a study group, which has to be a joke. He doesn't owe me an explanation if he just wants to hang with other friends, but it's not like him to pass up secret make-out opportunities.

I wonder if he's already losing interest.

I wish I didn't care so much. But I'm bummed. I thought I'd worked out the best kind of relationship—reliable, fun, and not completely without feeling, but without the public scrutiny that goes along with having an official boyfriend.

Instead I have Carson making all these public gestures, and I can't help but wish it was Andrew instead.

. . . . .

Later that night, I'm wide awake when Andrew sneaks into the guest room. We've never made out in here before, and never in a bed. We don't say a single word to each other, but the need to stay quiet makes everything feel more intense. More real. More like I'm communicating things I never meant to say.

We go farther than we ever have, until we're both sweaty and panting and I have to break the silence to say stop, even though we're both wishing for more. And he doesn't push it. But he doesn't stay. When we start falling asleep, he kisses my eyelids and stands up. It seems like he wants to tell me something, and I sit up because his expression makes me think I'll need to be solid and stable to hear it.

But a creak from downstairs sends him on a hasty escape. I lose another hour of sleep wondering if that was an *It's been nice, but it's done* kind of look, or . . . something else.

Both possibilities scare me.

Saturday, I use the constant stream of football games on TV as an excuse to ignore both boys and pretend everything is normal. The guilt of not telling Matt is starting to wear on me.

107

But suggesting Andrew and I go public means defining what we are. We're coming to a crossroads, and until I know which fork he's taking, I have to keep plowing straight ahead.

At eight, Asha meets us in the lobby of Spencer's dorm. She kisses everyone on the cheek and rests her forehead against mine. "I'm so glad to see yoooou!" She's obviously a few drinks up on us, as usual. Lucky.

We leave the car in the dorm lot and start the trek to Greek Row. Like a genius, I wore heels. High ones. And in other questionable decisions, my skirt is short, my shirt is tight, and my makeup is . . . well, enough that Matt commented, so obviously too much. But I don't want to stand out, and showing up in anything less would attract attention.

Liam meets us on the front porch, where four white columns pretend to hold up the roof. He waves Asha and Spencer in. "Richardson!" he says, beckoning to Andrew. "Come check out the house."

Andrew glances at me and I'm not sure what he's thinking. Does he want me to come with him? Then another frat boy steps in, hitting Andrew with some fancy handshake. "Come on, man, you're gonna rush, right?"

Andrew shrugs. "I dunno yet."

The guy laughs. "How you gonna get any pussy if you don't?"

My mouth flattens. I want Andrew to be the kind of guy that shuts that shit down, but Matt's the one who rolls his eyes. "How indeed," he says, stepping through the door.

Andrew just laughs. He sounds uncomfortable, I'll give him

that, but still. I'm not sticking around to hear more, so I go into the main room while Liam leads him to another part of the house.

Asha glances at me from the corner of her eye. I pretend to be very interested in the huge stuffed moose head hanging above the fireplace. It's wearing a white hat and a tie. Poor thing.

Across the half-full room, several girls perch on couches. One is wearing the same red top as me, and she's giving me the stink eye. Like I'm going to tell everyone she bought it at Target. The cluster of guys checking them out from around the keg wouldn't care, but those so-called sisters beside her might.

That'll be me next year, I realize. Still at these campus parties, playing these same games. Maybe with Asha and Spencer, but no Matt—and maybe Andrew, but as what? My secret high school boyfriend? And even that's only for a year. No matter what everyone else thinks, Andrew is smart. He's going somewhere else.

He won't be here. And I will.

"I need a drink," I say out loud.

"Spence," Asha orders, and he and Matt head for the keg. In their absence, she pulls her boyfriend's flask from her cleavage. "What was that?"

"What was what?" She passes it to me and I shudder as the whiskey hits my throat.

"That look, asking your permission. Are you Andrew's mommy now?"

I breathe like a dragon to get rid of the burn. "No."

She raises an eyebrow. "Are you Andrew's—"

"No." I tip the flask again, too fast, and choke. Matt returns just in time for me to grab his beer and chug it.

MATT

Andrew and I each have an arm, holding Raychel up as she stumbles back to the car. "Annnndreeeeeew . . ." she sings. "What did Liam want?"

We all know what Liam wants. He's hoping Andrew will be a recruit year after next, but they'd better start throwing cooler parties if he wants that to happen. "He gave me a tour of the house," Andrew says.

He was gone more than an hour, and since he volunteered to be DD for once, I drank several beers in that time span. But not as many as Raychel, who also helped Asha kill an entire flask of whiskey. She misses the step up onto the curb and falls, both knees hitting the concrete hard, and starts to giggle.

"Shit," Andrew and I say at the same time, and that sends her into gales of laughter. "I didn't know the puddle effect worked when you're walking," I say. She can't answer. We fold her into the backseat and stand by the closed car door.

"What now?" he asks, glancing at his phone. "It's early."

"You can drop us off at home and head to the Homecoming party at Trenton Montgomery's," I suggest. "Or you could drop us off and go to the Grove."

Andrew glances at the car and a gnawing starts in my gut. He looks so . . . concerned. "I dunno." He looks back at me. "Anyway, gimme your keys."

I hand them over. "Andrew's driving?" Raychel asks as we get in.

He turns around. "Your carriage awaits, m'lady." She cracks up and I roll my eyes again. "So where to?" he asks.

"Home," I say.

"No!" Raychel yelps.

"Taco Bell?" Andrew starts the car.

She makes an alarmingly realistic retching sound. My door's halfway open before she says, "No. No Taco Hell. Let's go to Trenton the Third's."

"That sounds like a terrible idea," I say.

"Annnnndreeeeeew," she says. "You want to go, right?"

He smiles into the rearview. "Sure. Let's go."

My stomach feels like that puking noise Raych just made.

RAYCHEL

It's way easier to walk if I watch my feet. People spill out of the house. Across the deck. Into the yard. Andrew and Matt greet them from either side of me. I watch my shoes. They are pointy. Our footsteps make a little beat: doot doot doot. Dootdoot doodoot doot. " 'Shakedown Street'!"

111

"What?" Matt sounds annoyed.

"That's my third Dead song."

"You've been thinking about that for three weeks?"

"'Don't tell me this town ain't got no heart,'" I sing, bobbing my head in time. "Doot doot doot. Dootdoot doodoot—"

Both boys disappear.

"What the hell?" They were right here, holding my arms! I'm not *that* drunk. I look to where some laughing girls are pointing and see both boys sprawled on the ground. Matt is rubbing his chin. Andrew sits up and rubs his neck. "What the hell?" I repeat.

"Clotheslined." Andrew points up, to the rope I easily walked under but those two giants hit full speed. I fall down laughing, in the grass right between them.

Matt glares at Andrew. "This was your idea."

Andrew shrugs.

MATT

"Andrew!" Raychel barks, drill sergeant–style. *"Will you get me a* beer?"

"No," I answer for him. She sobered up some in the car, but not enough. "Drink some water."

"Can I have a beer *and* some water?"

Andrew looks between us.

She reaches for his collar and I know he's done for. "Puh-leeze?"

He stands up, smiling a little, and goes inside.

"Damn, Raych." I dab at her knee with my thumb. "Why didn't you tell me you were bleeding?" Tiny dots of congealed blood speckle her cool skin. Last week's hundred-degree temperatures are gone. Why do girls insist on wearing nothing when it's cold outside?

She examines her leg. "It's no big deal."

I rub the blood off my hand in the grass, then pull her up, half dragging her into the house.

"Where's your brother?" she asks.

"Getting you a beer you don't need, remember? Seriously, you might want to slow down."

"And *you* might want to chill out," she says, pulling her arm away. The crowd inside smashes us against the wall. To my right, the dark living room throbs with dancers. "Holy crap! Trenton set up a disco ball!" she yells.

"You can barely walk, much less dance," I say, but she ignores me and keeps going.

I start to follow, but I can see Andrew cutting through the crowd to intercept her. "Fine," I say to no one. We have a DD, I have a decent buzz, and for once, I'm going to have fun at a party. Andrew insisted on bringing her here, and if he wants to be Mr. Responsible, then he can start by being the heavy for a change.

I turn around with a conviction I don't really feel. Maybe a few more beers will help.

RAYCHEL

Wow, that will suck to clean up. Mindy Merrithew just spilled red punch all over the carpet. I bet Trent gets grounded. No, I bet he has a cleaning lady to fix it before his mommy gets home. I picture Mom scrubbing his floor and my pulse spikes. Again. All I want is to have some freaking fun, but noooo, something always has to get in the way. Like Matt, always trying to tell me what to do. He's not my dad.

Ha. If he were, he wouldn't be here in the first place.

I laugh bitterly to myself. But a good song starts so I move toward the music, to the music. My hips already have a life of their own. Ghostly faces in the living room laugh and sing along speckled with light. Sparkling. Some I recognize. Smile. Say hi. Some say hi back. Others whisper when they see me.

Whatever.

A girl from chemistry seems friendly, so I make my way over to her. "You want some schnapps?" she offers.

Schnapps. High school kids are so cute. I can't remember her name. Karen? Carley? I thank her and take a sip. Ugh, peach, of course.

Everyone has to smoke outside, but the air still seems thick, more solid than normal around me. Chemistry Girl pulls me under the disco ball to dance. I catch a glimpse of Andrew leaning against the wall. He holds out a cup in my direction, so I dance over and take it.

"Water?" I ask him. "Really?"

"I've got a beer for you too." He pulls a bottle from his back pocket.

"Such a good boy." I kiss him on the cheek and go back to Chemistry Girl.

"Is that Andrew Richardson?" she yells over the music. "He is *so* hot!"

"Is he?" I glance back. He's smiling at us. And she's right. Andrew is pretty damn hot.

"Oh my god! Are you blind?" she squeals. "I have the *worst* crush on him."

My dancing slows. "You do?"

"Yeah." She sighs, pretending to pout. "We've actually been spending a lot of time together lately for school, but you know how he flirts with everybody." She seizes my elbow. "Hey, you're friends with him! Can you help me out?"

"Um . . ." Now what? Because seriously. Part of me wants to claw her eyes out.

But part of me wants to know where I stand. And why they've been spending time together that he didn't tell me about. "I—I don't know," I stammer. "We're not that kind of friends, really?" It shouldn't be a question, but I obviously don't know either.

"Oh, are you guys . . . Oh my god, are you guys together?" she yells. "Oh no, I'm so sorry!"

"No!" I shout back. We've both stopped dancing and the crowd knocks us into one another. Water sloshes out of my cup. "It's fine! We're not, I mean . . ."

"Oh yeah, you're his brother's girlfriend, right?"

The relief on her face is so tangible, I can't bring myself to break it. "We're all friends. We drove here together."

And this is the moment Andrew chooses to join us. "Hey, you know Keri?" he asks me.

Keri! That's it. Chemistry Girl is Hot Pep Rally Girl. Up close, she doesn't look much like Matt's ex. Hana's hair is lighter, and Keri's eyes are bigger. They follow Andrew's arm as it slides around my waist. "Hey!" I fake protest, pushing him off. "We have chemistry together," I tell him, and turn to her. "But y'all know each other?"

She blushes. Andrew gives an easy smile.

I tip my bottle toward him before either one can answer. "Dance with Keri. I have to pee."

And I leave them together. Don't look around to see where Matt has gone. Don't check to see if Andrew watches me go. Don't care.

Try not to care so much.

MATT

"Richardson!" Trent yells from the middle of a rowdy game of flip cup. "Help yourself, man." He gestures at the line of ice chests along the far wall of the kitchen.

The floor sticks to my shoes. I motion for a girl to scoot off a cooler lid, grab a beer, then grab a second for good measure when I see a decent label. "Where's the bottle opener?" I ask.

"Here," someone behind me says. It's Mindy.

"Thanks." I try to hide my surprise. She doesn't usually go to parties, and she looks alarmed as I pop both tops, chug one bottle, and toss it in the trash while swigging from the other.

Andrew comes in and fills a cup at the sink. "Is Raych with you?" I ask.

"She had to piss." His head jerks toward the hall. "You gonna dance?"

"No. You're on duty."

He shakes his head and leaves.

"Rough night?" Mindy asks.

I shrug. "How's yours?"

"Kind of boring." She plays with a strand of hair. "My Homecoming date already went home and my friends are all . . . busy," she says, eyes flicking toward the hallway.

"So you're . . ."

"Bored." She steps closer. "Are you sure you don't want to dance?"

"Pretty sure." I take another gulp of beer.

She crosses her arms at the wrist. It forces her boobs together and pops them up from the neck of her shirt, an awkwardly obvious move that makes me feel bad for her, and a little guilty.

Mindy is throwing herself at me. It wouldn't kill me to pay attention to her, and clearly no one else wants my attention tonight. "Well . . ." she says, and stretches her arms back, pushing her chest impossibly farther out as she steps forward.

My body pulls toward her, but something small pulls me away, a tickling feeling in my throat that I swallow. Then Trent busts back into the kitchen. "Who spilled red shit all over the carpet?"

Mindy grabs my hand. "That was me!" she whispers, and pulls me out of the room. "Come on!"

RAYCHEL

The line for the bathroom snakes down the dark hallway. This is why you don't break the seal. Then you have to pee every five minutes and spend the whole night in line. I scowl at the boys ahead of me, who should just go outside. I want the line to hurry so I can get back to Andrew. I want it to take a long time so I can see if he'd rather be with Keri.

Mostly, though, I just want to pee, and in a house this huge, there *has* to be more than one bathroom. I find the stairs and duck under a DO NOT ENTER sign. In the second floor hallway, the music is muffled enough that I can hear giggles and moans coming from behind the closed bedroom doors.

Since no one's in line for this bathroom, I take my time cleaning off my knees. The sting brings back memories of bike wrecks. Mrs. R. blowing on my scrapes. Dr. R. telling her that spreads germs. Why don't I have those memories of my own parents? I wash my hands, staring at myself in the mirror. That little girl was me, but this isn't her. I could wash this face right down the drain.

Someone pounds on the door, making me jump. "About time," a girl sneers as I step out.

I don't answer. I'm frozen to the spot. She huffs and pushes me out of the way, but I keep staring at the couple disappearing down the hall. I want to reach out, grab the backs of their shirts, tell them no.

But I can't move.

The click of their closing door breaks me. I take a step toward it, too late to stop the sound that follows. The lock. I feel like that sound—not a shatter but a pop. A snap. A sickening click of realization.

I take another step—and my high heel catches in the carpet. My ankle gives and I sit down hard, on the floor against the wall, staring at the door. The pain is sobering. Why do I want to stop them anyway? I don't want to take her place, and getting laid would do Matt a world of good.

I just want him to come help me. But I'm alone and I'd better get used to it. Matt and Andrew are both going to leave, and I'll have to fend for myself.

MATT

Mindy giggles a lot. "Matt!" she says, patting the bed beside her, and giggles again.

I probably do look funny, standing here with my hands in my pockets. *Move,* I tell my feet, and they take me to the bed. *Move,* I tell my arm, and it falls over her shoulders. *Move,* I tell my other arm, and it brings the bottle to my lips. My beer is hot. This girl is hot. She brings herself to my lips and pushes me back.

They say it's impossible to think clearly with your clothes off. But sometimes having them on doesn't make much difference.

Her hands move over my chest and down my arms, taking my beer away, taking my hands to put them where she wants them. Where I want them, I'll admit, but my mind and body aren't communicating very well. *Move,* I tell my hand. *Move!* And it clumsily unsnaps her bra.

She makes a noise in my ear, a half giggle, when I touch her boobs. *Pay attention,* I tell myself, but voices in the hall distract me. One sounds familiar, but I can't tell, and it's hard to think with Mindy writhing all over me.

I'm not complaining. I'm just saying.

RAYCHEL

"What are you doing?" He nudges me with his toe.

I don't look up.

He puts his hand on my head and tilts it back. "Hello?"

I push him away. "I'm just sitting."

Carson extends his hand again. "Need help?"

"No," I snap, trying to stand. I cannot believe I hurt my ankle again. Matt will . . .

Who cares what Matt will say or do. Anything he wants. He's not mine, after all.

A door opens closer to the stairs and a laughing couple stumbles out. The smell of beer and musky sweat follows them. "What happened?" Carson asks.

"I tripped." I press my hand flat against the wall for support. Nothing to hold on to.

He produces a fifth of Crown. "Want a painkiller?"

Of course. He's too good for regular whiskey. But it does go down smooth.

"You having a good time?" he asks.

"Not particularly," I say. He leans against the wall, blocking my exit. Trapping me in a corner. "When did you get here?"

"About half an hour ago. The Grove got busted," he says, shrugging. "Keg was cashed anyway." He gestures toward my leg. "I guess you don't want to dance, huh."

"How'd you know I was up here?"

"Richardson told me."

"Matt?" I ask stupidly.

"Andrew." He grins. "Lucky guy, he's got Keri Sturgis glued to his thigh."

Suddenly my bones feel unconnected again, but not in a good way.

"Listen," Carson says, "I've been trying to talk to you for weeks about this, but . . . I felt weird." He scuffs his shoe against the carpet like a little boy. "After what we did."

What you *did,* I want to reply, but don't.

"I shouldn't have said that," he says. "About, you know. The girlfriend thing."

My mouth opens and closes. "Apology accepted," I say, though he hasn't actually said sorry. And certainly not about the right thing.

"I just . . . I've had a crush on you for a long time, Raychel." He leans forward, tucking a strand of hair behind my ear.

If I close my eyes, I could pretend he was sincere. His gaze meets mine, and I realize with a sinking feeling that he *is* sincere, which is so much worse. "Carson," I start, unsure what to say. "You—you barely know me."

He half smiles, looking a little hurt. "Sure I do. I've known you since elementary school."

I cross my arms.

"You were scared of the monkey bars," he says. I try to protest, because I wasn't scared—the boys always tried to peek up my dress. But Carson goes on. "I know in fifth grade you convinced all the girls in Mrs. Silva's class that you could read their minds."

"Fourth," I correct, like it matters.

"And in junior high," he says, leaning closer, "you made the cheerleading squad, but then you quit because you were too cool for those girls."

I wasn't too cool. I was too poor and cheerleading camp is expensive. But it's still kind of flattering that he knows so much. Isn't it? Maybe not, if I know the same stuff about him. He was the playground tetherball champ every single year. He got caught kissing a girl in the junior high locker room. His Blazer's a replacement for the truck he wrecked at the lake last summer. Or *in* the lake, I should say.

Proximity doesn't prove anything. "You know just as much about half the girls here," I say, shaking my head. "Guys too, for that matter."

"But it's a start," he says. "Can't I get to know more?" His whole smile is charming. My brain and body are buzzing, reminding me how this all started in the first place—Carson is undeniably hot. That square jaw, shadowed with a little scruff, and those arms, Jesus. He knows he was a jerk. He apologized. He's been apologizing for weeks, it seems.

"Maybe," I say. "Why didn't you just say this earlier?"

He actually blushes. "I was nervous, and we were always in class . . ."

Relief spikes like adrenaline through my body. He didn't

mean to . . . force me. Carson is a nice guy with a crush, and I've been torturing myself for no reason. He's not after me for an easy lay. He just likes me. "So *are* you asking me to be your girlfriend?" I draw it out so he can play it off like a joke.

He smirks. "Maybe."

Oh. I'm positive my heart is visibly pounding out of my chest.

"Why don't we give it a test run?" Carson asks, leaning closer. "See how it goes."

He starts off slow, kissing me in ways I like—if I don't compare them to Andrew's. His hands move from the wall to me, and I suck in a breath, looking around. It sounds like someone is on the stairs.

"There's no one up here," he mumbles in my ear. "No one can see us."

Carson kisses me harder, pushing the length of his body hard against me. I do and don't want it to feel good. It does and doesn't. A whimper escapes my lips and makes him braver.

"You're pretty, Raychel," he whispers. I don't understand how I can be flattered and horrified at the same time. My skin crawls but it's hot and wants to be smoothed over. "I like girls like you."

"Like me?" I croak.

"The ones who aren't scared to get dirty."

My stomach flip-flops. "Wait."

"What?" He pulls back. "You want to go to a bedroom?"

I shake my head. I changed my sluggish mind.

I don't want this.

"You want to stay out here," he whispers, and doesn't wait for my reply. "You *are* dirty."

Suddenly there's no want except to escape. Every inch of me screams no. He shoves both hands into my shirt. His crotch pushes eagerly at mine. My tailbone digs into the wall, trying to create space that doesn't exist. I can't pull back and his mouth is on mine and there's no room for me to say anything until he pulls away. "No," I manage, trying to pull my shirt back down, but he swallows my protests with more kissing. His fly unbuttons in rapid succession, like a machine gun. I keep trying but I can't make myself heard around his tongue in my mouth.

Then he pulls away, putting his hand on top of my head, and pushes. Hard. It shoves me off-balance, forces me to the floor.

To my knees.

MATT

Mindy keeps doing her best, but voices are coming up the stairs, getting louder. "Hang on." I sit up and Mindy falls to the side, her hand still attached to an area I should be more excited about, considering that no one but me has been there in quite a while.

"What's going on?" she asks breathlessly.

"I dunno." We sit in silence, listening.

RAYCHEL

The carpet burns the scrapes on my knees. I can't believe that's what I'm thinking about while Carson is getting his dick out. When I try to get up, my ankle gives and he uses the other hand to keep me down. Everything is moving in slow motion but too fast. The whiskey-schnapps-beer-bourbon mix swells toward my throat.

"Raych?" a voice asks. "What the hell?"

I blink and look up, swiping at the tears running down my cheeks. It's Andrew. Keri and a bunch of other people hover behind him.

MATT

One of the voices is definitely Andrew's.

At least I know he's not in some room screwing Raychel.

That thought makes me scramble to the edge of the bed. The rest of my drink goes down fast, with a grimace and a shudder, but it doesn't take away the waxy taste of Mindy's red lipstick or the weight of her hand on my thigh or the fact that I shouldn't be in here with her.

The roiling in my gut isn't just hot beer. It's want, but not for Mindy. It's anger and greed and, most of all, guilt.

I push her hand away.

126

RAYCHEL

People are gathering, racing up the stairs to see the show.

Something loud comes out of Andrew's mouth—not really words, just sounds. His arm moves and for a split second I think he's reaching for me. I put my hand out to meet him.

Instead he grabs Carson's shoulder and throws him toward a bedroom door. Carson's unbuttoned pants leave everything hanging out, a hilariously useless weapon for this fight. I'm hysterical, laughing and crying at the same time, loud over the gasping crowd.

MATT

"Is that your brother out there?" Mindy asks.

"Sounds like it." And someone is laughing wildly.

She kneels behind me on the bed and runs her hand up my chest, but I squirm away. "Are you okay?" she asks.

"Yeah, I—"

A crash, and the door bows in for a moment, the sound of wood splintering almost lost under the yelling. Mindy shrieks and grabs her bra, stuffing it into her pocket as she scrambles for her shirt. I jump up, glance back just long enough to make sure she's covered, and jerk what's left of the door open.

A body falls at my feet with a grunt. Andrew lunges after him, pulling him back out into the hall, and I realize the guy's cock is hanging out. It's Carson Tipton. He lands a blow on Andrew's chin. Andrew's fist draws back.

"Wait!" I yell, rushing to get between them.

Andrew throws the punch anyway. It hits me in the nose.

RAYCHEL

Blood explodes like a gruesome firecracker. Matt holds his face, eyes wide with shock.

I lean forward and puke on Trenton Alexander Montgomery the Third's white carpet. I don't think peach will be any easier to get out than red.

MATT

The next few minutes are a blur. Andrew grabs Raychel with both hands, lifting her up and over Carson's body. Keri Sturgis is alternating between yelling at Carson and yelling at everyone else to back off, but everyone else is busy watching me chase Andrew and Raychel down the stairs.

Andrew bursts through the front door onto the lawn and

drags her toward the car. "What the hell is going on?" I yell after them.

"We're going home." He beeps the lock so the lights flash at the other end of the street.

"No," Raychel moans. "Andrew . . ."

"You want to stay?" He tosses her hand away. "What the fuck is wrong with you?"

"Take me to my house," she says, sobbing.

I finally catch up. "We can't take her to Mom and Dad like this."

"Fuck!" Andrew yells. He walks a few feet away and picks up a rock, throwing it hard at a tree. People are starting to emerge from Trenton's house. "Come on," he says. "Let's get the hell out of here."

I use my shirt to stanch the blood gushing from my nose while Andrew puts Raychel in the backseat. We drive in silence toward her duplex. "Andrew," she says quietly. "It's not what you think."

"You weren't about to suck Carson Tipton's dick?" he demands. I sit forward and cover my face, feeling like I'm on a roller coaster. "I thought you couldn't stand that guy, Raych!"

She doesn't argue. Her sobs are quiet, body folded in on itself like an animal that's given up escaping from a trap. The porch light is off when we reach her driveway. "Let us walk you in," I say, but she shakes her head. We watch her stumble-limp to the door and stab at the lock in the dark, not turning around when it finally opens.

Andrew pulls away before the light in her bedroom comes on. "Jesus, dude. What if she pukes in her sleep?" I ask, lowering the bloody shirt from my face.

"Then she can choke on it." He punches the power button on the radio.

I turn it off. "She hooked up with the guy weeks ago, man. You knew she had something going with him."

"No, I didn't," he says. "Not that it matters."

"Then why are you so pissed?" I demand.

"Because she's better than that!" he yells, taking a curve so fast that I bang into the passenger door.

"You think I don't know?" I shout back. "You think I like watching her hook up with random dudes?"

He doesn't answer, and it's the last thing we say to each other for two days.

RAYCHEL

I make it to the couch before I collapse. *At least one thing's gone right tonight,* I think, and pass out.

In the morning, I wake up to Mom feeling my forehead. "Dear god, Raychel, what did you do last night?" she asks. Tears immediately begin to leak from my eyes. "Oh honey," she says, sitting down and laying my head in her lap. "It's okay. Whatever happened, it's okay."

"I made . . ." I cough, hoping I can keep from throwing up again. "I made a mistake. I made a big fool of myself."

She smooths my hair. "It'll be okay, sweetie. It'll be okay."

. . . . .

Mom doesn't press for more details. We pretend I have the flu, and she brings me bowls of chicken soup and saltines. I ice and elevate my leg, watching football until it's late enough that I can reasonably go to bed. On Monday, my ankle feels better, but she accepts my excuse of still not feeling well and calls the school to tell them I'm staying home.

No one calls me. I don't call them. I don't even know what I'd say.

Mom starts talking about taking Tuesday off to stay with me, and I can't let her do that. I'll have to face the jackals sometime. So I get up, put on a simple outfit, and add some combat boots to make me feel tougher.

But at school, it's different from last time. Less giggling, no questions. Just stares and the conversations that float over and around me. I try to dodge between them, into silent spaces. There aren't many.

"*. . . was going to suck his dick! There in the hallway! . . . not like it's the first time, she totally had sex in his car . . . making out with Carson Tipton, in front of everybody . . . I know! . . .*"

The teachers eye me suspiciously too. I swear, even Eddie the janitor is watching me. His head turns as I pass.

"*. . . heard she's screwing him and both Richardson boys too, and*

they were all fighting over her, god, who knows why . . . everyone
knows she's a slut . . . everyone knows she's a whore . . . everyone
knows, everyone knows . . . everyone knows . . ."

Everyone knows something, but no one knows shit.

· · · · ·

Keri Sturgis grabs me the minute I walk into chemistry. "Are
you okay?" she whispers.

I blink hard. She's the first person to ask all day. "I've been
better," I mumble. Carson changed seats in calculus, but it just
made people whisper and stare at both of us.

"Raychel," she says, forcing me to look her in the eye. "I saw
what happened. You didn't want him on you!"

I start to tear up again. This was my one rule for today: no
goddamn crying. "How did you even . . ."

She scowls. "So I was dancing with Andrew—thanks for
that, by the way—and then Carson walks up and he's all
'Hey man, where's Sanders,' and Andrew's like, 'Not with
you, obviously,' but I didn't know he was such a jerk so I said
'She went to the bathroom, she'll be back in a sec.' And he
walked off but you had already been gone a long time, and
Andrew was acting all weird so I was like, 'Hey, I'll go find
her—'"

"Ladies," Mr. Monroe warns. I start working on the experi-
ment, but Keri just drops her voice to a whisper.

"So then you weren't in the line and someone said they saw

you go upstairs and then I saw him bothering you and I started downstairs to get Andrew but he had followed me halfway anyway and then—well, then you know what happened."

I stare at the Bunsen burner in front of us. I should have known Andrew wouldn't send Carson to find me.

Keri leans against the black counter, glaring at the classmates trying to listen in. "It's kind of sexy, you know?"

"What?" The glass tube I'm holding clanks against a scale.

Her hands flutter. "Oh no, not *that*. I mean boys fighting to defend you and all."

I don't see what's so sexy about it. It's like a sick fairy tale with too many swords.

"Hey, Sanders. *Psst*. Sanders!" A boy in glasses, a junior I don't know, leans over from his workstation. "You want to go in the back for a sec? Maybe a little, you know . . . ?" He makes a dirty hand gesture.

"No," I mumble. "Screw off." But Keri starts hissing a tirade at him and my answer gets lost.

MATT

Our parents, of course, don't fail to notice that I have a fractured nose and Andrew's jaw has swollen to a comical size. I do the lying, knowing they'll never suspect it from me. "It was really stupid," I tell Dad. "We went to a party at Trenton Montgomery's house and he still has this big jungle gym in his backyard, so we decided to play on the swings, only it was dark and we crashed into each other."

It's not the greatest story ever, but they seem to believe it.

The whole school is telling its own story, though never to our bruised faces. I'm probably missing a lot of the gossip, but what I hear is plenty: everything from a rumor that Carson got Raychel pregnant to a story that Andrew and I have been in an incestuous three-way with her for years.

The rumor most likely to be true is that the baseball team wants to kick our asses, even though Carson's fine. He just got a black eye (from Andrew) and some bruised ribs (from the door). It's hard to know if he deserved it, with Raychel acting like we don't exist. Monday morning, her mom texted that she was sick and didn't need a ride. I knew she wasn't, but I figured Raych would let me know when she felt better.

But today she's at school, and she's avoiding me. I don't know if she's taking different routes to class or what, but I didn't see her before second period like usual, and she was nowhere to be found at lunchtime. She came in late to Senior Seminar and left before I could catch her. After school, I wait with Andrew at his car, expecting her to catch a ride with him to work, but instead we see her getting in a small red convertible. "Whose is that?" I ask.

"Keri Sturgis," he says, like I asked who ate the last cookie.

"Oh. I didn't know she and Raych were friends."

"Yeah," he says, tossing and catching a lighter over and over. "Me neither."

"Aren't *you* and Keri 'friends'?" I ask, making air quotes.

Andrew snorts. "We're in the same SAT prep class together."

"Oh." I didn't even know he was in a class. "I thought you hooked up last year."

"You shouldn't believe everything you hear." He stretches his neck like he's sore. "What about you and Mindy?"

"There's no 'me and Mindy,'" I say, shamefaced. After the fight, I was so focused on Raych that I didn't even realize I'd left Mindy without a goodbye until I pulled up to school yesterday morning. "I have to see her in a few minutes though."

"Bummer," he says, and starts tossing his lighter again.

We watch the convertible get in line to leave. "Have you talked to Raychel yet?"

"Nope." He catches the lighter.

"Are you going to try?"

Andrew opens his car door. "She knows where to find me."

He pulls away and I stare, wondering where the hell my goofy little brother has gone.

· · · · ·

I knew our StuCo subcommittee meeting was going to be hard, but it sure doesn't help that when I get there, Trenton Alexander Montgomery the Third refuses to call me anything but "Champ" or, occasionally, "Ali." He keeps trying to hold my hand up like a prizefighter. Mindy walks in at the last minute and keeps her eyes away from my side of the room during the whole meeting. When we start discussing projects, I find out she's taken on blood drive decorations, leaving me on my own with the catering.

When the meeting's over, I have no choice but to throw myself on the grenade. "Mindy," I say, interrupting her and Rosa as they're leaving. "Can I talk to you?"

She turns as slowly as possible to fix me with a withering glare. "Rosa, I'll meet you in the car," she says. Rosa shoots me a hateful glance and I try to look sufficiently contrite. "What do you want?" Mindy demands.

"I just . . . wanted to say sorry." My hands are suddenly in my way. I can't figure out where to put them.

She tucks her hair behind her ears, like she's getting ready to tackle a big job. "Sorry for what?" she asks, voice overly sweet, even for her.

"Um . . ." *Because it's uncool to leave a girl in bed while you get in a fight with the guy who's putting the moves on your crush?* Probably not the best phrasing. "For . . ."

"For leading me on?" she says. "For letting the entire party see me half-naked? Or—"

"All of it," I say quickly, knowing better than to argue that I made sure she was covered. "Everything. It was just—"

She stops me. "I was there, okay? I remember."

"I'm sorry," I say again, studying the floor tiles between us. I never realized how truly worthless that sentence can be.

"Listen—I understand, about the party," she says. "I mean you couldn't help that Carson came through the door." His name makes my teeth grind. "I mean, maybe I'm stupid for thinking you could like me more than Raychel, you know? Everybody knows you've been hung up on her for years." My surprise pisses her off. "Seriously, you think it's not obvious?"

"I . . ." I have no idea what to say. "You know, we're friends, so . . ."

Mindy laughs, mean and sad. "No, you and I were friends. You and Raychel are . . ." She shakes her head. "I don't know what y'all are."

"Neither do I," I admit, running a hand over my head. "But not that." I look her in the eye. "I wouldn't have used you like that. Or her."

"Well, you used me like something." She steps closer. "If you're not screwing her, then you're either totally whipped for no reason, or you just really like being at her beck and call. But either way, it's pathetic, and you should like, look into some new hobbies or something."

She turns and walks out before I can argue, but I'm not sure I could have anyway.

RAYCHEL

Mom speeds around the house Wednesday night like a five-year-old's remote-control car. She crashes into the table, knocking half of my homework to the floor. "Mom, it's okay," I say, hoping she'll stop trying to pick it up. I haven't had the energy to clean, and she's making the mess worse. "Go get ready."

"I'm sorry!" She jumps up as I smooth the wrinkled papers.

When Mom comes back, keys in hand, she's added more eyeliner. One eye is crooked and brown makeup cakes the wrinkles at one corner of her mouth. She's ten years younger than Mrs. R., but looks like the older of the two. "This base won't blend right," she says helplessly.

"Close your eyes." I rub her cheek, then smudge the eyeliner until it's even. "Why are you so nervous?"

"We're going to Johnson Mill," she says. "And I'm late."

"Wow." That's a four-star restaurant. And it's priced like a five.

She pats her hair. "Do I look okay?"

"You look great," I lie. She kisses my forehead and heads for the door. "Mom," I say impulsively. "Why don't you invite him over here?"

She stops at the threshold and glances around at the mess. "Why don't you have Matt over more?"

I fake laugh. "Point taken." She looks like she expected a real answer, so I shoo her out the door. "Have fun."

She hesitates. "You will meet him soon, sweetheart. I promise."

"Whenever you're ready." I'm not in the best position to argue for honesty about dudes at the moment. "Now get going."

Mom still waits. "You should call Asha."

"She's busy." As usual.

"What about that Mexican girl? Briana?"

"Bree's away at college, like all my other friends, remember?" I say. "And her folks are from Chile, not Mexico."

"Oh. Okay," Mom says contritely. "I might be late . . ."

"I won't wait up." I close the door behind her and rest my forehead against it, trying to absorb the calm left in her wake. Minutes could have passed, or hours, when something scuttles outside. Probably a leaf. I flip the deadbolt anyway, and the click echoes through the empty room.

Click. You're alone.

Again.

I flop back onto the couch, trying not to think. Sick of thinking about it. Sick of Carson invading my space. One minute I'm fine, and the next, some random detail puts that night on replay in my head—the smell of artificial peach, the shoes I was wearing, the song that was on. Suddenly I'm back on my knees, swaying. Weak. Why didn't I get up? Why didn't I grab him by the balls and teach him a lesson?

Because you wanted it, a voice says in my mind.

No I didn't.

Yes you did. You couldn't have your first choice, or even your second, so you went for that instead.

That's not quite true, but it's a humiliating fact to face: I wanted to be Andrew's girlfriend. I *still* wish I could be his girlfriend. But worse is that I was jealous of Mindy, and not because I want to date Matt—I just like being his favorite. I always knew I came first, no matter who he dated, and I always knew Eliza had reason to hate me. Because I can count on Matt to be there for me.

Until next fall, when he leaves. And Andrew won't be far behind him.

The truth is that I'm scared to be alone. I'm scared for everyone to leave Big Springs and leave me here with no one but Mom, who sees her boyfriend more than she does me.

That's why I wanted to believe Carson.

I wanted to believe someone liked me enough to claim me. Call me theirs. Keep me around. And sober, I can see the flawed reasoning, but drunk, I wanted to say yes this time so last time's no wouldn't count. So the scene in Carson's truck would take on a different meaning. So some part of this stupid situation would be under my control.

But I said no this time. And he didn't listen.

I think Matt will listen, once I work up the nerve to tell him the truth, but Andrew was so angry. I understand why, but . . . I wasn't his girlfriend. He never asked me to be. We never made anything exclusive or official. And maybe I shouldn't have kissed Carson—god, what an understatement—but it's not like Andrew wasn't down there with Keri.

He probably thinks I was lying about Carson from the very beginning. And if Andrew's mad enough that he confessed to Matt . . . Well, at least I won't have to be the one to do it. *Every silver lining's got a touch of gray.*

140

That song really does suck.

It's only nine fifteen, the clock's hands making a flat face like "Sorry, still lots of night to go." So I put a pillow over my head and lie on the couch.

"Lie" is passive. I'm actively lying. Lying to myself that everything will be okay.

MATT

My mom waits until she's tricked me into going to the grocery store Wednesday evening before she springs the question. "Are you sure Raychel's okay?"

"She's fine."

Mom glances at me over a bunch of bananas. "Fine. Even though she keeps calling in sick to work and hasn't hung out with you in days."

"I'm not in charge of Raychel," I say. It might be the truest thing I know at the moment. "Call her mom if you're so concerned."

"That'd go over like a ton of bricks." We never discuss it, but we all know that Raychel's mom is not our family's biggest fan. Mom bags some pears as if this is casual chitchat. "What happened?"

"Nothing," I say, just as nonchalantly.

She gives me a fake smile and head tilt to show she's wait-ing. I pretend to be fascinated by the variety of peppers. "Matthew," she says, stepping closer so the nosy old woman buying bagged salad can't hear. "I'm not completely clueless. I know you and your brother hit that Tipton boy."

"What?" I drop a poblano, and she smirks. "How?"

She taps her temple. "I hear things."

Of course she does. Two of the other professors in her de-partment have kids at Big Springs High. "I didn't hit him," I mumble. "I was too slow."

She sighs. "I don't know why his parents aren't pressing charges—"

"They can't."

"Who is the law professor here?" She glares at me. "You could be charged with assault."

"So could he," I say petulantly.

"Did he start the fight?"

"Sort of."

Mom exhales loudly and we have a staring contest, but the produce spritzers come on, startling us out of our stalemate. "Look, it doesn't take a genius to figure out that Raychel was in-volved," she says, pulling a plastic bag from the dispenser. "And unless you explain, I'm going to assume that you lied because you should be in trouble."

"No," I insist. "I just wasn't sure how much she'd want me to say."

Mom levels her gaze at me. "If someone hurt her, you need to report it. Period."

"I don't—" Her eyes narrow as soon as I say it. "No, I mean, I'm not sure."

"So you and Andrew teamed up on an unarmed boy because you thought—"

"We didn't team up," I argue. "I was in a different room and walked in at the wrong time." I touch my nose self-consciously. "I never hit anybody, I just pulled them apart."

"But why were they fighting in the first place?"

"Because Andrew threw him through a door."

Mom stops and squeezes her temples. "Matthew, tell me right now, or—"

"Because he had her cornered," I say too loudly. The old salad lady raises her eyebrows. Mom wheels our cart to the ethnic food aisle, where there are fewer shoppers to eavesdrop. "Carson had Raychel cornered," I say again, when we're alone. "With his fly down. And she was . . ." I cannot say "about to give him a blow job" to my mother. "In a compromising position. And she was crying," I add. "I don't know if that was the alcohol or embarrassment or what."

Mom closes her eyes, then opens them to survey a wall of rice, as if jasmine and arborio might present her with a game plan. "You were drinking."

"Raychel and I were," I admit. "Andrew wasn't."

She doesn't bother to hide her surprise, but it clearly changes her thinking. "Okay. And what does Raychel have to say about all this?"

"She doesn't." I drop a box of noodles into the cart too hard. "She won't say anything."

"Have you asked her?"

"No, because she's avoiding me, and because she and Carson have, um . . . This isn't their first . . . you know."

Mom nods. "So they've been dating?"

I don't want to make my mom think bad of Raychel, but I don't want her to think bad of me either. "No, definitely not. She barely talks to him."

"Okay," Mom says again. "So you have good reason to believe, then, that she was assaulted."

"I wouldn't call it that, but—"

Mom holds up a hand. "If he was forcing her to do something, even if they *were* dating, it was assault."

"Fine." Naming it as a crime makes it all seem ten times worse, and casts a lot of other things in a different light too: the way her mood fell after the pep rally when Carson talked to her, the way she seemed extra drunk all of a sudden at the toga party, the way she snapped at anyone who asked . . . She wasn't watching him, I realize, all those times I caught her looking.

She was watching *out* for him.

"I don't normally approve of solving things with violence," Mom says, passing me a jar of spaghetti sauce. "But this may be the one time I can say you made the right choice in that re-spect." She gives me a tight smile. "I'm proud of you for being a good man."

I duck my head. I don't feel good, and I don't feel like a man. I feel like complete and total crap. I feel small enough to ride in the cart, and I kind of wish it was an option right now. Letting Mom be in charge would be a relief.

RAYCHEL

With Mom gone on her date, I'm so pathetic that I'm rereading The Handmaid's Tale *just for something to do.* But a knock on the door startles me. I didn't hear a car pull up, so it's either someone on foot, which means stranger danger . . . or it's Matt's hybrid, which I can see through the blinds.

I stand in the middle of my room, paralyzed by indecision. I hope it's just him. But I also hope Andrew's with him.

Maybe I can pretend I'm not here.

The phone rings.

Maybe not. "Come answer the damn door," Matt says when I pick up.

"I'm . . . at Asha's."

He turns to face the window, and I can hear the eye roll in his voice. "I can see your shadow on the blinds, genius."

MATT

Damn. Raychel looks like hell. Her eyes don't meet mine as she hovers at the door, but I can tell they're red. "Hey."

"Hey." She steps back to let me in. Laundry, magazines, plates, and all kinds of chaos litter the room. There's no place to sit, so I wait, hands in pockets, as she closes the door and stands stranded in the entryway. "It's a pit," she says, one hand flopping toward the mess.

I can't argue. "Where have you been?"

"Here."

I snort. "Bullshit. If you'd been here, this place would be spotless."

She doesn't even scowl, and that's when I realize I still had hope that I was wrong about the party. "Raych—" I take a few steps toward her and stop when she steps back. "Hey." I've never seen her like this. "What's wrong?"

She gives a choking laugh. "Seriously?"

I flush. "I mean—it's just me. I should have . . . I don't know, I'm sorry. I shouldn't have waited so long to come over."

She shrugs. "I could have called."

"No, see . . ." I close the distance to take her hand. "That's the thing. It took me a few days, but I get it."

" 'It,' " she repeats cautiously.

"It wasn't your fault," I say.

She steps forward, pressing her face against my chest, and her arms clutch my waist. Her body shakes a little and I pull her closer, flush against me, petting her hair and whispering soothing nonsense, doing anything to calm her down.

If I'd just told her, all those goddamn nights she was lying right beside me, that I wanted her to be *my* girl, maybe none of this would have happened. I was too scared to lose her friendship, yeah. But I also wanted her to pick me.

No. I was insulted that she picked everyone else. I wanted her and tried not to, because so many others wanted her too, and she said yes to so many of them. I was embarrassed by her. Even though I knew, all along, that she fits just right, nestled under my arm, cheek pressed to my chest. I picked my pride over my girl, who's sweet under the spicy, soft under the harsh. She doesn't think I see it, but I do, and I want to tell her.

But I can't, not right now. There are other things to say first, and my words aren't smart enough, my lips aren't brave enough, for more. Not yet. But they will be, once we're past this, because she's my girl, stumbling and running, drinking and laughing, dancing and falling.

She's my girl, in the sunshine smelling like coconut, in the rain smelling like weed.

She does this to me, makes my thoughts come in funny lines and spurts, all crushing and dramatic and obvious.

She's my girl and I've never told her I know, that I've known it all along, but she's my girl and I've known it all along.

RAYCHEL

I cry all over Matt's shirt. When I've calmed down, I feel raw, shredded and open. He brings me ice water and a roll of toilet paper since we don't have tissues. I'm so grateful he's listening that I don't even think about asking him about Mindy. Or Andrew.

Instead I tell him about Mom using my college money, and about Carson. Not the horrible details, the ones that keep me awake at night, but the basics—that I went willingly, both times. That I tried to change my mind, both times. That Carson didn't know he'd done anything wrong and probably still doesn't. Matt hugs me again. "Have you talked to him since?"

I let out a weak laugh. "Um, no. He's staying far, far away from me." I hope it stays that way. "Have you?"

"Um, no," Matt says, also laughing halfheartedly.

"Did you get in trouble with your folks?" I've been so convinced I'll get fired that I haven't even stopped to think about whether the boys are grounded forever.

"Nah." Matt runs a hand through his hair. Only he could make a fractured nose look good. "We had to tell Mom a little."

I flinch, but I understand. "Yeah, mine too. As little as possible."

"Really?"

"She's been great," I say defensively. "But your dad must be super pissed at me."

He shakes his head. "Mom talked to him. I haven't said anything to Andrew though. He's been too big an asshole."

I try to say "Andrew has a right to be mad," but my throat makes a clicking sound, and I can't do it. "I'll talk to him soon," I manage.

•   •   •   •   •

Talking to Andrew is easier said than done.

Thursday morning, Matt drives me to school just like always. We walk together to English, ignoring the stares and whispers, and eat lunch as usual.

But Andrew is completely missing in action, so it's no surprise that he doesn't offer me rides to work. I take the transit instead. Friday afternoon, I hear him slam the garage door, but he's up the stairs by the time I reach the kitchen. I decide not to follow.

I hope to catch him Saturday, but Mrs. R. catches me instead. She and Dr. R. have been totally understanding and played along with the story that I've been sick, since that was my excuse when I called in. "Working on the weekend?"

"Just making up the time I missed," I say, pushing my hair out of my eyes.

She smiles. "Do you have a minute? I'd like to talk to you."

I follow her apprehensively out to the deck, where she's set two glasses of iced tea next to the lounge chairs. "Have a seat." She waits until I'm comfortable. "There's no easy way to broach this," she says, "so I'll just come right out with it. Matt explained about the fight at Trenton Montgomery's house."

149

I stare at the deck railing. "What did he say?"

"That the Tipton boy was assaulting you."

I flinch. Sometimes I forget Mrs. R. is a lawyer, not just a professor. But I kind of like how she refuses to use Carson's name, like he doesn't deserve it. "I guess," I say quietly. "He . . . we, um, we've . . . you know. Hooked up. Before."

"Had sex?" Mrs. R. pulls no punches. "Heavy petting?" she asks when I shake my head.

I'm not sure what heavy petting entails, but this isn't the time to point out she's old. "The first time he . . . made me do some stuff," I say, closing my eyes.

It doesn't hide her quiet intake of breath. "Did he rape you, Raychel?" Her voice is steady, but she can't mask the feeling behind it.

"No." I make myself look at her so she'll know it's true. Birds chirp a mismatched soundtrack above our scene. "It was just . . . oral." I barely get the last word out, but she hears it.

"You didn't agree to it?"

"He didn't exactly ask."

"So you didn't say yes." When I shrug, she says, "Raychel, listen to me." As if I have a choice. "What he did was wrong. Penetration of any kind without consent is rape, and it is wrong."

I study the polka-dot pattern on the chair cushion. "But I didn't really say no, either. At least the first time."

"But you didn't say yes. You didn't give your consent."

I blink back sudden tears. "But I said yes to . . . stuff before that." My chin quivers.

"Inviting someone into your living room doesn't give them permission to go through your underwear drawer."

I laugh involuntarily and drop my forehead into my hands. "I just . . . I don't know," I say. "Carson said a bunch of nice stuff and I wanted to believe him. I wanted to think someone . . ." A few tears escape but I make myself go on. "That someone . . . actually liked me, you know?"

She puts her hand on my arm. "I want you to listen, and really hear what I say," she says, pulling back to hold my hand. "You made some bad decisions. Everyone does. But that *doesn't give him the right.*" Her face is just like Andrew and Matt's when she's angry—all twitchy and full of fire. "No one has the right to touch you without your consent. I don't care if you parade down the street naked and stand three inches from his face—no one touches you unless you say so. And even if they've *had* your permission, they stop when you say stop. That's your right. Not his. Yours."

I nod tentatively, trying the idea on for size. It doesn't quite fit, but maybe I can stretch it into shape.

MATT

I don't know what Mom said to Raychel, but when we play a few rounds of pool in the afternoon, she seems calmer than she has in days. She goes home to have dinner with her mom, but

Sunday, she invites me over to watch football and do homework. The duplex is spotless again and everything feels as normal as it possibly can, except that I haven't manned up and told Raychel the truth about how I feel.

So naturally, I decide to do it in the least manly way possible.

When I get home, I retrieve an empty photo album from my desk and flip it open. It's a cheesy gift, and she will either love or hate it, but I'm hoping for the former. I mean, it's just pictures in plastic sleeves and white sticker labels, none of that scrapbooking crap.

I'm surprised by how many pictures there are of us together though. Hiking trips and random parties and choir performances and ridiculous-ass junior prom, hamming it up in formal clothes at Brenda's Bigger Burger. The Nuge at the Mulberry, pulling Bree and Raychel up to dance beside him. Us with Andrew, piled on the couch the day after Thanksgiving. All three of us with Spencer and Asha in a university skybox, courtesy of the football coach, who's one of my dad's patients. All the girls lined up at the bottom of Twin Falls. All the guys lined up at the top of McNair Mountain. All of us blurry at Eagle Point because Nathan's phone fell off its makeshift rock tripod.

I sort them out, deciding to put them in chronological order. The last page will be blank. I've debated leaving a letter there, or a giant question mark, or . . . something. I'm not sure how to say, "By the way, I'm in love with you and always have been, but no pressure if you don't feel the same way."

I try not to consider what happens if she doesn't. And I really try not to consider what happens if she does, because once I let the fantasies start, they won't turn off. I feel bad about some of them: Raychel at the lake in her bikini, untying it when I sunscreen her back instead of just pulling the straps aside; Raychel on my bed, but lying back beneath me instead of sitting with a pillow on her lap; Raychel leaning in to kiss me on the mouth instead of the cheek like she always does.

But mostly they're benign. Just me and her, doing the same stuff we always do, and all of it meaning a little more.

· · · · ·

Mom gave me some tips on helping Raychel recover, so I don't take it personally when she lapses into quiet spells or seems sad. I keep an eye out for Carson, but he stays away, probably because Keri Sturgis has been talking some mad trash about him at school. Raychel's not the only one taking the brunt of this gossip cycle, now that Keri's got other people whispering that maybe what happened wasn't mutual.

I thought Andrew would ask me for the truth, but he's barely been around. When I do see him, his eyes are so bloodshot I'm surprised they work at all. He sleeps most of the time he's home, and I heard my parents discussing whether or not to take away his car. Raychel said she'd talk to him, but she hasn't. Not that I'm in a hurry for them to become best buddies again. I know it's selfish, but I was starting to get really worried that their friendship might become something more. And now that I have her to myself, I'm not looking forward to sharing again.

I'm not going to wuss out on talking to her, though. Tomorrow's a teacher work day so I think I'm going to give her the photo album over the three-day weekend. But first I have to get through today's blood drive. When I pick her up, Raychel's having one of her quiet mornings, so I blather a little about college applications and how my dad wants me to do early admission at Duke. "It's due November 1," I say, "which is ridiculous. And even regular admission is due by mid-December if I want an alumni interview."

"Huh," she says. "That's early."

"Have you started yet?" I ask. "Regular admission is January 1 at most of the good schools."

She looks up. "I thought I told you—we're using my money for rent now."

I know she doesn't want to hear this, but I have to ask. "Isn't there any way to contact your dad? I mean, there has to—"

"I wouldn't take his money even if he had some," she says.

She should sue him and take it all, but I can tell it's not a good time to press. "I still think you'll get scholarships."

Raychel sighs. "My grades are good enough for a state school, but . . ."

"Yeah and your financial situation will probably help, so you're kind of lucky," I say, trying to sound positive. "I mean, you have guaranteed money here, but that doesn't mean it's your only choice."

"I didn't say I wasn't applying anywhere else," she says, words clipped. "Most applications aren't due until March."

"True," I admit. "You'll get in better places though, if you try."

"Thanks," she says, and I can't tell if she's being sarcastic or not.

. . . . .

At school, Raych goes to class, and I go to the gym to help set up for the blood drive. Everyone's so busy that I don't even have to try to avoid Mindy.

I wait to give blood myself until fourth period, the same time Raychel comes to donate. "Hey, Trent," I call. He looks up from a cookie tray he's organizing with Rosa. "I'm going to get in line." He gives me finger guns, nodding at Raychel, and I join her. "How's your day?"

"Fantastic," she deadpans. "Yours?"

"Not as bad as I expected." The line moves forward. I know she doesn't weigh enough to meet the requirements, but I also know enough not to mention a girl's weight, ever. Her eyes cut toward the tables, so I try to hear what she's listening to.

"Have you had male-to-male sexual activity?" a worker asks one of our linemen, who makes a big show of laughing and looking around as he sputters his denials.

"Methinks the meathead doth protest too much," I whisper, but Raych doesn't even crack a smile. Maybe this weekend won't be photo album time after all.

RAYCHEL

I'm glad it's blood drive day. Getting stabbed with a needle sounds oddly cathartic.

Last night, Mom and I sat down with a budget and tried to find a loophole, but the numbers are nothing but a noose: I'm stuck here next year, unless I can get a full ride somewhere else. I'm trying to feel okay about it. At least I get to go to college. But Matt's little lecture this morning about "better" places sucked the wind right out of that.

I step forward when he does, waiting for my turn to bleed. Student Council really decorated for the occasion. I mean, they decorate for every occasion, but this one is a doozy. Red streamers everywhere, as high as someone on a chair could reach. Smiling red poster-board blood drops dangle from the basketball goals like morbidly happy rain. There's even a kid dressed as a plush blood drop carrying a giant stuffed syringe. I'm afraid to laugh. I might not be able to stop.

Matt's arm bumps mine. I can tell he's about to put it around my waist, so I lean over to scratch a pretend itch on my leg. He's been extra affectionate lately, and I'm sure he's just trying to make sure I'm okay, but it's getting a little annoying.

When it's our turn, I answer each question in a normal voice. Might as well make the eavesdropping easy. No recent vaccinations. No sexual contact with a prostitute. "Have you ever had sexual contact with a male who has ever had sexual contact with another male?" the nurse asks.

"Not that I know of."

She gives me a dirty look. "From 1977 to the present, have you received money, drugs, or other payment for sex?"

"No." She won't think beer for boobs is funny. It's funny to me—funny that it makes the most sense of all my recent sexual encounters. It's not all that different from tempting blood donors with free food. Surely veins are more intimate than chests.

"Are you sure you weigh enough?" the nurse asks, eyeing me.

"Of course," I lie, faking a smile. She shakes her head but writes it down. I'm only a few pounds low, and I'll do anything to miss an hour in the same room with Carson. Talking to Mrs. R. helped, but it doesn't change the fact that I have to see him every day—or that I'm likely to keep seeing him every day for the next four years. He probably signed his soul to a fraternity in fifth grade.

I was worried that Mrs. R. would be legally obligated to report what happened, but she promised not to. "To be honest, you'd never get a conviction," she said. She did make me promise to tell my mom, but I'm in no hurry to follow through there.

The nurse preps my arm. "You might want to look away." I don't. "Tiny veins . . ." She taps my inner arm. "Let's try this one. Little stick . . ." The needle looks huge, but doesn't hurt that bad. "Just lie back and relax," she says, pointing to the TVs they've set up with old Disney movies. I can see both *Cinderella* and *Snow White and the Seven Dwarfs* from my chair.

I watch the bag instead. It fills slowly, blood thinner than I expect. Beside me, Matt's watching *Aladdin* and drinking bottled water, his bag slightly darker than mine. "What's your blood type?" I ask.

He glances over. "A positive."

Of course.

MATT

The nurse pulls the needle out of my arm. It hurts worse coming out than going in, but I'm ready and manage not to wince. Raychel doesn't either, and shows me her Disney princess Band-Aid with dark humor, but when she stands up, her eyes roll back in her head. "Crap!" I move on instinct and grab her under the arms before she hits the floor.

"Oh dear," the nurse says blandly. "I had a feeling that might happen." When I glare, she glares back. "I bet she learns her lesson."

I bet she doesn't.

· · · · ·

The nurse approves Raych to leave in time to make Senior Seminar. Ms. Moses, our teacher, might understand if Raychel missed, but since she told me I couldn't skip for StuCo responsibilities, I doubt she'd make an allowance for Raychel responsibilities. "How do you feel?" I ask as we leave the gym.

158

"Okay. Wobbly." I offer my arm but she waves it away. "It was worth it for the cheese dip."

"It is pretty good," I admit, humoring her. "But Raych . . ." I grab her hand and pull her to a stop. "You know that was a bad idea. I could have just brought you some queso."

"I'm a big girl," she says. "It was fine."

"You're *not* a big girl. That's why it wasn't fine." I smile, hoping she'll take the joke and the warning and let it go without getting mad.

She lets go of my hand to adjust her sleeve. "It was no big deal. It's fine."

Fine.

· · · · ·

Every week, Ms. Moses gives us a topic to discuss that's common to all our projects. Today we're discussing gender equality, which should be fun, given Raychel's mood. When I'm called on toward the end of class, I mumble something about men and women being inherently equal, but Raychel levels a glare across the room. "You're just saying that to be PC," she says, and the rest of the class goes silent.

I put on my calmest face. "So if I say women and men aren't equal, I'm a chauvinist, and if I say they are, I'm . . . still wrong somehow?"

"There's a difference," she says, taking her pencil out of her mouth, "between equal and identical."

"Well yeah, but that doesn't mean one is better."

"No, but one inherently has the upper hand."

I shrug. "If you say so."

She scowls, pissed that I'm folding before she can win. "Think about it, Matthew." The girl beside her snickers at the way Raychel spits my name, like it tastes bad. "What's the one difference between girls and boys? What can you force me to do that I can't do to you?"

I squirm, trying to think of a way not to answer. "Guys can get raped too," a kid across the room volunteers, not looking at anyone but Raychel.

"Yeah," she says, frowning in sympathy. "But that's not what I meant." She turns back to me. "Say that happens. Are you going to get pregnant?" She waits, staring me down. She's going to make me answer, make me say it.

"No."

She points the sharp end of her pencil at me. "Can someone force you to abort a baby you want to keep?"

"No," I admit again. She's not only going to make her point, she's going to use it to stake me through the heart.

"Can someone force you to have a baby you don't want?"

"No." I can't look at her. She's right, of course, but I don't have to like it.

"Can you hop off, scot-free, and pretend like that baby's never been born?"

Like her dad. "I . . . I mean I wouldn't . . ."

"So don't tell me," she interrupts, jabbing the pencil in my direction, "that everyone is equal. Don't tell me you know what it's like, to know that no matter what you do, how powerful you are, some prick could attack you—" Ms. Moses coughs but Raychel doesn't even pause. "You can do everything right, be careful, become a nun and intend to die a goddamn virgin, but at any moment, some dickhead could not just hurt you, but create another life to ruin at the same time, and you get held responsible for both. Don't *tell* me you understand that."

No one speaks. My mind races, realizing Raychel is both people in this hypothetical: the woman attacked and the abandoned child. But I can't put the words together quickly enough to beat the bell. Everyone rushes to escape the room, including Raychel, who leaves me behind still trying to say "All I want in my goddamn life is to keep that from happening to you."

But I couldn't even say it in time, much less do it.

RAYCHEL

Just when I think Matt's starting to get it, he demonstrates in spectacular fashion that he doesn't. Maybe I was too hard on him in class, but goddamn—he's a rich white dude with his future wide open, and he wants to lecture me about not trying hard enough for college and how much I weigh while whining about his own opportunities? Excuse me if I'm not interested in sitting through his insights on gender roles.

He's walking a safe ten feet behind me, but I slow down when I notice Andrew farther ahead. His arm drapes around Keri as they leave the lobby. His other hand shoots out to touch Cowboy Chester. He doesn't notice Carson breaking off from a group across the patio.

I speed up, pushing outside into the crisp afternoon.

"Richardson!" Carson barks. Andrew looks up. "You a senior now, or just think you're such a badass that rules don't apply to you?"

Andrew replies with something I can't hear, but I see his casual smirk. Keri backs away from them, stopping beside me. "That jerk," she whispers. "I hope Andrew kicks his butt again."

I don't. I start forward but Matt catches me by the shoulder. "What are you doing?"

I brush him off and take another step, slightly sideways, so I can see both boys' faces. Carson, twice as wide but nowhere near eye level, even on tiptoe, gets closer and closer to Andrew. He pokes Andrew in the chest. "You think you're hot shit, junior?"

Andrew scoffs. "I kicked your ass, didn't I?"

"Two on one's not a fair fight." His spit sprays Andrew's shirt. "Your big brother isn't here to defend your ass."

Matt coughs. They both turn to glower at him. "This isn't your—" Andrew starts, but Carson sucker punches him in the gut and the word "fight" comes out in a wheeze. "Fight!" someone yells for him, and another voice takes up the chant. "Fight! Fight!"

Blood rushes in my ears, deafening me to anything resembling sense. I start forward and Andrew straightens up to grab my arm. "Raych," he warns.

His fingers dig into my flesh. He's not scared to hurt me like Matt is. "Damnit, let go!"

"Stay out of it, Sanders." Carson reaches like he's going to push me away. In a movement so fast that I miss it, Andrew lets go of me and pops him in the mouth. Carson yells, guttural and furious. His hands cover his lips. Blood seeps between his fingers. "I'll kill you!" He sounds like a cartoon character, words all spongy and exaggerated.

The lobby doors burst open. "You," the principal shouts, pointing at all three boys. "In my office. Now." He gives me a long stare but leaves me alone. The boys follow him into the building without a backward glance.

The crowd buzzes around us. I'm so furious that I'm shaking. I spin around, looking for someone or something to hurt, but a hand touches my back. "Raychel."

I blink. Keri links her arm through mine and tugs me gently through the crowd.

MATT

"You boys think I don't know what goes on after school?" Mr. Johnson paces in front of us. Plants fill the window of his office

and a young girl smiles from a frame on his desk. "You think I don't know you had a fight a couple weeks ago?"

"No, sir," I answer. "I mean—"

"I know what you mean," he cuts me off. "What's you boys' problem?"

We glance at one another warily. I mentally will Andrew to keep his mouth shut, and dare Carson to open his, because if he says Raychel's name, I might break his face. Good guy or not, I would enjoy it, no matter what Mom thinks.

Carson speaks up from behind an ice pack. "Just a little disagreement, sir."

"About?" Johnson demands. The guy is huge, at least six foot five, and completely bald, so of course we call him Big Johnson. No way was he going to avoid that nickname. "A girl?"

We all look in different directions. "Not really," I lie.

Big Johnson stares us all down, glaring at the top of my brother's head until he looks up. "Tipton, Richardson—Andrew," he amends. "You're both suspended for three days."

"What?" Carson shouts. Andrew rubs the back of his neck.

"Matthew," Johnson says. "I expect better out of you. I'll let you off this time since I can't prove you were involved, but next time it's a suspension." I nod, meeting his eyes, and start to stand. "Sit down, son." He shakes his head. "I know that Sanders girl is your friend, but don't go ruining your future for her."

Carson guffaws, and Big Johnson whirls on him as he tries to cover it with a cough. "You got something to add?" His lips purse as Carson's eyes widen. "Good. Get out of here before I kick you off the baseball team for good measure." He looks at all of us. "I'll chat with your folks this evening."

RAYCHEL

The Mardi Gras beads on Keri's mirror sway hypnotically. I don't notice where we're going until we pull up to Coffee Depot. "My treat," she says, smiling.

We order and find a seat on the deck, waiting for our drinks to cool. Autumn is finally making an appearance, with gray clouds hanging over the first of the yellow leaves. I try not to look at the lawn or think about who mowed its neat edges. Or why I ordered a drink I've never had before.

"Here's the deal," Keri says, folding her hands. "I know about you and Andrew."

"What?" I yelp, with absolutely no attempt to play it cool. I literally cannot take one more thing today. Not one.

But she laughs. "It's okay. I mean, it was kind of obvious when he tried to fight Carson. For the second time."

"Keri," I start, stalling for time. "It ended at Trent's party. It wasn't since you and I have been—or you and him have—"

She waves me off. "Me and him are nothing. We take test prep together, that's all."

I look up cautiously. "So you're not mad."

"No, I understand." She twists her short black hair. "Does Matt know?"

"No," I admit. "And there's no reason for him to find out now."

"He'd be really jealous," Keri says. "That kid has loved you forever."

I shake my head. "We're just friends." My fingers trace the mosaic in the tile tabletop. "To be honest, there was a time I wished we were more, but after all this? I really like knowing that at least one guy likes me for my brain and not my body." I look up. "He'll be mad we lied, but the jealousy will just be about us spending time without him."

"Well, either way, I won't tell him." She holds her cup up for a toast. "God, boys are more trouble than they're worth."

We both drink to that.

· · · · ·

The first time she gave me a ride, I made Keri drop me on campus and claimed I was meeting my mom. Today I don't even have the energy to be embarrassed by my cracked driveway and peeling paint. "Can I use your bathroom?" she asks.

I can't exactly say no. At the door, I get my keys out, but the door isn't locked. "It's right through there," I say, flipping on the light.

Two very surprised and guilty faces freeze mid-make-out on the couch. "Raychel!" Mom yelps.

The guy beside her looks up. All I want to do is shove Keri

out the door and slam it behind us. But she's polite despite her shock. "Hi, Mrs. Sanders," she says. "Hi, Eddie."

I'm not dreaming. It *is* Eddie.

My mother is on top of the school janitor.

Keri squeezes my arm. "I can hold it. I'll see you tomorrow?"

"Yeah. I'll . . . um . . ."

"I'll text you later," she says.

I nod mutely, wishing I could go with her. Mom finds a less compromising position and clears her throat once Keri's gone. "Ed," she says, her voice fake and perky, "this is my daughter, Raychel."

"We've met," he says, and smiles. "I'm pretty popular up there."

"Really?" She waits for me to nod. "Well . . ."

I stare at a spot over her head. "I think I'll, uh . . . do some homework." I rush to my room. Safest bet would be to sleep. Sleep means I don't have to discuss this with her.

Because what the actual hell.

My mother and the janitor.

Don't think about it. Get in bed. Never mind that it's early. Emergency napping in progress. But the click of the front door tells me Eddie's left, and a moment later, Mom knocks on my door. "Raychel?" She takes a seat on my bed. "So. You, um . . . you know Ed?"

"Everybody knows him."

That makes her smile. "He's a great guy. I wanted your first meeting to go . . . differently . . ."

"That's who you've been with this whole time." I sit up. "The janitor."

She jerks as if she's been slapped. It's sort of satisfying. "What?"

"Eddie." I shake my head. "This whole time, you just couldn't bring yourself to tell me the truth."

Mom straightens her back. "You think I'm embarrassed?"

I shrug.

"Because he does the same job I do?"

"That's different," I say, cringing. "I just—what happened to 'do better'? 'Make something of yourself'?"

She slaps me across the face.

Mom has never slapped me. Ever.

"Not all of us get the opportunities you will," she hisses. "I don't expect you to respect what I do, even if I do it for you. But Ed is a better person than your father ever *thought* about being."

"I didn't pick my father!" I yell as she storms out. "You did!"

She slams the door.

MATT

Dad's voice carries up the stairs and through my open door. "Until the end of the semester!" he yells. "And maybe not even then!"

"You can have the car back when you demonstrate some maturity!" Mom adds.

When Andrew stomps up the stairs, I jump to close my door, but he barrels through it anyway. "Did you hear that shit?" he demands.

"That sucks."

He's not impressed by my sympathy. "And you get off free and clear, as usual."

"Hey, I had your back," I argue. "But I was trying to keep Raychel out of it."

"No you weren't," he says. "I should have let her take a swing."

"It might have helped," I agree sarcastically. "She was pretty bitchy today." I fake laugh. "Not that it's different from any other day."

Andrew stiffens. "Take it back."

"Why? Because it's true?"

"You're supposed to be her best friend," he says, his voice rising.

"What about you?" I yell back. "You haven't even talked to her!"

"Boys!" Dad barks from the door. We jump.

"What the hell is the matter with you?" Mom asks from behind him.

Andrew runs a hand over his chest, watching me warily. "You haven't even bothered to ask her what happened," I say.

"I know what happened," he snaps.

"Yeah? And you're still treating her like trash? You're an even bigger asshole than I thought, then."

I can tell he's confused. "You don't know what you're talking about."

"Really? I don't know that Carson forced himself on her? Twice?"

Andrew looks like I've kicked him in the stomach. But Mom gasps. "Matthew! You didn't even tell him to call her?"

"What?" I jerk backward. "Why do I have to be his conscience?"

"You should have at least—"

"Mom," Andrew interrupts, and I've never seen my brother look so shattered. "I know you just took them, but I need my car keys."

She doesn't say a word as she hands them over. He rushes out, and Dad shakes his head. "I'm disappointed in you, Matthew."

"Raych didn't want me to say anything!"

"You didn't have to give him details to make clear that he should talk to her."

I sit down, knowing he's right, and wondering if I feel bad for being selfish, or just bad that someone noticed.

RAYCHEL

I grab my backpack from the living room and start shoving clothes into it. "What are you doing?" Mom demands.

"I'm packing. I'm not fucking staying here." And I mean it. Not tonight, and not next year. I am not staying in this duplex and I'm not staying in this town. I'll go somewhere else and get a job and a cheap apartment. Maybe I'll go right now.

Mom stands up and stalks out, slamming her bedroom door. I return the favor as I exit through the front.

But then I stand there, stranded on the porch. I don't actually have any money to leave with at the moment. And who am I going to call? Matt, who I chewed out a few hours ago? Andrew, who hates my guts? I decide to walk to Asha's, but I'm only a house away when a horn honks.

I turn around. Andrew's in my driveway. He gets out of the car and rushes over, slowing when he takes in my expression. "Raych . . ." he starts, and that's all it takes for me to burst into tears. "Hey," he says, pulling me to his chest. "Hey."

"I'm sorry," I sob, grabbing his shirt.

"I know." He tugs me toward the car. "Me too. Come on, let's go home."

· · · · ·

After a short explanation, Mrs. R. takes me to the guest room, telling both boys to let me sleep. They follow her advice, and so do I. In the morning, she comes in quietly. "Hungry?" she asks, balancing a tray heaped with food.

The smell makes me push the blanket off my face. "Is that bacon?"

She nods. "And hash browns, eggs, fruit, and coffee."

"Wow, thanks." I sit up, trying to do something with my hair.

"Don't thank me," she says. "I'm just the waitstaff."

"Still . . ." I don't remember the last time I had breakfast in bed. My birthday, probably, a few years ago—Mom made waffles and . . . and last night comes roaring back.

Mrs. R. watches and adopts a false smile. "Here." She pulls the legs of the tray down and sets it over my lap. Only the Richardsons would have a special tray for breakfast in bed.

"Thanks," I say again, and start on the bacon as she circles the bed. She sits carefully beside me, not speaking until I finish. It's kind of hard to eat with her watching.

"So you want to talk about it?" She picks up the tray and puts it on the dresser.

No. I don't want to talk about anything. Ever. "I'd rather brush my teeth."

"Fair enough." But I'm not off the hook yet. "Honey, have you told your mother what happened?"

I shake my head. She sighs, and I'm about to tell her Carson started the fight yesterday, not Andrew or Matt, but she speaks first. "Look, you know I love you like a daughter. It's unacceptable for her to slap you and I won't defend that. But you have to talk to her. Nothing's going to change if you don't communicate."

I nod, not sure if I'm trying to convince her or myself. Mom and I can communicate all day long, but there are some things that no amount of talking can change.

MATT

Raychel doesn't venture out of the guest room until late morning.
I try to intercept her before she goes downstairs, but she picks
the one minute I'm in the bathroom to leave, and judging by
her expression when I catch up to her in the kitchen, it was
probably on purpose. Before I can ask her about last night or
anything else, my dad is pulling a stool up to the bar. "What
are you kids doing with your day off?" he asks.

Andrew belches from the playroom and it sounds like he
says "pooool," but it's hard to tell. "I thought we were grounded,"
I say.

Dad studies me. "I thought spending the day with your old
man might be a good punishment."

"Old?" Raychel repeats, perking up. "Who's old?"

"Suck-up!" Andrew shouts, coming into the room. "I dunno,
old man. Depends on what you're offering."

Dad pulls out his wallet and peeks inside. "Well, I'm on call,
but I still have two free passes to the mini-golf course at Speed-
way Station, since I am such a master—"

"What?" Raychel squawks. "I totally beat you!"

He holds up the passes. "But *I* got a hole in one."

"So did I!" She jumps for one of the passes.

He lets her have it. "Looks like you boys are paying your own
way," he says, grinning.

RAYCHEL

It's pretty obvious that Dr. R. is just doing this to cheer me up, but both Matt and Andrew play along without complaint. I'm grateful for the reprieve. Dr. R. gets us a zillion tokens. Andrew drags us to the go-carts and demands to race me, but it turns out what he really wants is to talk while Matt and Dr. R. take their turn. "So hey," he says. "Are you okay?"

"I'm fine." I was so wrapped up in my own drama that we didn't even discuss why he showed up at my house. "Thanks for, you know. Taking care of me last night."

He rubs the back of his neck. "It's the least I could do. Jesus, Raych, I just— About the party. I didn't know."

This is not the reprieve I was hoping for. I start to say "It's okay" or "I should have told you," but instead I find myself saying, "I wish you had asked."

"I should have." He leans against the railing. "I was . . . My feelings were hurt. I thought you and I . . ."

I blow a piece of hair out of my eyes. "I mean, I get it. We never really got clear on, like . . . what we were."

The final bell rings. We look at the track and see Matt watching us. Dr. R. takes advantage and passes him at the last minute. Andrew grins, at them and then at me. "Well, let's get clear," he says, pulling me toward the gate.

I drag my feet. "Right now?"

He laughs. "Tonight," he says, and gets in his go-cart. "Let's talk after dinner." He revs his engine, like he can't wait.

MATT

After racing, Raychel insists that we have a skeeball tournament. The volume in the building is right at "dull roar," which makes any conversation that's not trash talk impossible. She throws the wooden balls viciously, staring down the rings like they've burned and pillaged her village or something, but every time the light on her lane goes off, she breaks into an enormous smile.

So I can't be too annoyed at my dad for stealing our whole day. But I'm plenty annoyed with Andrew, who's basically monopolizing her time now that they're friends again.

When we're out of tokens, she turns to me with that smile and tears off my strip of tickets. "Mine's way longer," she says gleefully.

"Not as long as mine." Andrew lets his strip unravel to his feet.

Dad clears his throat. "Tee time, kids."

· · · · ·

On the way out to the golf course, we stop at the photo booth and cram inside. "Take a serious one for your mother!" Dad says from outside the curtain.

"Okay," Raych says. But all the photos end up ridiculous.

On the golf course, there are a lot of jokes about balls and holes. Dad pretends like he's not listening, then like he's not with us, and then like he's showering under the fountain shaped like an elephant. When we reach the Hippo Hole, which causes more snickering, Dad and Andrew are both through in two shots, but I purposely miss a few times. "Go on," I say, waving them away. "We'll catch up."

Raych stands behind me, waiting. "Don't miss," she says right as I swing.

"I have a club."

"That you don't know how to use."

I prove her right several times before I prove her wrong. Finally it's her turn, and I wait until she's lined up before I say, "So what happened last night?"

Her shot veers left. "Oh. Um . . ." She walks over to her ball. "I got in a fight with my mom." Her next shot goes way right. I stand between her and the hole, so she spins her club against the ground.

I nod, waiting. I heard that last night before Mom took Raychel upstairs.

"And . . ." She lets the spinning stop. "And she slapped me."

"Damn, Rauch." I move my feet apart so she can putt between them, realizing a moment too late that I'm exhibiting a whole lot of trust. But she just shoots and writes down our scores. I'm trying to think of a tactful way to ask what she's going to do about her mom when she looks up.

"Why didn't you tell Andrew? About Carson?"

I look at my feet. "It didn't . . . I mean, I wasn't sure what you'd want him to know. I figured it was your story to tell."

She nods slowly. "I'm sorry about yesterday, in class. I mean, I meant it, but . . . it's just been a really hard year."

"Oh, yeah, I mean . . ." Now I'm the one fumbling for words. "No big deal. I mean . . . you're my girl, Raych. I get it." I try to keep the words light, let her make what she wants of them.

I must say it too earnestly, because she studies me for a moment before handing over the scorecard, shaking her head. "We should talk more, later," she says. Her eyes meet mine again and for a heartbeat, I picture kissing her.

But we're in the middle of the mini-golf course, and my dad is shouting "Hole in one!" while doing an embarrassing victory dance by the windmill behind her, and I have to step back. Just like always.

RAYCHEL

All in all, it ends up being a pretty nice day—as good as can be expected, under the circumstances. Dr. R. never gets called in to work, the boys manage not to pick at each other for a few hours, and hopefully Andrew and I will snag some time alone to sort things out later. There was a weird moment with Matt on the golf course, but I think I'm just so hyperaware of boys making advances that I read too much into it. Matt's never made a single move on me. I can trust him.

I'm hoping for a short dinner, because I have to admit—I can't wait to straighten things out with Andrew. But Dr. R. wants to talk about college applications. He badgers Matt about early decision at Duke. Matt, trying to take the attention off himself, turns to me. "Have you thought any more about early applications?"

I stare at the steak bleeding on my plate. "A little. I'll probably just do March."

"What?" Matt demands. "Why?"

"It's expensive," I say. "The less I spend, the more I can help my mom. And I can always just go to the university here."

"There's nothing wrong with staying," Andrew says.

"Of course not!" Mrs. R. says from behind my chair, then serves me some potatoes. They hit my plate with a wet slop. "I teach here, after all."

Matt snorts. "Because they were the only ones that offered you tenure." It's true—she's told us that many times, as a cautionary tale against relying on academia for employment—but the room falls silent until he looks up. "What?"

Mrs. R. has laser eyes. "I'm sorry, I didn't realize my job was such a disappointment to you."

"What?" Matt says again, looking to Andrew and me for help. "I'm just saying—"

"Oh, I know what you're saying," Mrs. R. interrupts. "What I can't figure out is where you get off saying it." Matt doesn't have a chance of defending himself once she gets rolling. She grabs the salad from the counter and comes back to the table. "Where do you think you're getting the education that's preparing you for a fancy school? Here, in Big Springs. Where you can take university classes at fourteen. Where a National Book Award winner lives down the street. Where an internationally known pianist gave you lessons, and a president went to school, and plenty of smart people, myself included, *choose* to raise their children because it offers so many advantages."

He tries again, but she puts the bowl down and points a serving spoon at him. "You have this town, and our jobs here, to thank for your future, and you'd do well to recognize it." She sits and puts her napkin in her lap with an angry flourish.

Andrew, to his credit, stays quiet. But Matt tries to laugh and says, "Wow, have a little overreaction, Mom."

"Go to your room," Dr. R. snaps.

"What?" Matt looks at him in disbelief. "Fine." He throws down his fork and storms out.

· · · · ·

After an awkward and silent dinner, I excuse myself to head upstairs, and tap on Matt's door. "Come in," he calls.

I close it quietly behind me. Matt's lying on his plaid bedspread, tossing a foam football into the air. "You should apologize to your mom," I tell him.

"I will. Later." He waits for me to sit down, but I stay next to the dresser with my arms crossed. "What?" he asks.

"You don't have anything to say to me?"

"You know what?" He catches the football. "Yeah. I do. What the hell, Raych?"

My mouth falls open. "Seriously?"

"You're just giving up?"

"I'm not giving up," I say, hands on hips. "I'm making the best decision for my situation."

Matt tilts his head like I'm being thick. "I just . . . I worry about you, you know? You're so smart, Raych. You're meant for good things. Big things."

"I can do good things with a state-school degree," I argue. "And I didn't say I'm *definitely* staying here. But it's Big Springs I want to escape, not the university."

He sighs. "I just don't want you to end up flipping burgers or scrubbing toilets or something."

My hackles rise again. "You know my mom scrubs toilets, right?"

"I just meant—"

"No, I know what you meant." I step toward him. "I embarrass you. Just like my mom embarrasses me."

"No—"

"No, I get it. This is the exact same conversation she and I had last night when I walked in on her and Eddie. She's right, I'm the one being a—"

"What?" Matt says. "Eddie the janitor?"

And then he does the one thing I can't forgive—the one thing worse than my own reaction.

He laughs.

MATT

How? How have I managed to screw this up so royally?

Raychel stormed out of my room. I just sat there, confused, until I heard her talking to Andrew. Then I decided to escape the insanity before they could team up on me.

Now the headlights shine on one tree at a time, like stop-motion animation, like the thoughts I can't isolate in my brain. I flip through my music, suddenly understanding why Andrew says it sucks. There's nothing remotely angry enough for tonight.

I've never considered why my brother wants angry music all the time. Or maybe he only wants it when he's with me.

I settle for a Doors marathon on the classic rock station, consoling myself with the fact that Jim Morrison was a way bigger screwup than me.

I don't understand what happened. Even putting aside my disappointment that Raychel is giving up, which means we definitely won't be at neighboring schools, I'm still not seeing why I'm in the wrong. Raychel's never wanted to stay here, and she's spent years planning ways to leave. But now she's staying, and she acts like it's by choice, even though it's clearly because her mom blew all her money. Yet she's still defensive about her mom, even though that's the one person she's never wanted to be like.

I try to see it from Raychel's point of view. I guess I'd be mad if she talked trash about my mom.

Kind of like I did at dinner.

Damn.

I'm dipshit.

Flashing blue lights in my rearview rudely inform me that local law enforcement agrees.

RAYCHEL

I stand in the hallway, debating whether to hide or go home. I don't really want to face any other Richardsons right now, much less my mom, so I open the guest room door.

But Andrew's lying on my bed.

His fingers are crossed behind his head, legs at the ankles. He sits up when I wave him off. "I called shotgun," he says. I give him a weak smile and his fades. "Are you okay?" He moves over, patting the space beside him.

"Yeah," I mumble, propping a pillow against the headboard.

He starts to stand up. "You want me to go kick Matt's ass?"

"No!" I say, surprised at how loud it comes out. "Jesus, stop punching people and sit down." I pull my knees up and hide my face.

His touch on my hair surprises me. "I'm sorry," he says. "I shouldn't have punched Carson either."

"Why did you?" I ask.

"He hit me first."

I roll my eyes. "You know what I mean."

Andrew looks around uncomfortably. "I don't know. I was jealous, but . . . At the time, I could tell something wasn't right, you know? I knew he was hurting you. But then once we left, you didn't want to talk—"

"I was drunk," I interrupt.

"I know," he says. "I mean, I realize that now. But when you didn't call or anything after . . . I dunno. I should have realized you were upset, but I started to doubt myself and whether you really liked me and it was just . . ." He sighs. "It was easier to be mad than it was to admit I had screwed up."

We're both silent for a moment. Then Matt's door slams and his feet pound down the hall.

Andrew whistles. "He's really pissed, huh?"

"I don't care."

He snorts and moves closer. "So. Tell me what happened."

I look up. "With Matt?"

"No," he says, shaking his head. "I mean everything. From the beginning."

"Why?"

He exhales, insulted. "Because I want to know, genius." He squeezes my knee. "Because I screwed up, and I want to make it right. I care about you, no matter what else happens with . . . you know"—his cheeks flush—"with us."

I think for a minute. I hate that my brain immediately goes to Matt—what he'll think, how he'll feel, if Andrew and I get back together and make it official. He won't understand. He'll make fun of me.

But I'm tired of Matt always trying to tell me what's best. "Us, huh?" I say. "Is that on the table?"

Andrew's mouth twitches. "I won't make the obvious joke about having *you* on a table, but I want you to admire my self-restraint."

I laugh. "Oh yes, very admirable." But the laughter is short, because I know that what's coming isn't pretty. "Are you sure you want to hear all this?"

Andrew nods, making a big show of settling in. "All of it. Let me have it."

.   .   .   .   .

When I'm finished, Andrew stares at me. Finally he blinks. "He did *what?*"

"He . . . he made me . . ." I can't say it again.

"That's wrong," Andrew says, reaching for my hand. "You know that's wrong, right? Like, illegal wrong. Like you should press charges wrong."

I half laugh, half cough. "Like anyone would believe me."

"That's rape, Raych. You can't let him—"

"It's not," I interrupt. "I mean, it is, but even your mom admitted we'd never get a conviction. My word against his, and everyone thinks I'm a slut anyway."

Mrs. R. never said that last part, but Andrew doesn't argue. I kind of love him for not trying to lie. He pulls me into a hug and mumbles again that he's sorry. I bury my face in his shoulder, take a heaving breath, and try not to cry. I'm really tired of crying. But he kisses the top of my head and I can't help it. "Hey," he says, patting my back. "It's okay. You're going to be okay."

"It helps that you know," I tell him. "Just hearing that another person thinks it's messed up."

"Of course it's messed up!" he says. "You're blaming yourself for that shit?"

I pull at a loose thread on the bedspread. I know Mrs. R. would want me to say no. "I mean . . . I said yes."

"To sucking his dick?"

I grimace. "No!"

"Then what?"

"To going to his car. To getting *in* the car. And at the party, I—"

"None of those things say, 'I want to go down on you,'" he scolds, shaking my shoulder. "I make out with lots of girls, but I don't stick my dick in their mouths uninvited."

Hearing it so bluntly from Andrew somehow makes it sink in. He's not spouting stuff he learned in lawyer school, or offering vague platitudes like Matt did. He's just agreeing without even having to think about it. It makes me tear up again, and he rushes to apologize. "Wait, I'm sorry, I should watch my mouth . . . I mean . . . shit." He pulls me into another hug and I don't know what else to do, so I wrap my arms around his back and squeeze.

"I want . . ." He runs a hand under my hair, making me shudder. I try again. "I want it all to go away. I want everything to be . . ." I cough-laugh again, rubbing my nose. "I don't even know what I want."

Andrew pulls back to look me in the eye. "Well, I do," he says, and I've never seen him more serious. "I want you."

I'm crying again. "I don't see how you can."

He touches my cheek. "Then let me show you."

MATT

One two-hundred-dollar speeding ticket later, I'm on my way home. I drove a lot farther than I thought, and now I have to watch my speed on top of it, so the drive home takes forever.

Dad is waiting at the breakfast bar, his gin and tonic sweating a small ring on the counter. He flips the TV off when I come in. "Have a seat," he says. It's less threatening than I expected, but I still try to get out of it.

"I'm really tired." I fake a stretch and give a real yawn.

His eyes follow my hand. "What's that?"

God*damnit*. I brought the ticket in with me. "Nothing."

He looks tired, not mad. "How fast?"

I sigh. "Seventy in a fifty-five."

He takes a sip of his drink. He doesn't ask where I went or what I was doing, at least. "Have a seat," he says again, and this time I obey. "You want something to drink?"

"Are you offering one of those?"

He snorts. "I was thinking more like iced tea."

"I'm good."

We sit in silence for a moment. I know what's coming and cringe when he clears his throat. "You don't have to go to Duke if you don't want to."

"What?" That's not what I thought was coming.

He gives me a sad smile. "You don't have to go to Duke. If you want to go somewhere else, that's fine."

I stare at the counter, drumming my fingers. "It's not Duke, specifically. It's just . . . big." I hate rushing from the high school to my calculus class on the far side of campus. I hate the frats and the sorority girls and the party culture and the stadium-sized lecture halls. "I know what big is like and I'm tired of it already."

"Do you have something else in mind?" he asks.

I shrug. "Just something smaller." A stab of guilt twists my gut. "Is Mom still pissed?"

Dad shoves his drink toward me and I take a big gulp. It tastes like Pine-Sol. "Matt," he says, swiveling to face me, "we both know Raychel's too smart to stay here."

"But—"

"But your mom's right. There's a reason we chose to move here, to raise you kids here and not in Chicago or Houston." Dad did two residencies, a normal one at Northwestern and then a special fellowship type of deal in Texas, because he's that smart. "Raychel will be fine. And she doesn't need you making it harder for her."

I want to put my head down on the counter, but I sit back, tipping my chair on two legs.

"Where are you thinking about?" he asks.

I hesitate, lowering my chair. "There are a couple . . . Amherst, maybe? Or Pomona and Middlebury are good." Dad looks concerned. "There are some closer ones, too. Austin College is in north Texas, and Sewanee and Rhodes are both in Tennessee."

He nods. "I have a friend at St. Jude's Hospital, there in Memphis, whose wife works in admissions at Rhodes. You want me to talk to her?"

"Sure."

He sighs. "Look, I know you're frustrated with Raychel, but all you can do right now is be there for her," he says. "Be her friend."

"I don't seem to be very good at that," I admit.

"You've been at it for more than a decade." Dad watches me. "Unless you want to be something more than her friend."

I exhale. "I don't know *what* I am, exactly."

He flattens his lips and pops them apart. "Have you asked her?"

Bastard. He might be super smart, but he got that one from Mom.

RAYCHEL

Andrew's mouth is erasing my mind, but one more important question pops up. "Wait." I push him back. "Keri. You guys really weren't hooking up?"

Relief floods me as one side of his mouth rises. "No. We were taking an ACT prep class together." He shrugs at my surprise. "I decided to take your advice."

"I'm glad," I say quietly. "And I'm glad there's nothing with Keri. Even though I like her."

"I like her too," he says, smiling, "but not like I like you."

I would blush, but something else occurs to me. "But didn't she tell you? About Carson? She's told half the school."

He grimaces. "At the party, she just said I should come with her, but it was too wild for explanations. She kept trying to talk to me later, but I thought she was just trying to pass me a message from you." He looks down. "I should have just listened. I hated being mad at you. I hated not being with you."

"I hated it too," I whisper. He leans forward and puts his mouth on mine and I'm so grateful to have him back that after a minute I fumble with the button of his pants.

He stills my hands. "Not tonight."

"'Not tonight' what?"

He looks at me, his dark hair flopping into his eyes. "I don't know. What did you have in mind?"

I can't answer. I have nothing in mind. That's the whole point.

He sits back up, then rolls onto his side. "If you're trying to forget Carson with me, it won't work," he says. "I don't want you to, uh, do to me what he made you do to him."

"I . . . thanks," I say, trying not to tear up again. "But that wasn't . . . I just wanted to . . . get closer."

"Closer," he repeats, and smiles. "You tell me the limits," he says. "I don't want to do anything wrong."

"I just want you," I mumble. I don't care. Suddenly I don't care at all. "To hell with everything else." This is my life and my body and my chance to do what I want, when I want.

And I want Andrew.

I pull him to me and fumble with his pants again. He raises his eyes to my face. "Have you ever . . . before?"

His eyes widen when I say no, and it's his disbelief, the impossibility of me still being a virgin, that pushes me over the brink. This is mine to give, and if Andrew really wants me, let him really have me.

Let him take it before someone else decides for me.

I flip off the light and reach for his belt again.

MATT

Exhausted, I stumble upstairs from my talk with Dad, and Andrew almost barrels into me. "What the hell, man?"

"Left my phone in the car," he calls over his shoulder.

I don't know who he's calling at 1 a.m., and I don't care. I just want to talk to Raychel. But when I stop outside the guest room, I can hear the fan through the door, and no light shines beneath it.

Andrew bolts back up the steps while I'm still deciding, and Dad follows. "You find it?" I ask.

"I think it's in my room." Andrew rubs the back of his neck. "If not, I'll find it tomorrow."

"Good night," Dad says, ruffling his hair. Andrew messes up Dad's comb-over and disappears into his room. "Raychel already asleep?" Dad asks me.

"Yeah."

"You can talk to her in the morning," he says.

I nod. Everything always seems easier in the morning.

RAYCHEL

I lie perfectly still, scared to breathe until Andrew tiptoes back into the room. "Did you find one?" I ask.

"Yeah," he says. He gets back in bed and lowers himself over me. "Are you sure?" he asks again.

I put my mouth on his to answer. He puts his body on mine.

Romance novels always talk about the guy "sliding" into the girl, but there's no sliding here. It's damp hand squeaking over a balloon, peeling static cling skirt from sunburned leg, slowly sanding rust off of metal.

191

But it's ours and it's awkward and that's how it's supposed to be.

"Is this okay?" he asks, breathless, and I want to crack up. So I do, as quietly as possible. He stops. "What?"

I bite my lip and shake my head. He stares down into my eyes, gently brushing a piece of hair off my forehead.

Andrew's not taking. He's giving too.

"I've wanted to do this for a long time," he whispers, laughing.

I crack up again. "I'm glad we did."

MATT

I wake up alone.

I knew she wouldn't come to me, but I guess I still hoped.

At breakfast, I return her watery smile, trying to let her know we're okay. Andrew keeps staring at her and it's so irritating that when Mom leaves the table, I kick him in the shin.

"Son of a—"

"Watch your mouth," Mom scolds from the sink.

Andrew glares at me, but his expression softens again when he glances at Raychel. It pisses me off. "Nathan and Eliza are in town," I say, trying to distract her. She makes a face. "Do you want to go hiking today?"

Mom clears her throat. "Have you talked to your mom, Raychel?"

She pokes at her pancakes. "This morning. She's working all weekend and said I should come home tomorrow and talk." I think Raychel's lying, but Mom nods and they exchange a look that's almost as annoying as Andrew's staring.

"So you want to go?" I ask. Raychel shrugs and turns to Andrew, who nods. "Great," I say, pretending not to be annoyed. "I'll grab some supplies."

I didn't want Andrew to come. I wanted to talk to her alone, somewhere neutral and chill, and in the car after a relaxing hike seemed ideal. But my little brother still follows me everywhere like a shadow.

RAYCHEL

I don't regret a single thing, except for one: I woke up beside Andrew, and at first I thought he was Matt.

It made me realize that we still have a thing or two to work out. I need to tell Andrew about the post-nightmare bed sharing. We need to have a real discussion about what our relationship is going to be, and how we're going to tell his brother and his parents.

But while I'm not looking forward to telling Matt, it sounds better than hiking—I'm sore and bleeding a little, and still wearing the same jeans from Thursday. Matt goes upstairs to get dressed and I take the opportunity to glare at Andrew. "Hiking?" I whisper.

"Sorry!" Andrew squeezes the back of his neck, leaving his elbow next to his face. "I thought you wanted to go!"

"Not really," I say. "But look—we have to tell him," I say firmly.

Andrew lets go of his neck to pinkie swear. "Tonight."

·　·　·　·　·

I wash my face and spend a few minutes puttering in the bathroom. Thank goodness Mrs. R. keeps tampons and pads under the sink. She started stashing them there after I had to ask, humiliated, for supplies and a change of shorts when I was fourteen. Worse, she wasn't even here—I had to ask Dr. R.

Matt's waiting in the hall when I emerge. "You ready?"

I can't meet his eyes. "Yeah."

"We can go to Roger's Hollow if you want," he says, stepping forward.

I shake my head. "Eagle Point's fine."

"You sure?"

"Yeah."

He coughs. "I'm sorry. About last night."

"We need to talk about it—" I start, but he interrupts.

"I didn't mean to insult you, or your mom." He squeezes his

eyes shut and opens them. "It's just that I . . ." He's leaning closer to my face. Alarm bells start to ring in my head, but I can't believe their warning.

Matt wouldn't try to kiss me.

Still, I step back on instinct, bumping into the wall. "We can talk later, okay?"

"Okay." He closes the distance and kisses me on the forehead, which is somehow more devastating than the lips. "We'll talk after the hike, okay?"

I nod, but panic starts to rattle in my stomach. Yeah. We'll talk. But it won't be the conversation he's anticipating. And so much worse than the one I expected.

MATT

Dad hands me the speeding ticket as we leave. "You're paying it."

"You got a ticket?" Andrew bellows, whooping.

"Yeah." My face flushes, as if it's not already red enough from botching yet another opportunity to kiss Raychel. At least she didn't seem to notice.

"For jaywalking?" Andrew asks.

I flip him off. "For speeding."

"Last night?"

I don't answer and no one speaks much from that point on,

not on our way through town, and not on the twisting high-way that takes us east into the National Forest. Raychel gave Andrew shotgun and they both stare out their windows. For once, he picks something mellow to listen to, a folksy band perfect for a gray fall day, and everything feels okay. I know it's not yet, but it will be.

· · · · ·

Nathan and Eliza meet us at the trailhead, which is really just a wide spot in the gravel road. The threat of rain means the trail is mostly ours, with just two Subarus, a truck, and a Hummer besides our cars. Raychel hangs back, digging through her pack, while Andrew and I greet our friends.

"Aw!" Nathan reaches up to give Andrew a noogie. "You're getting so big!" he says in baby talk.

"Hell," Andrew says, pretending to twist Nathan's arm behind his back. "I could've kicked your ass three years ago." Nathan is short, with a chest as wide and hairy as a gorilla's. I wouldn't take bets on the winner if he and Andrew did tangle for real.

Eliza stands to the side, kicking pebbles. "Hey guys," she says when the roughhousing ends. "How's it going."

It's not a question, but I answer anyway. "Good. You?"

She shrugs. I'm sure Nathan had to sweet-talk her into coming. "Where's Asha and Spencer?"

She never says Asha's name right, pronouncing it *ash-uh* instead of *ah-sha*. "Couldn't come." I hoist my pack higher and adjust the straps. "Asha flunked some midterms, so they're studying."

"Hm." She points to my back. "Did you pack your whole house in there?" Before I can answer, her birdlike face twitches into a closed-mouth smile. "Raych!" she says, arms flung out. "Look at you!"

She probably doesn't mean that in a nice way. Raychel looks like hell. Puffy eyes, hair messy, wrinkled jeans, Andrew's shirt hanging out under her hoodie. I want to slide an arm over her shoulders like a shield against backhanded compliments, which are the only kind Eliza gives, but Nathan buries her in a bear hug. "How's my girl?"

Her eyes flicker to me for a millisecond as she hugs him back, making my face flush. After a moment, he holds her at arm's length and stares. "How's your ankle? I heard you hurt it."

"It's okay now."

"Yeah? You sure you can keep up?"

She gives him a playful shove. "To hell with my ankle," she says. "Let's go."

"To hell with it," Andrew echoes, and laughs. She gives him a small smile.

"Attagirl." Nathan winks and swings an arm around Eliza. But Andrew stays with me, patting his pockets.

"What's wrong with you?"

"I lost my pipe."

"Only users lose drugs," Nathan calls, starting down the trail. Andrew snorts and follows him. I stop Raychel as she passes.

"You don't have to carry a pack," I tell her. "You can put your stuff in here if you want."

She shakes her head. "I can carry it."

"You sure?"

Her eyebrow rises. "You want to carry my tampons?"

She knows I don't care, but Andrew makes a weird sound, so I make a face. "Fine. You win."

RAYCHEL

The valley spreads out below us, white fog floating among the orange and red and yellow. Green-gray stone juts out against the lighter gray sky. Eagle Point sticks out the farthest, like the beak of a limestone bird above the trees and clouds, refusing to let water and wind wear it down.

To the right, the hills meet, closing off the valley. To the left the valley dead-ends into another, forming a T in the earth. A choice of direction. Upriver or down. Uphill or down.

My friends' voices float down the tree line and Nathan's laugh rings across the hills. Its echo seems mocking. Everyone else has gone on, down the trail to the next vantage point, leaving me alone on this small outcropping. If Eagle Point is the beak, this is a wing bone, protruding like a fossil over the treetops below. My shoe dislodges a pebble. Sends it flying over the cliff.

I listen to it clatter down the rock face, unable to tell when it reaches the valley floor.

The straps of my pack dig into my armpits, making me sweat despite the chill. I should have just put some supplies in Matt's pack and been done with it. But I don't want him carrying anything for me.

All this time, I thought I was just a friend. And Matt thought I could be something more—"his girl." I don't mind when Nathan says it affectionately. I'd be . . . slightly annoyed but also sort of happy if Andrew said it.

But I am not Matt's girl. Not like that. He's supposed to be my friend.

And if Matt's not my friend, who is?

I drop my backpack, just to make myself feel lighter. My toes line up with the treacherous, crumbly edge. The wind buffets me, trying to tip me over the edge, and I press against it to prove I'm tougher.

"Raychel," Andrew says, startling me. "Sorry, didn't want to scare you." His hands steal around my waist, underneath my sweatshirt to the thin fabric below, and stop. Left or right. Up or down. He'll choose whatever makes me squirm most. Whatever gets me the most bothered.

I turn around and he's ready, face already lowering toward mine. His breath is sweet, minty and not labored from our hike.

I put a hand between our faces. "We have a small problem."

He pulls back. "You regret it." At my confused expression, he adds, "Last night."

"What?" I shake my head. "No." A terrible thought occurs to me. "Do you?"

"Hell, no." Andrew looks over my shoulder and tugs me away from the edge.

"Well, that's a relief." He tries to kiss me again but I stop him. "I think telling Matt is going to be harder than we thought."

He shrugs. "He'll get over it."

"No—I mean . . ." There's no good way to put this. "I think he tried to kiss me this morning."

Andrew rubs the back of his neck, staring out at the trees below for a long minute. "Did you want him to?"

I step away, insulted. "Maybe when I was fifteen, but not now."

He grabs my hands. "I didn't mean—I just wanted to make sure, you know?"

I do know. That's what I love about Andrew. We understand each other, which has been the blessing and the curse all along.

But he still looks confused, so I stand on my tiptoes and bust out the cheesiest line I can think of. "I'm only interested in kissing one person these days."

He grins and starts to answer, but a branch snaps. We jerk apart.

MATT

I know Raych didn't really want to hike today, but everyone has an element, a place where they belong. Raychel's has always been the woods, and so has mine. So I wait and watch, hoping her shoulders will straighten and her face will open up, but she stays closed, small and quiet.

After we talk, I'll send her home with the photo album that's hidden in my trunk, my apologies and promises folded into the last page. I wrote them out at four thirty this morning. Then I'll let her make the next move.

Everyone else has headed down the trail, hurrying toward the big crag, but I hang back. I wait to stand by myself for a minute, breathing in the crisp air. It's refreshing, almost purifying.

But the sound of voices disappoints me. I start to move on when I realize it's Raychel and Andrew, and push aside a branch to join them.

RAYCHEL

Matt's mouth hangs open and when he looks at me it's shock, but when he looks at his brother, it's a pure rage I've never seen on his face. "Matt—" I start, but he's advancing, coming at us, and Andrew backs up.

"You said you weren't screwing her," Matt says, his voice low.

Flat. Like a snake you can't see in the grass until it's too late. And it makes me angry—angry that he thinks he has the right. Angry that Andrew and I didn't tell him weeks ago. Angry at my luck and myself and most of all, the fact that he's blaming his brother and ignoring me.

Andrew takes another step back. "Bro," he says, hands up, "it's not—let me explain." He looks to me for help and I reach out, but Matt keeps advancing on him. "Matt, wait," Andrew says.

MATT

"You said you weren't screwing her." If I could growl like a dog, like a wolf, I would. I'd tear his throat out. I'd tear his mouth off for having touched her.

"Bro," he says, hands up, "it's not—let me explain." He glances at Raychel, who's reaching for him, and I want to tear his eyes out for looking at her. "Matt, wait," he says, stepping backward, buying time. "Hang on—"

His eyes widen, then go wider, almost comically.

And then they disappear.

He doesn't even scream.

But Raychel does.

RAYCHEL

"Hang on—" Andrew says.

But that's all he says. Because he falls.

He steps backward and it's too far.

He falls.

PART II

AFTER THE FALL

"Is that how we lived, then? But we lived as usual. Everyone does, most of the time. Whatever is going on is as usual. Even this is as usual, now."

—The Handmaid's Tale *by Margaret Atwood*

MATT

My fault. My fault. My fault.

RAYCHEL

The service is ridiculous.

Nothing the minister says has anything to do with Andrew, whose name is like punctuation between Bible verses. A few friends take turns sharing memories, but they're sanitized. Stripped of life.

As dead as Andrew.

No one says anything about the real Andrew. He was annoying. Never knew when to quit teasing. Merciless at *Mario Kart*. Amazing at kissing. Preferred homegrown to Mexican. Bottled beer to kegs. Loved sports. Sucked at pool. Wanted to grow up, in lots of ways.

These are the things that matter and no one will say them. Least of all me.

Matt sits beside me. He doesn't take my hand. I don't take his.

Keri sits on my other side. Tears flood her face, over her chin, down her neck, into her dress. She makes no effort to dry them.

I don't cry. Even when Matt breaks down in great silent sobs, I remain dry-eyed. I sit in silence, taking the pain as penance.

MATT

My fault.
   My fault.
   My fault.

RAYCHEL

We form a line in the aisle, like the world's unluckiest bridal party at the world's worst wedding. We take turns saying farewell to the shell that's no longer Andrew.

Matt stays behind me. Ladies first.

So I step up to the coffin, onto a small ledge before it, because let's do this right. Let's really see what we've done. Somehow, they've made his head almost normal. You can't tell, unless you look too close, that he cracked like an egg on his way down.

His face survived mostly unscathed, but that's what finally breaks me. They've put makeup an inch thick on him. It looks like Mom's expired base. But he'll never have wrinkles. I don't realize I'm shaking, making a keening noise, until arms wrap around me, pull me away from the edge.

They aren't the ones I want. They're not Andrew's and they're not Matt's and they're not even my mom's, who's still sitting in the back next to Eddie. They're Mrs. R.'s and she's whispering, "That's not him, honey, it's okay. That's not him." I want to scream, "Why are you comforting me? He was yours and I took him! Don't you know this is my fault?"

But of course she doesn't. Matt would never tell her. He loves them both too much for that.

So I don't either, because I love them too. I take her comfort. Cry on her shoulder. Hug Keri. Cry on hers too. I take and I take and I take because I've never had anything to give.

MATT

My fault.
My fault.
My fucking fault.

RAYCHEL

The night after the funeral, we have an unofficial wake at the Grove.

Our whole crew has come home from college. Stanton drove in from Lawrence, and Fischer flew in from UCLA. Bree stopped in St. Louis and picked up The Nuge and his new boyfriend on her way from Chicago. Nathan and Eliza don't even have to miss school—they don't have to be back in Texas until next week. They've all been circling us, unsure how to take my detachment from Matt, but no one's asked questions. Bree knows something's up, though. She and Asha won't leave my side, and it's both annoying and welcome.

Matt and I haven't been back to school, except for the so-called memorial service there today. It was also ridiculous. Everyone and their dog jumped on the opportunity to skip class. No one close enough to Andrew to deserve to talk was capable, so we got heartfelt but lame platitudes from the school counselors and Big Johnson.

Cowboy Chester has become a makeshift memorial, with flowers and candles and knickknacks tossed at his feet. I wonder how long the school will let that stuff sit there. Until it rains, maybe. Or until someone notices there's a lighter and a package of Zig-Zags among the offerings.

Tonight has ended up a more exclusive event. The entire basketball team is here, and Keri and the non-devout half of her youth group. A big chunk of the football team shows up after the game, along with Trent Montgomery, Rosa Gallegos, and most of the other cheerleaders. "We had a moment of silence," Rosa tells me. "Some of the girls wanted to do a tribute to him, but I told them it was lame." I thank her, although a twenty-one-pom salute would probably have cracked him up.

Only a few people show up expecting an actual party. Carson came to the funeral with the rest of the baseball players, but he either has the common sense not to crash this, or lacks the balls for it. Mindy is here, but she stays away from Matt. I almost wish she'd go to him, comfort him, since I can't.

The boys have him sitting on a hay bale near the bonfire. He's like the guest of honor. The Nuge climbs up in the back of someone's pickup, stands on the truck box, and hoists a bottle of Beam. The crowd falls silent. "Tonight," he announces, "we remember . . . a man." Firelight dances off the back windshield, giving The Nuge's wild hair and eyes an orange glow. It's the perfect mix of otherworldly, making serious what should sound cheesy. "He was our friend, our teammate, and our brother. He went out the way he would have wanted—livin' it up in the wilderness with friends. Tonight, we honor him the way he would have wanted—by drinkin' it up with friends. To Andrew!" He raises the bottle into the air, then tips it back.

We all do the same.

MATT

Spencer and Fischer keep my cup full. Eliza sits by my side all night, but she doesn't talk, and I appreciate it. I'll never forget the way her scream echoed up the rocks when she and Nathan reached Andrew's body. Nathan wouldn't let me look. He pushed me and Raychel back, almost to the edge of the river, to keep us there until help arrived.

I could have gotten around him, if I'd really wanted to. But I didn't want to see what I'd done to my brother.

Raychel did. She shoved past him after a minute, ran to Andrew's side, and collapsed on the ground beside him. I didn't want to see that either. She came back covered in his blood and that was when I lost it.

"Matt. Hey." I open my eyes. Spencer holds a bottle toward me, all teeth and glasses in the firelight. I nod my thanks and take a swig. The inside of my knuckle taps against the glass and I wonder which is stronger, glass or bone.

I try not to watch Raychel, but it's hard when years of party experience have me trained to keep an eye on her. A flashlight beam catches the can in her hand and I realize it's maroon. She's drinking Dr Pepper.

Not me. Nathan brings me another drink, this one in a plastic cup. "Is this moonshine?" My words slur.

Nathan laughs. "Moonshine? I feed you Crown and you accuse me of rotgut?"

"S-s-sorry." He claps me on the shoulder and sits down on Eliza's other side.

A parade of people offer condolences. Most of them did the same yesterday at the church, but tonight the liquor has loosened my mouth enough for me to answer. "Thanks," I say over and over. "Thank you. I appreciate it. He would have loved it. We'll all miss him." Trent doesn't call me "Ali" or shadowbox. He just gives me a bro hug and walks off, wiping his eyes. It hurts worse than an actual punch.

If I didn't know better, if I could let myself pretend, I could think Andrew was here. Maybe if the crowd quieted down, I could hear him sneaking up behind someone in the woods, the way he always did at parties. Maybe if I squint the right way, I'll see him holding Fischer's legs up for a keg stand.

Someone brought a guitar, and someone else produces a bongo drum, because in a college town, someone always has a guitar and a bongo drum. They play a little, drawing people toward the fire, until most of the crowd has gathered in a large circle. I squint across the flames. The guitar player is Cruz, and he nods at me. "Any requests?" he calls.

Raychel stands off to one side, flanked by Keri and Asha and Bree, and I try not to look at her. I fail. "You know anything by The Band?" I croak.

He shakes his head. "No, but . . ." He strums until he hits a familiar chord.

Close enough. A Crosby, Stills, Nash & Young song, in

four-part harmony, that we sang for last year's spring choir concert. Raychel's alto shakes over the fire, joined by Nathan's tenor, and some of the crowd come in on the chorus. Maybe if I listen really carefully, I'll hear my brother's bass in the trees, rising up with the smoke.

Does he know how much I hate him right now? Does he know how much I love him?

Maybe he can see the bonfire from wherever he is: not a pyre, but a beacon that will guide him to us, just for tonight. He never could resist a party.

When the chorus comes around again, I join in too.

RAYCHEL

Matt is trashed. At the Richardsons', Nathan leaves Fischer and The Nuge *playing air guitar in the car and helps me drag Matt to his room.* "You got him?" he asks from the doorway.

"Yeah." Matt's sprawled across his bed, fully dressed. I take off his shoes and line them up in the closet, the way he'd do it himself. "We'll talk to you tomorrow."

Nathan gives me a quick salute, two fingers over the eyebrow, and heads out. Behind me, Matt groans. "Do you need something?" I ask quietly. "Water?"

He nods without opening his eyes.

"There's a glass here." I help him sit up, then pull some

Tylenol from the drawer of his bedside table. "Here, take these too." He gulps them and lies back down. I flip the light off and sit beside him, watching him breathe. Hoping he doesn't puke. When I'm fairly sure he's in the clear, I touch his hand and stand up.

"Raych," he says in a half moan, and holds his hand out. "Stay."

I don't know which would be more selfish, to go or to give in. "Are you sure?"

His fingers twitch. I take his hand and sit. He pulls me toward him, and we sleep curled together, my head on his chest.

When I wake up, he's gone.

MATT

In the days that follow, as the hangover wears off and reality sets in, I can't look at her, even though I know she's not the one who lied. I never bothered to give her that chance.

If I'd asked, she would have told me the truth. But I didn't want to hear it, and I don't want to hear it now.

I don't want to hear anything.

Actually, what I want to hear is my brother thundering down the stairs, breaking for a game of pool, yelling across the house for Mom, asking to borrow my clothes. Anything. Even if it was him saying "I'm hooking up with Raychel." I'd give anything to hear him say it. And I never would have pushed him for it, even if he'd said it and laughed.

I wanted to, but I wouldn't have. But he's dead either way. And either way, it's my fault.

RAYCHEL

We're playing pretend, playing normal, for our parents' sakes. The Richardsons would wonder why if I wasn't around. I have to be there for Matt even if he pretends I'm not there. They think he's ignoring me because he's upset and ignoring everyone.

He can get away with it—he lost his brother. Playing along is the least I can do. I don't deserve special treatment, and don't expect it. No one knows I lost my boyfriend and my best friend, and I don't even know who fits which description any more now than I did two weeks ago.

And it doesn't matter. I've lost them both.

· · · · ·

Asha is suddenly a really good friend, but school still keeps her busy. My school is a goddamn joke. Our parents have the idea that routine is good for us. Like sleepwalking from class to class will somehow restore a semblance of normalcy to our lives. I clean out Andrew's locker and tell the Richardsons that Matt took care of it.

Whispers follow us down the halls. I hear but don't acknowledge them.

"heard he jumped . . . heard his brother pushed him . . . he was drunk, you know . . . heard his head split right down the middle . . . that's what happens when you get stoned on a cliff! . . . how did Matt let that happen? . . . I heard they were fighting over Raychel . . . I heard, I heard, I heard . . ."

I could scream in the middle of this hallway, let it echo off tile and metal, and no one would hear a goddamn thing.

· · · · ·

I wake up screaming at night, but Matt's not there to comfort me. My mom tries her best. I can't bring myself to detail what I'm reliving: Andrew falls. Nothing else moves for a long second. Then the crash. The crunch. The sound of bone on stone, skull on wood, leg on I don't even know what, oh my god, and I'm torn, tearing in half for good—I can't climb down without leaving Matt here and what if he tries to follow the same way Andrew went?

He throws himself onto his stomach, arms stretched over the cliff's edge, yelling for his brother. But I know he won't answer. "Matt," I say, voice cracking. "Matt. Matt. Matt!" I finally get my voice to yell. "Matt!"

I should be glad to wake up, but it just makes me remember what's real. What's here.

And what's not.

· · · · ·

At school, I don't look for Andrew in the hallway. Don't look at anyone—keep my head down, avoid people's faces. Answer teachers' condolences with downcast eyes and thanks. Be grateful they don't call on me.

Everyone seems to be giving us a wide berth, but after sixth period one day, Matt stops in the bathroom and I go to my locker alone. A few acquaintances say hi, and one even stops to ask how I'm doing.

The berth has been for Matt. Not me.

Which is unfortunate, because I could use it, with Carson lingering down the hall from my locker. His friends crowd around him and their silence creeps me out more than hollering would. The last thing I want to do is kneel to reach my locker on the bottom row. So I pretend to search for something in my backpack, eyes flicking up every couple seconds to check the group's progress toward me.

"Move on," a voice says, shooing them away. "Get to class."

I whirl around and meet Eddie's eyes, trying to tell him thank you without speaking. He nods. And later that day, I pass him cleaning up the Cowboy Chester memorial. "What will you do with all that stuff?" I ask.

He sucks his teeth. "Dunno," he says finally. "Anything you want to keep?"

I shake my head, but he catches my gaze lingering on the small red glass pipe. His hand shoots out to cover it, and slides it into his pocket with a wink.

MATT

Every single day, something happens to make me think, "Oh man, I gotta tell Andrew about this."

And then I remember that I'll never tell Andrew anything again.

Every single day, I wake up alone. I don't mean in my bed, though that's true. I mean I brush my teeth alone. I don't fight anyone for the shower. I have all the cereal to myself. No one left an empty OJ carton in the fridge. The dishes are always done. No wet towels on the bathroom floor. My clothes stay in my closet.

My life is the most immaculate mess you've ever seen.

· · · · ·

I go to school, and I go home, and I don't really know what happens in between, but in class I pay attention like my life depends on it. Like two lives depend on it: the one I'm living and the one my brother should have had. Mom and Dad expected two graduations, two college tuitions, two senior proms, too much, maybe, of both of us. But now all my accomplishments mean more because they'll be the only ones, and less because his absence will always take something away.

Mom wants me to stay here for college now. She hasn't said it, but I can tell by the way she looks at the school brochures that are still showing up like clockwork. But I can't stay in this town where every single thing is tied to Andrew. I'd almost rather die, if I didn't know so goddamn well what I'd leave behind me.

So I focus on that: Mom will be sad, but she'd rather miss me from a few hours away than for forever. I can nearly convince myself I'm doing her a favor, focusing on nothing but applications and grades. I study more than I've ever studied before, so much that I end up screwing myself because I read ahead and then I'm bored in class.

Then my mind wanders, and I can't let that happen. Not with other people around.

They think I don't hear them, but I do. They think I pushed my brother. I don't tell them I might as well have. I don't tell them how much I wanted to kill him, not knowing what "dead" really means. I don't tell them how it happened, or why, but that much, the worst of them have guessed. The rumor slips around the school with a whisper like a belt through loops.

I don't correct them. It's not that I lack the energy, or the strength, or the give-a-damn. It's that I have too much of the latter: I don't want anyone to know the truth, because they'll know that Raychel picked him, not me.

I want to protect her. They'll pick her apart and relish the meal.

But I'm also protecting myself. I can't stand to let her go, but I can't stand myself for keeping her. I can't stand being with her, but I can't stand being away.

By the end of each day, I can barely stand up at all.

RAYCHEL

A week goes by, then two, but Matt and I still don't discuss anything. Not the accident, not the aftermath, and certainly not the other things that day revealed. I've tried to approach it in a roundabout way, but Matt shuts me down every time.

"Just give him a little time," Keri says in chemistry. She's been a godsend at school—fending off questions I don't want to answer and listening when I need to vent, though I haven't told her any of the worst details. I haven't told anyone. "We learned in psych that there are . . . here, wait." She gets out a textbook and looks in the index, then flips to a page with a flowchart. "There're all these steps to trauma recovery. Right now, it's like he's the soda bottle and his feelings are the Coke," she says, pointing to a picture of a spewing bottle. "He's all shaken up, and unless he takes the cap off slowly, he'll just blow his top."

"That'll be fun." I read over her shoulder. It says the first stage is shock, and describes trauma as causing "circuit overload," which is more how I feel—like all of my fuses have blown and my wires aren't reconnected yet.

"I guess you just have to be there for him and hope he'll open up a little," she says.

"Yeah." For once, Matt needs me for support. I feel indebted, and almost relieved to have a chance to pay him back. But I also haven't forgotten that Matt always expected a refund of some kind. If being his friend wasn't enough before, maybe I'm crazy to hope it can be enough now.

But there's no other option. Losing him and Andrew both is too much to contemplate.

MATT

Dad's taken a leave of absence, but Raychel keeps working for him because my parents want her around. She makes the void less glaring, for them.

I've been trying to keep my distance when she's here, but today my brain has Eagle Point on instant replay, so I hang out, pretending to read, as Raychel types up records that are decades old.

But it doesn't help. Nothing helps.

I keep seeing Andrew disappear from view. I stretched my hand out. I tried to catch him. I knew it was too little too late. For the rest of my life, some part of me is going to be on that rock, trying to undo what I've done.

What I *haven't* done is tell my parents the truth. I'm not sure I ever can.

I should have told them that day, but nothing made sense at the time. Andrew fell, and Raychel dragged me back from the edge. Other hikers heard her screaming and immediately ran to the top of the mountain, trying to find a signal so they could call 911, but the helicopter still took over an hour to reach us.

Not that it mattered. Andrew was dead on impact.

Even when I saw his crumpled body on the stretcher, I tried to convince myself there was still a chance. They flew him to the closest trauma center, here in Big Springs, but we had to hike back to the parking lot. Nathan drove my car home, with me in the passenger seat, Raychel collapsed in the back, and Eliza trailing in his Jeep. It was almost three hours before we reached the hospital, and I managed to believe that Andrew was still alive until the minute I saw my parents.

Then I knew.

And that's when I should have told them.

But Mom was sobbing. Dad was shaking. Even Raychel's mom hugged me, patting us both like she couldn't believe we were real. Everyone asked, "What happened? What happened?" Raychel glanced at me. She waited for my lead.

And I couldn't take it. I couldn't tell them the truth.

So I just said, "He fell." And she nodded.

Weeks later, Raychel's still following my lead, or lack thereof. I haven't said a word about what happened, and neither has she, not even to each other. We've barely spoken at all. We couldn't even comfort each other at Andrew's sham of a funeral.

He never wanted a funeral. He didn't want a coffin. "He wanted to be thrown off Eagle Point," I blurt, voice rough from disuse.

Raychel's hand jerks, knocking a cup of water off the desk onto the floor.

"He wanted his ashes thrown off the cliff." There's a laugh, and with dull horror, I realize it's mine. "That's ironic."

Raychel stares. Right when I think she's going to ignore me, her mouth opens, closes, and opens again. "That's what you wanted," she says. "He just agreed."

I laugh that horrible laugh again. "It's the only thing we ever agreed on, then."

She slowly closes the laptop. "You guys are more alike than you realize."

"Well, I guess you'd know," I snap, annoyed by her present tense.

She looks up slowly, more sad than angry. "Yeah," she says. "I guess I would." And she walks out of the room, leaving me with yet another mess to clean up.

RAYCHEL

After hiding in the bathroom to cry, thanks to Matt, I decide I've done enough work for today. But instead of a break at home, I get Mom waiting at the kitchen table. She has two Dr. Thunders sitting out, and a snack—crackers, string cheese, and grapes she's cut in half like she did when I was little and my windpipe was just their size. I've been expecting this talk, but every time Mom tries to have a heart-to-heart, I've managed to turn on the waterworks and slide out of the room.

Until today. "We need to talk," she says.

I'm tempted to make a joke—*Sorry, Mom, no more money for you to take!*—but I only have so much fuel and that anger has burned itself out. Life could be worse, I'm learning. It could always be worse.

She taps her fingers on the table as I sit. "I know a few weeks have gone by, but you still need to know that I'm sorry I slapped you."

"I know." I pop some grapes in my mouth to avoid talking about it a few seconds longer.

"I have no excuse." Mom studies the ceiling, gathering her thoughts like they're balloons that have floated away. "But there are some things I want you to understand anyway."

"Okay." I open the string cheese. Peeling the plastic apart is very satisfying.

"I was very young when I had you," she starts.

"I know," I say again.

"Before your father left . . . he had a major drug problem," she says. "He pretty well burned through everything we owned. He left us with . . . nothing, basically. Which you know," she says, before I can. "But you were too young to understand how ruthless he was. He took all my jewelry. My grandmother's pearls. The earrings his mother had left you. Everything."

I use the grape halves to make the string cheese pieces into flowers. This conversation should hurt more, but I don't explode or deflate anymore. The constant pain is too solid, and not even unexpected stabs of grief can puncture it.

Mom's gaze moves to her hands folded on the table. "I should have told you that," she says. "I should have told you my own mother slapped me when I acted up. That's why I've always tried to use words with you. But I haven't tried hard enough lately."

"Why didn't you tell me about Eddie sooner?" I ask.

She leans forward, reaching for my hands. I let her take them. "I was embarrassed too."

"I'm not embarrassed anymore," I tell her. "I'm proud of you." It's true. I've thought a lot in the past few weeks about my mom, and how she lost my dad but kept herself together for me. My grudging admiration comes with yet more guilt— for never realizing that before, and never thanking her for what she's done.

But now's not the time for that conversation. "I'm proud of you too, honey," she says. "And I'm sorry if you thought you were the reason I didn't bring him around. I am allowed to have secrets, but he wasn't the right one to keep." I sit back, digesting that fact. Her eyes start to fill up and I have to look away. "I feel unfairly lucky in all this."

"Lucky?"

"Yes," she says. "It's hard to watch someone lose a child. To realize I could lose *you*." She rubs her nose. "The Richardsons are good parents. So good I've always been jealous that they can give you what I can't. But somehow, I did a bunch of foolish things, and my punishment is having you stay close to me for another year. And it makes me happy, even though I know it's the last thing you want."

"It's not the *last* thing I want," I say, trying to be funny. "I can think of tons of things I want less. The problem is that I already have most of them."

Her sad smile fades, and so does mine. Just when I think there can't possibly be room for more guilt, another stone hits the pile. No wonder I don't explode or deflate. There's no room for air.

MATT

For the first few weeks after Andrew died, I couldn't believe time kept moving forward. I expected it to stop, to freeze at the point when it ended for him, but of course it didn't. It keeps plowing forward, running over and over again.

My email and voice mail were both full at first. People said things like "No need to reply, just wanted you to know I'm thinking of you," or "I'm praying for your family," or "Let me know if I can do anything." I know they meant well, but I wanted to reply, "Don't. Don't think of me at all." Why should they suffer for no reason? It doesn't do any good. If everyone who's praying would get to work on a time machine, maybe that would be helpful. But I know what praying and thinking really mean: *I took time to thank God I'm not you.* And they don't even know the whole story.

So I haven't been answering, and now they've dried up. Everyone has stopped trying. My parents have their own crap to deal with, and Raychel just goes about her business like I'm part of the furniture. She's spending less time here and more with Asha and Spencer. I guess she's decided to be their third wheel for a change.

Of course, I always thought Andrew was our third wheel, but it turns out that was me. Or maybe we were a tripod and can't stand on two legs.

I can't wait until next year to leave. I have to get out of here as soon as possible. And if I can't make time stop, maybe I can speed it up.

· · · · ·

I catch Dad in his office before dinner, not that dinner is much of an event anymore. It's always silent, except for clinking and chewing and the occasional "please" or "thank you." "Hey," I say, knocking on the open door.

He looks up. "Dinner?"

"I haven't put it in yet." We've eaten enough frozen lasagnas and casseroles to feed a small army for a year, but people keep bringing them because Mom's department set up a Feed-the-Richardsons schedule but neglected to coordinate what they were feeding us. It's kind of them, but I think it would do Dad some good to get back in the kitchen, though I'm probably not the one to be handing out coping tips. "Can I talk to you?" I ask.

I expect him to be relieved, to think I'm finally opening up, but he just seems tired. "Come on in."

I close the door. "Did you ever talk to the lady at Rhodes?"

He rubs his forehead. "Matt, I'm so sorry—"

"No, it's okay." I rock back and forth on my heels, trying to work up the nerve. "When you do, could you . . . maybe ask her about this spring semester?"

RAYCHEL

I'm still reeling from my conversation with Mom when Asha calls, sobbing so hard I can barely understand her. I manage to get "Spencer," "stupid," "asshole," and "broke up." I've avoided campus completely so far by making her come to the duplex, but I head for her dorm immediately. Her roommate fled the sexfest weeks ago and moved in with a girl down the hall. I guess that was a premature move. "What happened?"

Asha blows her nose and flops across the beds. She's pushed them together to make a king-size. It's like the Hilton of dorm rooms. Or at least the Motel 6. "I don't even know," she says. "He won't come to my sister's wedding and then it turned into

'We're too young' and 'Why do we have to talk about marriage' and 'You're insane.' "

"What did you say?"

She grimaces. "I told him if he thought he could keep screwing me through college and dump me at graduation, he should think again."

Even I cringe. Everyone knows that's not Spencer's plan. He's been hung up on Asha since kindergarten. "Why wouldn't he go?"

"He's 'too busy' that weekend."

"But it's not until May." She won't look at me, and I make the connection. "Isn't that when his big family reunion thing always happens?" Spencer's family is as big as Asha's—it's one reason they get each other so well. And everyone knows they're meant to be together, so much that we've always said "when you get married," not "if."

Asha lies down, arms crossed over her face. "I know," she wails. "I'm horrible. But do you know how many aunties have called me every week since my sister got engaged? I got *four* last week, wanting to know if I'm next or if they should start setting me up with their friends' sons." Her arms move back and forth with her head. "We're only eighteen! No guy wants to deal with that!"

I pat her leg. "Are you going to call him?"

"I don't know." Her arms muffle her voice. "What should I do?"

"You're asking *me* for relationship advice?"

She laughs and sits up. "We should go out tonight."

"No." I cross the small space to the window. "Not up for it."

"Why not?" She joins me and points across the courtyard. "See the room with the pirate flag? They're having a Halloween party."

I would ignore Halloween altogether if I could, but it's soon, so there are lots of costumes and decorations at school and around town.

Asha nudges me. "Come on—whatever happened to the Terrible Twosome?"

I snort. We've never called ourselves that. "Don't get mad," I say. "It's just . . . a bad idea. For me."

"Wow." She walks back to her boat of a bed. "Never thought I'd see the day."

"Please," I say, turning around with another snort. "You party every bit as hard as me."

She holds up a peace sign. "We've been to two whole parties this year."

"Yeah, together, but you . . ." I trail off as she shakes her head, looking down. "Then where were you?"

She shakes her head again.

"You blew me off to screw Spencer?" It's not like it's the first time, but at least she was honest about it before.

Asha huffs. "Like you don't blow me off for Matt all the time?"

I start to protest that Matt *and* I blew her off, but realize she's right. And that's not even taking Andrew into account.

"And for your information, no, we weren't screwing. Usually," she adds, as I start to roll my eyes. "I know you think this is a crappy school, but it's still way harder than high school, okay?"

"You were *studying*?" I regret it even before her face scrunches up. "I didn't mean it like—"

"No, I get it," she says, standing up. "You guys are all super smart. I only took hard classes to tag along. Remember when I dropped AP Psych?"

I don't, but I nod.

"It wasn't because Mom wanted me to spend more time on orchestra. I just needed an excuse because I was flunking."

"But . . ." There's nothing I can say that doesn't make me look like a bitch. I had no idea Asha had so much trouble in school. I thought all her excuses about Spencer tutoring her were made up . . . and I never considered that maybe she stayed here because she had no other options.

That maybe Spencer stayed to be with her, and not the other way around.

"You know why this is a crappy school?" she says, looking at her bulletin board to avoid me. "Because there's way more work, but there're also way more people in your class, and hardly any chance to talk to the TA, much less the professor." She straightens a concert ticket. "It's not like Senior Seminar with Ms.

Moses, where you can waltz in and have tea and chat. They don't give a crap about your life. They just want you to hand in papers and get out."

"I . . ." I still don't know what to say. "I'm sorry. I didn't know."

She turns around. "Well, it's not like you ever *ask*, Raych. You were so wrapped up in the Richardsons that I started not to even call you."

My face flushes. I do ignore her phone calls sometimes, but I thought she would understand. "You sound like my mother."

"Well, maybe somebody needs to!"

Then neither of us speaks. Asha picks at her orange fingernail polish. I stare at the scuffed toes of my boots. Music blares and quiets as a door slams down the hall. A toilet flushes. Someone yells to a friend. Finally I make myself look up and admit what we both know. "You're right."

Asha's cheek twitches. "Did I seriously just hear Raychel Sanders say that *I'm* right?"

"I'm sorry," I add, rubbing the back of my neck. In the mirror, I recognize it as a habit I picked up from Andrew, and I have to inhale hard to keep the tears back.

"I'm sorry too," Asha says quickly, thinking she's made me cry. "I know this is hard, with everything, I didn't mean—"

"I know." I pace the room, blinking hard. "But I mean— you won't even talk to him?" I try to change the subject away from me. "I mean, think if Spencer fell and that was the last conversation y'all had? You can't imagine how . . ." My throat closes up.

Asha tilts her head. "But you and Andrew—you weren't like, that close . . ."

Despite everything, I laugh. "We were a little closer than you think."

"I knew it!" she says loudly, making me jump. "Sorry. But I totally thought you were hooking up at that last party." She sits on the bed and gestures for me to join her. "Come on. Time to spill."

I take a seat. So much for changing the subject.

MATT

Friday morning, Raychel texts that she stayed over with Asha and doesn't need a ride to school. I send back "k." Not even "Say hi to Asha" or "See you tomorrow" or even an entire word. Just "k."

I know I'm being an asshole, and it's not entirely on purpose. It just keeps happening. And now that I might be leaving early, there's also a kind of savage pleasure in being the one with a secret for a change.

Plus if she's glad I'm leaving, it might be easier to go.

It's hard not to worry about her, though. She's been chewing her nails, and I haven't seen her do that in a long time, not since her first choir solo, sophomore year. I remember because after that, she took up chewing gum, and I used to sneak packages into her locker.

The memory irritates me.

Everything irritates me. Especially me.

RAYCHEL

I spend the whole weekend with Asha. Selfishly, it's a relief to have the time away from Matt, but our weekend apart seems to do him some good too. Monday is uneventful, and that night I hand out candy at Asha's dorm, while the Richardsons turn off their lights to avoid trick-or-treaters. On Tuesday, he follows me around silently while I try to work, which is annoying, but bearable.

But Wednesday he gets weirdly pissy that I have plans with Asha and can't stay for dinner. And Thursday morning he's immediately mad at me for running late, which gives someone else time to steal his parking spot. He doesn't say anything as we hike up from the gravel lot, even when Eddie says hello at the lobby door, squeezing my shoulder in greeting. The pipe he saved is hidden in my jewelry box, but I don't use it. It's just a talisman, a memento. A tiny piece of Andrew that stays with me.

A wolf whistle meets me at the stairs. "Sanders!" someone calls down. "Eddie the Janitor your new boyfriend?" I don't know the voice, but there's no mistaking Carson's booming laugh in response.

I ignore them. Matt ignores me. And we both ignore the fact that no matter what everyone else expects, things will never be normal again.

·　·　·　·　·

Matt stops giving me the silent treatment by the end of school, but within a few minutes I'm wishing he'd shut up. "Are you going out tomorrow?" he asks, not glancing away from the road.

"I don't know. Probably not."

"What are you going to do then?" he asks. "Hang around my house?"

"If you don't want me to, then no."

"What if I do?"

"Then I will, Matt, god!" I have no idea what he wants from me. Not that I ever did—a fact that's getting harder to ignore as he takes his grief out on me more and more. Is he still holding out hope that we're going to be more than friends? Are we really even friends at this point?

I consider just taking the afternoon off, but I need the money, as usual. I spent my last paycheck on some clothes to replace the ones I threw away after Eagle Point. I also went on an impulsive card-buying spree—I'm going to send one to everyone I love. I even found a Thanksgiving one for The Nuge with a farmer holding a turkey by the neck. It plays "Stranglehold" when you open it.

By the time we reach the house, I need some air and a few

minutes alone. But Matt follows me out onto the deck, into the gray and chilly afternoon. I tuck my hands inside the sleeves of my hoodie and rest my arms on the rail, looking out at the backyard. At the garden Mrs. R. abandons halfway through every summer. At the lawn the boys take turns mowing.

Took turns.

Just one boy now.

Andrew was a much bigger part of my life than I realized, even before we were together. His house is nothing but a minefield of memories. It's impossible to be here and impossible to leave.

I shake my head, refusing the tears I don't deserve. The sky gives me a few of its own, raindrops sprinkling on our heads. I pull my arms tighter and curl in against the damp. I'm not just sad, I'm mad. At Matt, for being jealous, for being possessive, and for continuing to be mad at me.

And at Andrew, for falling. For stepping backward instead of forward. For being stupid enough to kiss me in public.

For leaving me here by myself.

MATT

It starts to drizzle, but I ignore it, the same way I ignore Raychel's shivering. I hate that I don't care enough to hate that I don't care.

There's just not room when my guilt overwhelms everything. How many times did I warn them to stay back from the edge? How many times did I warn him to be careful? I tried and tried to be responsible, but it wasn't enough.

I can't say I'd give anything to have him back, because it's a pointless exercise in thought, playing poker with invisible cards. But looking at Raychel now, it's not hard to imagine her in his place. We're not that high up, but high enough, and I fight the urge to pull her back. "How long?" I ask.

She turns slowly and squints through the rain. "What?"

"You and Andrew," I say. "How long were you . . ."

"Not long."

I exhale loudly, making a puff of steam.

"It started that weekend you and I fought about books," she says, and pauses. "With a break, and then . . ."

I reach out, the first time I've purposely touched her since the Grove, and pull her back toward the center of the deck where it's safer. "Does Keri know?"

"Yeah." I expected to be mad when she said no, not furious at her yes. Other people knew, but not me. "They weren't together. But she and I talked about it a day or two before he . . ."

"Died." Everyone keeps pussyfooting around it, saying he "passed" or "walked on" or "went to be with Jeebus," but Andrew fucking died. Because of me.

She starts pacing. "We were going to tell you. That's what we were talking about, when you walked up."

God. "At least he died happy," I say, unsure which of us I'm trying to hurt more. Her face crumples and I want to pull her to my chest, but I don't.

"I'm sorry," she says, and she waits for me to reply, but I don't do that either. I'm carrying enough blame. I can't take hers too.

RAYCHEL

Matt watches the drizzle slowly stain the deck. I'm afraid that if I let the conversation end, it'll be months until we have another.

"Matt," I start, waiting for him to look up. "What happened . . ." I want to say *It wasn't your fault,* but I can't, even if I don't blame him entirely. And if I know Matt, he's blaming himself plenty already—which is why I've put up with his attitude this long. "You can't keep living like this," I say instead.

He glares at me. "How am I supposed to live then? Pretend like it never happened, like you're doing?"

"I'm not pretending that. I'm just trying to get through each day."

He snorts. "Yeah, well. You'll find a replacement. I don't get another brother."

"A replacement?" I repeat. "For Christ's sake, Matt." That's a low blow, even for his current state.

"You'll be fine," he says.

"Fine?" My voice rises. "I'm not *fine*. I miss Andrew. We spent a lot of time together."

He snorts again.

Anger steams its way past my patience. "I'm sorry that was a shock to you, but the truth is that I liked your brother. A lot." How this news can still surprise him, I'm not sure. But he looks devastated, which just pisses me off even more. "Would you rather hear I was just using him?" I demand. "Or that he was using me?"

Matt shrugs sadly. "I guess . . . that's what I assumed."

"That's a hell of a thing to think about people you care about."

"At least I cared!" he says back, louder. "At least I wasn't sneaking around!"

I stop and take a breath before this can get nastier. "Listen. I can't go back in time and erase anything. And you know what? I wouldn't erase what happened with Andrew even if I could. So you're either going to have to get over it, or . . ." I'm not sure how to finish the sentence. We can't *not* be friends.

Matt looks like he's going to cry. "How am I supposed to get over it? You slept with my brother, Raychel!" He waits, and after a moment, I realize he wants me to deny it. But I don't. "I can't believe you slept with him," he repeats, almost to himself.

"It wasn't your business. It's still not your business. You're not my dad." *Or my boyfriend,* I add mentally. "You're supposed to be my friend."

He steps under the eave, out of the rain. "I just . . . I don't know how to do that now."

I push past him and open the door. "I'm not sure you ever did."

MATT

Mom watches wide-eyed as Raychel stalks through the kitchen and into the front hall. "What in the world?"

"We had a fight."

"I can see that." The door closes loudly. "Is she walking home in the rain?"

"She'll take the transit."

"She'll get soaked on the way to—"

"I don't care, okay?" I bang around, trying to make myself a glass of iced tea, until Mom takes the breakables out of my hands.

"Matthew." She makes me turn to face her. "I know it feels easier to push people away, but you can't just—"

"Why do you always take her side?" I yell. I know I'm being irrational and immature, but it's true. I'm always wrong, and

Raychel's always right, even when we've both screwed up. "I'm your son!"

Mom waits, lightly rubbing my upper arm. "Why don't you tell me what really happened?" she says finally.

"You don't want to know." I move out of her reach and try again to make a drink.

She waits until I have a full glass and take a sip. "I know that you and Raychel are both struggling," she says slowly. "But you need each other to get through this."

"She doesn't need me," I say, unable to hide my bitterness.

"Honey." Mom goes for my shoulder this time, squeezing it gently. "I know how you feel about her."

I laugh hollowly. "I don't think you do."

Mom gives a ghost of a smile. "It's pretty obvious."

Hearing that gets worse every single time. Everyone thought I should end up with Raychel, even my mom. I feel like I've let her down. "I can promise you, she doesn't feel the same way."

"How do you know?"

"Because I know!" I shout, then lower my voice. It's petty, but the fact that I'm here, taking the heat for my brother's lies, pushes me into tattling on him one last time. "Because she liked Andrew."

Mom stares at me. "What?"

"She liked Andrew," I say, defeated, but also relieved to finally admit the truth, or at least part of it. "They were sort of . . . dating. Before."

What I don't expect is for Mom's entire body to stiffen. "What do you mean, 'sort of dating'?"

"I mean . . . I don't know, Mom, they were hooking up. They liked each other. But they kept it secret."

Mom straightens, her lips pinched. "Were they 'hooking up' under my roof?"

"I don't . . . I don't know."

"For how long? Right here under my nose?" Mom won't give me a chance to answer. "I cannot *believe* that she would abuse our trust this way!"

I'm not sure what to say. Mom never used to lose her cool like this, and it's freaking me out to see her explode instead of setting me straight with logic.

"We've done nothing but help that girl and she—I just cannot believe—" Mom is so mad she's sputtering, then she bursts into tears. "How could this happen?"

"I don't . . . I don't know." It's the same question I've asked myself a million times. All I've learned is that Andrew's just as much to blame as Raychel, but it's a lot harder to be mad at a dead person.

But Mom doesn't really want an answer. I tentatively put my arms around her, and she cries like Andrew's just died again, not letting go of me until Dad gets home to take my place.

RAYCHEL

I don't hear from Matt that night, which is no surprise. When I text him not to pick me up for school, Dr. R. replies instead.

> Raychel—Come to the clinic tomorrow instead of the house. Thx—Dr. R.

· · · · ·

Matt ignores me all Friday, so I return the favor. But he's no-where to be found after school. I'm late to the clinic after catch-ing the transit, and when Dr. R. waves me into his office, I assume I'm in trouble for that. Instead he takes a seat in his big leather chair. "I think it might be better," he says carefully, "if you work here from now on."

"Okay . . ." I wait for some explanation, but none comes. "Did something happen?"

He sits back and gazes at me sadly. "Raychel, were you . . . dating Andrew?"

My hands ball into fists. I knew Matt was mad, but I never would have guessed he'd go this far to get back at me. "Sort of. We weren't really official until . . . We were going to tell every-one. The day he . . ."

Dr. R. leans forward. "When did Matt find out?"

Matt wants to tell my secrets? Fine. Two can play that game. "That . . . that morning, Matt, um . . . he tried to kiss me that morning, so he was really mad when he saw me and Andrew . . ."

I don't have it in me to be this cruel, and tears start to prickle. "It was an accident. He acted like he was going to hit him and then . . . and then . . ."

"He didn't push him."

"No," I hiccup. "It was just . . . terrible."

Dr. R. is quiet for a long time. "Accidents happen," he says finally, his voice shaking. "He should have been more careful." His shoulders heave. "We all should have."

I can't stand to watch him cry. "Is Mrs. R. mad?" I ask. He doesn't answer, and my stomach sinks. "I'll go apologize. Right after work."

He waits until I'm about to walk out before he says quietly, "I don't think that would be a good idea."

MATT

On Friday night, I try to blank out in front of a football game, but Mom and Dad come in and turn off the TV. "We need to talk to you," Dad says.

My entire life feels like one big talk right now. "About what?"

They take seats on either side of me. "We want to hear your version of what happened on the hiking trail."

I rest my elbows on my knees, clasping my hands like I can squash my panic between them. Dad must have talked to Raychel today. She probably told him the truth, because it's bad enough without embellishment, but does he hope she was lying?

Or does he think she left stuff out to cover for me?

From the corner of my eye, I can see Mom's hands shaking, and her fear spurs me into spilling it all at once. "I . . . Everyone else had gone ahead, but I heard voices, so I looked out on a little outcropping and . . ." My voice drops. "And I saw Andrew kissing Raychel," I say dully.

"And?" Mom asks.

"And I got really mad. I was yelling, and I kept stepping toward them, and Andrew didn't realize how"—I swallow as hard as I can—"how close he was. So he . . . he stepped off."

I expect Mom to look horrified, but her face just settles into resignation, which is even worse. She's already prepared herself to believe this was my fault. It freezes me in place until Dad clears his throat. "Okay. That's what Raychel said too. Okay."

"I'm sorry," I say, trying not to cry. "I . . . should have told you. I just . . . couldn't."

"We understand," he says, taking my hand. I doubt Mom agrees, but I let him say it anyway. "Of course you would be hesitant to explain. But we know you would never have hurt him on purpose."

"I was so mad . . ." I start, and can't finish. Finally I cough out, "I *would* have hurt him. But not . . . not like . . ."

"There's a difference between wanting to hurt someone and actually doing it," Dad says.

"Is there?" I burst out. "Because the end result's the same."

246

He tries to argue, but I have to release the thought that's tormented me since my first day back at school. "I mean, Carson didn't *intend* to hurt Raychel, but he did and I don't . . . I don't see how I'm . . ."

Mom stands up abruptly.

I look up at her through my tears. "Mom. I'm so sorry. I—"

She doesn't look at me. "There's a difference between being a murderer or a rapist and just an asshole," she says over my head. "Your actions contributed to an accident. They weren't the incident itself." She stands there, pinching the bridge of her nose. "But I'm still pretty damn upset to realize I raised an asshole."

Dad squeezes my hand. I stare at my reflection in the blank TV screen and realize Mom hasn't been taking sides at all. She's just stuck with me as a teammate.

RAYCHEL

Against Dr. R.'s advice, I try to call Mrs. R. Friday night. I leave a message, but she doesn't respond.

Asha does, though, and so does Keri. They both come over to keep me company, which is a little awkward at first because they barely know each other. But they're both so mad on my behalf that they buddy up within an hour. "Like, are you kidding me?" Keri gestures with the nail polish brush in her hand, and I almost tell her not to spill the jar until I realize that bright pink with sparkles would only improve our couch. "The least she could do is answer your phone call."

I shrug. I'm not a fool—Andrew and I knew all along that sneaking around was wrong and we'd have to apologize. I just never imagined I'd have to do it alone, much less that Mrs. R. wouldn't let me. "She did lose a kid," I say. I don't explain the rest—that Dr. R.'s probably told her Matt's role in that. As angry as I am, I'm not ready to hear our friends condemn him for it. "I doubt she's feeling the most rational right now. But I can't make her listen."

"You shouldn't have to. She's the adult here."

"It's Matt that really gets me," Asha says, handing me the bag of M&M's. "Where does he get off treating you that way?" She looks at me almost apologetically. "To be totally honest, I'm kind of glad it happened this way. Matt has never really liked me, so—"

My mouth falls open. "What?"

"Come on, you know he doesn't."

"He's never said that to me." But he does roll his eyes a lot when she's around.

"He's not, like, *mean* to me," she says. "But if it weren't for Spencer, we definitely wouldn't talk." She shrugs. "Honestly, I'll be surprised if he even stays in touch with Spencer once he leaves for school."

"Really?" I shake my head at the polish she holds up. Not red. I have enough nightmares about blood as it is.

"Look, don't ever tell Matt I said this," she says, putting the bottle down. "But Spencer's take was always that Matt—he means well, you know, but kind of in the way that like . . . old hippies and guys on the Internet mean well." She grabs a bottle of gold glitter from Keri and starts painting the nails on my left hand. "Like, they 'don't see color' and think girls should be equal but 'boys will be boys,' as if those aren't huge problems themselves. You know?"

"Yeah . . . I guess so." I never really thought about it like that. "It goes with his taste in music."

She points at me in agreement. "But it's always little stuff," she says. "Not *quite* worth calling out because you don't want to make a scene, or you know he doesn't mean it 'that' way."

Keri nods enthusiastically. "Or they'll say you're 'overreacting.' Even when they're the eighty-seventh person to tell you that all Asian girls look alike."

Asha makes a puking noise. "Or 'You should be smart since you're Indian.'"

"Oh my god, same, except Chinese, and I'm freaking Korean." Keri pretends to fist-bump Asha, careful not to smear anything.

"You seem plenty smart to me," I say. Whereas I feel exceptionally stupid at the moment. "God, if I say shit like that, you'll call me out, right?"

Asha laughs. "Do you not remember the collards joke?"

I blush hard. Once I suggested that the theme of her and Spencer's wedding should be collards and curry. To be fair, lots of people eat collards in Arkansas, and Spencer's mom happens to make the best. But yeah. It wasn't funny, and she let me know in a hurry. I still feel terrible about it.

"Not to be rude," Keri says, "but it's not really our job to tell you. I mean, *I* totally would, but just like . . . don't expect it of people, you know?"

"Yeah," I say immediately. "Yeah, for sure. Okay." I think about all the times I've let sexist jokes go because I didn't have the energy to argue at the time. Or Matt's homophobic meat-head joke at the blood drive.

"Anyway," Asha says, "I'm not saying Matt is a horrible dude. He wants to do the right thing. He just . . . screws it up a lot."

Keri laughs. "Rosa hates him because every time she suggests something for StuCo, he has some other 'save the world' idea that makes her feel shallow."

I snort. "He's good at that."

"Speaking of," Keri says, reaching for a bottle of top coat. "Have you seen Rosa's new car?"

She starts describing it to Asha, but I zone out, overwhelmed by how much I've missed. So many things I should have known about so many people around me. I can't stand to think about all the things I'll never learn about Andrew. But I thought I knew Asha. I definitely thought I knew Matt. And I always hated that Matt thought he knew everything.

Turns out we're both pretty clueless.

MATT

After our discussion, I move past my mom in silence, never knowing when one innocent comment might set off a squall. But there's still something I have to discuss with my dad. I catch him sweeping the driveway while Mom's at the store on Sunday. "What's up?" he asks, brushing dead leaves away from the garage door.

I don't even try to ease into it. "I got into Rhodes." The email came Friday afternoon.

Dad leans on his broom. "Are you going to accept?"

"That was . . . kind of the point."

He studies me. "I thought actually facing the decision might change your mind."

It has made me reconsider, but I don't want to admit that. "So you think I should stay?"

"I can see it both ways." He starts sweeping again. "You have a lot of problems to face here, and I'm never a fan of running away from those. But on the other hand, having something of a clean slate could do you good." The leaves join a growing pile. "Sometimes you can't put the pieces back together, even if you get them picked up."

"That's deep, Dad." I really just want him to tell me what to do.

"How do you plan to tell your mom?" he asks.

I've been trying not to think about that. "I'll . . . I guess I'll wait until I'm one hundred percent sure, and then I'll just . . . tell her." He looks disappointed. "I know she'll be upset, but . . ."

He straightens up and leans the broom against the wall. "She won't be okay if you just drop it on her."

"Not at first, but—"

"Matthew, I've known the woman longer than you've been alive. Don't you dare act like this is a casual decision that's not going to destroy her."

I don't want to hurt my mom, but the anger I'm always trying to push down strikes at my dad instead. "She thinks I'm an asshole. She's not going to miss me."

"That's bullshit and you know it." My dad hardly ever cusses at me, and it's startling enough that I forget my planned comeback. "Look," he says. "Sometimes being a parent means doing what's best for your child, even if you hate it." He picks up the broom again, pushing the leaves all the way back across the driveway. "I want to say that this is your decision, and you should have to break the news to her. That would be best for you, from a character perspective." The leaves are starting to disintegrate into flakes. "But your mother is dealing with enough and I'm not going to do that to her."

It occurs to me that Dad's dealing with just as much, which gives me a surge of unwanted respect. "So what do I do?"

He stands up and faces me. "Let me talk to her first. I'll tell her it's a possibility you're considering and that I made the contact thinking you weren't serious."

My newfound respect is joined by huge relief.

"I should have told her that in the first place." He glances down the road at an oncoming car. "We'll give her some time to adjust to the idea, and you think some more on the decision."

"And when I choose . . ."

He sighs. "Then you can tell us both. And we'll go from there."

RAYCHEL

After weeks of the silent treatment from Matt, going to school without him isn't much different. Keri starts giving me a ride in the morning and introduces me to her lunchtime crew in the drama room. They're all friendly and perfectly nice, and I try to remember their names and pay attention. It's easier than being alone with my thoughts, and before long I'm comfortable eating there even when Keri has other stuff to do.

It's amazing, really, how fast you can settle into a new reality.

Mom and I manage to coordinate schedules so she can drive me home from work. The ten-minute trip becomes a daily catch-up time, and I think we're both surprised by how much difference it makes to touch base on the daily. After a few days, I find myself confessing the details of my exile from the Richardson house. She nods thoughtfully until I'm done. "Well," she says, "you sure stuck your foot in it, darlin'."

I snort. "And then I tracked it all over the house."

"What're you going to do?"

"I don't know what else I *can* do," I say. "I tried to apologize to Mrs. R., and Matt—I mean, I know he's upset, but this isn't all my fault."

"Sometimes," she says, her drawl stretching the word, "people just aren't ready yet. They'll remember that you tried, when they get there."

"What if they never get there?"

Mom glances away from the road to half smile at me. "Then you go on without, and you prove 'em wrong."

MATT

Dad tells Mom on Monday. I can hear them arguing through the vents, something that hasn't happened since the days he was working emergency room hours. Andrew used to come to my room when they fought because arguments upset him more than me, and I always told him everything would be okay. I honestly thought it was true.

After she finds out, Mom pretends nothing is wrong, making an effort to be civil but little more. But she and Dad make me go see a therapist. I don't want to cooperate, but Dr. Shin has a sneaky way of turning "I don't want to talk about this" into me spilling my guts. "I just can't believe Raychel hasn't tried to apologize," I admitted at our first session. I didn't add that I'm also a little disgusted with myself for expecting it.

"Is it possible," Dr. Shin asked, "that you're just looking for reasons to be mad at her?"

"I think I have plenty of reasons," I snapped.

"I'm not negating that," she said. "But being angry might be easier than dealing with other emotions at the moment."

Which of course just made me angrier. But I have to admit: my other emotions are all over the goddamn place, and without Raychel to fight with, my brother's absence is impossible to ignore. He's not even in my dreams, which should maybe be a relief, but I feel cheated. At least it would feel like I was spending time with him again, for just a little while. I never spot his lookalike in a crowd and try to catch up, or imagine a glimpse of him on television, or have that moment of believing I've been hallucinating the whole thing.

I don't really deserve dream time with him anyway. What I deserve are the things that keep popping up to remind me in no uncertain terms that I'm now an only child. There's a card on our fridge addressed to "the Richardson boys," and I move a magnet to cover the *s*. The ugly frames in the hallway that display our school pictures from every year have my senior portrait, but will never have his. Big Johnson calls me into his office to check up on me, mumbling the entire time about "this horrible tragedy," and all I can do is stare at the family photo on his desk. I've always been the big brother.

I don't know what I am now.

RAYCHEL

Not all my life's changes are so easy to accept.

Being in the Richardson house seemed hard, so surrounded by memories of Andrew, but now I realize what a comfort that was too. At least I rarely forgot he was missing. Everywhere else, it's too easy to forget that he's not a phone call away, and I have to remember over and over that he's gone. Sometimes I pull up our old text thread and cry, but I only send messages to his ghost via email—long lists of things we didn't get to say and questions we never got to ask or answer. I hope his parents never find out the password and read all of my pathetic-ness. Although maybe it would make them see how I really felt about their son. Both of their sons.

There's no chance of telling Dr. R. about it at work. The job at the clinic is much different from the one I enjoyed. I'm no longer on my own schedule with my own project, and I have to take orders from everyone else in the office. I don't think my co-workers realize I used to be part of the family.

Past tense. I've been disowned. There's some stupid saying like "It's the family you choose that matters," but what do you do when they un-choose you?

I feel like I've been thrown away.

But even trash has its uses.

I seriously considered quitting. The last thing I want is another handout from the Richardsons, but this job isn't charity. I work hard for Dr. R. Maybe I didn't deserve it at first, but I've earned it since. My paycheck may be the only thing I've ever deserved from them.

Besides, I keep thinking about another saying—"When the only tool you have is a hammer, every problem looks like a nail." Well, when your body is the only tool you have, you either get hammered or nailed.

So I didn't give up my job. Dr. R.'s one condition was that I see the therapist in the office next door, which felt insulting until he told me Matt has to go too—not to the same one, thankfully. I've been once so far. I don't feel amazingly better or anything, but it helped to talk to someone with an outsider's perspective. My nightmares are as strong as ever, but the therapist reassured me they're a perfectly normal response to trauma—and always have been. She also convinced me to apply to some of my long-shot schools, because you never know until you try. That's all she wants me to do right now. Just try. One step at a time.

Which, right now, means covering the front desk until the receptionist is back from a break. I wave the next patient forward. "Why so blue, darlin'?" he asks.

I try not to scowl at the old man. I'm not blue. I am gray. Black. The complete absence of color. "Your co-pay is twenty dollars," I say brusquely.

He doesn't take the hint. "It can't be that bad," he says. "Smile!" He gets bitch face instead and it sours him immediately. "Jeez, that time of the month?"

"Yeah, actually," I snap. "And it's a gusher."

His horrified expression earns that smile.

MATT

The weekend before Thanksgiving, I'm brushing my teeth, feeling as close to normal as I ever feel these days, and I realize Andrew's toothbrush is still in the holder, right next to his disgusting razor. The next thing I know, I've emptied the cabinet and dumped all his stuff in the trash.

A moment later, I pull it all back out and wrap it in a towel. He doesn't—*didn't*—have much. He always used mine. I stalk down the hall to his room and throw open his door for the first time since the day after he died, when I found his stash and gave it to The Nuge. I was afraid Mom would find it.

It made sense at the time.

Our rooms are almost identical, his green where mine is blue, but it's still like being punched in the gut. Everything remains untouched. It's where we've been dumping all the Andrew artifacts, all the things we stumble across in the house and need to move behind a closed door because it hurts too much to look at them. But it hurts to look at what's not here too. He's not sprawled across his bed eating Oreos, or sitting at his desk, working on the models we loved making as kids, the ones that still hang in a corner. He's everywhere and nowhere and it makes me so angry that I throw the bundle across the room. It falls to the floor with an unsatisfying clatter.

I close the door and slide to the floor, head between my pulled-up knees. The guilt has made it hard to really feel the loss, and when I do, the loss makes me feel guilty for treating even his smallest possessions like trash. For always treating *him* like trash. It just circles, around and around, like a drain that can't be bothered to suck me down.

Crying makes me angrier, so I stand and walk around the room, taking in his lasts: the last shoes he took off, still lying untied in the corner. The last pillow he slept on. The last gum wrapper he left on his dresser.

I stare in his mirror, trying to see him in me, trying to see myself in him. I stare into my own eyes until they're blurred with tears, and I tell myself over and over: *Your brother is dead. Your brother is dead. Your brother is forever and truly dead.*

I wonder if I'll ever really believe it.

RAYCHEL

My estrangement from Matt has had one unexpected perk: it gave Carson the perfect opportunity to weasel out of the spotlight as new rumors replaced the old ones. Andrew's death and its aftermath are proof that Carson was right: I'm crazy, or a drama queen, or your run-of-the-mill slut. But he's not stupid enough to flaunt it and risk dredging shit up again. He laughs if his teammates taunt me, but otherwise, he pretends I'm invisible. Just like old times. Except now it seems unbelievable that I ever wanted anything but his indifference.

Now I have it back—and Matt's to go with it. But Matt's not

as good at looking through me, and sometimes I think he's going to crack. We've been friends too long. Old habits die hard. I keep finding myself looking forward to the day after Thanksgiving, when we always camp out on his couch for a leftovers-and-football coma.

But then he looks away, and I'm forced to remember that this year's holidays will be nothing like any before. Still, when I'm at my locker on the last day before break, my heart leaps to hear someone behind me. Until he speaks. "Hey, Sanders."

I stand up slowly, hoping someone will interrupt. But no one is staying at school one minute more than they have to. Carson stands well away from me. "I just want to talk," he says, glancing around.

I bang my locker shut with my foot. "I don't have anything to say to you."

"Listen," he says, pulling his hat lower over his eyes. "I just want to apologize, okay?"

I've heard this before. I'm sure not going to help him along.

"I just want to say . . ." He clears his throat. "I'm really sorry. Andrew was a good guy," he says, shaking his head in sympathy. "I would have backed off if I'd known y'all were together."

I should argue. At least pretend he's wrong. But that ship has sailed since Matt stopped speaking to me—half the school knows, or thinks they know, about me and Andrew. Instead, I stare at the bill of Carson's cap. "Wow," I say finally. "So nice of you to respect his wishes." *Without giving any thought to mine,* I'm about to add.

But Carson has no idea I'm being sarcastic. He gives me a cautious smile. "I mean, don't you think he would have wanted us to call a truce?"

I can't even laugh. "You're serious."

"Yeah," he says, his smile sliding away.

I never let myself picture what it might be like if Andrew were here to be my actual boyfriend. It just hurts too damn much. But for a moment, I imagine him coming around the corner. Spotting Carson here and grinning at the chance to cause trouble. His memory slips an arm around my waist and tightens until I can't breathe. "He would have told you to fuck off," I say, hoisting my backpack to shake off the pain.

Carson's jaw drops. "We had a little misunderstanding," he says, dumbfounded, "but Richardson was my friend too."

If getting punched in the face didn't prove he's wrong, nothing will, and giving Carson's ego this tiny bruise offers little satisfaction. But I say it anyway. "He wasn't your friend," I tell him, wrapping my own arms around my waist as I turn away. "And neither am I."

MATT

I still haven't committed to Rhodes when my diminished family goes skiing for Thanksgiving, unable to face our first holiday at home. Dad accidentally told the hotel clerk there's four of us.

He calls the front desk to remove the extra rollaway from our room, and we watch it go like a hearse wheeling into the hall.

When we get back to town, Dad wipes Andrew's laptop clean and sells it, then finds a buyer for his car. It's a compromise: Dad thinks it's best to move forward, while Mom clings to every single scrap of the past she can. So the bedroom stays, but the car goes, and I watch from my window as Dad shakes the new owner's hand. I hope she gets to drive it more than Andrew did.

· · · · ·

When Dr. Shin asks me in late November how things are going with Raychel, I don't know what to say. "She still works for my dad," I start.

"How do you feel about that?"

I shrug. "He's pretty careful not to mention her, so I guess it doesn't affect me."

"Does it bother you that he still pays attention to her?"

"What?" I almost laugh. "No. God, somebody has to."

"Does it bother you not to be that person?"

"No." I cross my arms, then uncross them. "Yeah. Of course. But I get it's not healthy or whatever." Amateur self-analysis has turned out to be that new hobby Mindy suggested I find.

Dr. Shin smiles. She has very straight, shiny teeth. "How are you feeling otherwise?"

"Like crap," I say, running a hand through my hair. "Like something's sitting on my chest." Andrew used to do that plenty, once he got bigger than me.

"That's normal," she says, and it takes all my willpower not to say "Duh." "Tell me, do you feel like the depression is unmanageable?"

"Like what? Like, am I going to throw myself off a cliff?"

She doesn't think that's funny.

"I feel . . . low," I say, looking away. "Like, literally low. Flat. It's not . . . sad, exactly. I mean, sad too, obviously. But that's a different feeling, I guess."

She nods. "There's a reason it's called 'depression' and not 'chronic sadness' or 'manic sorrow.'" She picks up a foam stress ball and squeezes it, leaving imprints of her fingers. "Depressions like these are holes left behind by a physical force. With mental depression, the force can be chemical or situational or both, but it doesn't just make a hole—it presses you into one that feels impossible to escape."

"Yeah," I say, trying not to picture Andrew in his own hole in the ground. "It's a lot like that."

RAYCHEL

One step at a time. Wake up, school, work, study, bed. Start over again. Any deviation is a chance to get knocked down, so I don't go anywhere else if I can help it. Mom and Eddie and I went out for Mexican food on Thanksgiving, and she's made me come to the grocery store once or twice. Keri's invited me to a few movies and football games, but she always accepts my excuses or ends up coming here.

Asha, on the other hand, is very persistent about trying to make me leave the house. She calls again as I'm walking home from work one Friday early in December. "Rayyyyych," she sings.

"No," I say immediately. This is her new thing. Just like everyone else, she's decided I need to move on—no more babying Raychel. Back on the horse. "Cowboy up." She seriously said that.

"There's a fiesta this weekend and you are my date," she informs me. She and Spencer still haven't gotten back together. I thought for sure they would, but now I don't know. I'm not the best judge of relationships, as it turns out.

"Don't you have to study for finals?"

She huffs. "Yes, but Dead Day is Monday, so tomorrow we're going out."

When I was younger, I always thought Dead Day was a big concert. Finding out it's just a day with no classes was disappointing. "*You're* going out."

She makes a buzzer noise. "I'm going out, and you're coming with me."

I hold the phone with my shoulder as I open the door. "What are the chances I can talk you into a movie or something instead?"

"Negative one zillion. Get your ass over here by seven or I'm coming to get it for you."

We hang up and I drop my stuff next to Mom, who's folding laundry. "That stack is yours," she says. "I still need to sort socks."

"You want help?"

She shakes her head. "Almost done. Go do your homework."

It's really weird, Mom suddenly caring about things like homework. "Asha wants me to go out with her tomorrow," I say, hoping she'll suddenly care about curfews too, but she smiles.

"I think that'd be good for you. You barely leave the house."

I don't bother to argue. She's right about the second part, anyway. Some of our friends came home again for the Thanksgiving break, but hanging out with them was awkward. Not because of Matt, who was out of town, but because their being more his friends than mine was too obvious. The boys didn't come out and say it, but if forced, they'd take his side.

The girls are still friendly, except Eliza, but we never really had that much in common. We were mostly friends by proximity, thrown together by our connections to boys we knew. Just a group of girls occupying a weird space in the middle.

Spaces in the margins, I think, remembering a line from early in *The Handmaid's Tale*. "We lived in the gap between words," or something like that.

Now I live in the gap between my old life and my new one. Asha has a place in it, but I don't know where everyone else will fit.

The doorbell rings, and I hear Mom greeting Eddie. He has

a spot in this new life of mine. First he was invisible; now he basically lives here. I try to show that I don't mind by being extra friendly, laughing at his jokes, that kind of thing. I'm about to come say hello when Mom brings the sock basket to my room. She sets it on my dresser and I'm about to thank her when she gasps. "What is this?"

My head jerks up. She's holding the baggie with Andrew's pipe. "It's not mine," I say reflexively.

"Really?" She throws the socks down. "You just keep drug paraphernalia around for fun?"

"No!" I say, trying to take the pipe from her. I was in a hurry this morning and left my jewelry box open, like a genius. "It's all . . . it's all I have," I say out loud.

"You think it makes a difference whether you have one pipe or several?"

"No!" I say again, desperately. I'm petrified she's going to break it. "I mean that's not what it's for, it's—"

"I work in a college dormitory, Raychel!" she shouts. "I know what it's for!"

"No!" I yell back. "I mean it was Andrew's!"

That shuts her up for a moment, but she's still livid. "I don't care why you have this or where it came from," she says, her nostrils flaring, "but you cannot expect to live in *my* house—"

"I gave it to her."

I whirl around. Eddie's standing in the doorway. "What?" Mom yelps.

"It was part of a memorial at school," he says, stepping into

266

the room. "Kids left all sorts of stuff. Administration wanted it cleaned up, but I couldn't stand to throw it all away, so I gave it to Raychel."

"But why in the *world* would you choose to give her *this*?"

He takes it from her hand and gives it to me. I close my fist around it tightly. "Kids smoke," he says. "But I knew Raychel wouldn't use it."

She looks between us, seething, then marches out of the room. He stops to glance over his shoulder at me. "You okay?"

"Yeah. Thanks," I say quietly.

He shuts the door and I sit on my bed, holding the pipe for a long time. I open the baggie and breathe in the dank smell of my time with Andrew. I miss him so hard that every bone in my body aches.

This smell, skunky as it is, will fade. So will pictures and memories and even this pain, so everyone says. But I don't want it to. I want Andrew to always be as loud and bright and painfully great as he was in real life.

And there's not a damn thing I can do about it. He'll still fade, even if I smoke and drink and play his music and movies . . . He'll never see the end of that vampire series, and what a stupid damn thing to make me choke up, but it does.

I wipe my eyes and drop the pipe back in its bag, then put it on a shelf at the top of my closet, in a shoebox full of other memorial detritus Eddie gave me for safekeeping. It seems wrong that I'm the one to keep it all.

It seems wrong that they're the only things I get to keep.

MATT

I drive to school and back in silence because I can't stand my own music and I can't handle Andrew's. I eat lunch alone in Ms. Moses's room, while she takes a break in the teachers' lounge. I quit all my extracurriculars, I only work out when the weight room is empty, and I've read through a solid half of the books on our living room shelves. I've even finished my Senior Seminar project, which isn't due until finals week.

Dr. Shin says I should stop "socially isolating" myself, but the truth is that without Raychel and Andrew, I have no friends left in Big Springs.

Mindy gives me sympathetic looks once in a while, but they're clearly pity, not an invitation. Raychel got custody of Asha in our divorce, which means I should get Spencer, but he claims he's decided to buckle down and study all the time, when it's obvious I just make him uncomfortable.

I make myself uncomfortable, and I'm not alone in that. There were the initial sorrys and sympathy hugs, but since then everyone at school seems afraid to talk to me.

Everyone except for Trenton Alexander Montgomery the Third, anyway.

"Ali!" he says, stopping me in the hallway and grabbing my hand like a winning prizefighter as always. He let it rest for about two weeks after the funeral, and then it was back to "You *are* the greatest!" and "Float like a butterfly, sting like a bee!"

It's the most normal thing that happens to me anymore. "How's tricks?" he asks.

"Have you ever considered that maybe you were born in the wrong era?" I ask, extricating myself from his grasp.

He nods solemnly. "All the time, man. All. The. Time." We move so we're not blocking a doorway. "Speaking of—how do you feel about the eighties?"

"The decade? Or like, geriatrics?"

"The former." He pulls out a flyer. That frat that wanted to recruit my brother is having an eighties-themed party. I wonder if they know he's gone. "My band is playing this scene tomorrow," Trent says. "You should come."

I shake my head. "I don't think so."

"Aw, come on, dude." He punches me in the arm. "It'll be fun!"

"No, it won't. I've been to parties there before." I try not to remember.

He pops his collar. "Trenton Alexander Montgomery the Third will *make* it a party."

I can't help but laugh, just a little. "I'm not sure even Trenton Alexander Montgomery the Third can save that place."

He leans in, lowering his voice. "Dude. It's going to be a total bust, okay?" he says, very seriously. "We're trying to get high school kids to come because we're going to look like such chumps up there with no crowd."

Chumps. I'm not sure the crowd is Trent's real problem. "Any takers?"

"None. I even tried to ask Rosa, but . . ." He whistles, miming a diving plane and its explosion.

I know that feeling. I pretend to study the flyer for a long time. "Okay," I say finally. The alternative is another Saturday night in my mausoleum of a house. "But I'm not going to wear a costume."

"No need, brah." He gives my clothes the once-over. "You're totally working that eighties' emo-goth look anyway. Get you a shirt with The Cure on it and you're good to go."

· · · · ·

At dinner, I try not stare at Andrew's empty chair and missing plate. I just want to fast-forward my life until it's time to leave for Memphis. Maybe even a few years past that.

We all pick at leftover takeout from the meal we barely ate last night. At least now that Mom and Dad are back at work, they can have some banal conversation about their days. Then they pretend to care about mine.

I shrug. "It was fine." I think of Trent popping his collar and force a weak smile. "A friend wants me to see his band play tomorrow night."

I thought Mom would be against me going, but it's Dad who's worried. "Where?"

"At a frat," I say, grimacing.

"On campus?"

I look at him sideways. "That's where most frats are."

"Are you sure that's a good idea?"

I shrug again. The more he bugs me about it, the more determined I'm getting, and I don't even want to see this show in the first place. "I've been to parties there before."

"You did lots of things . . . before," he says, glancing at Mom.

She pretends not to notice. "No drinking. Be home by midnight."

"Okay," I agree, surprised at us both.

Dad's still shaking his head. "It'll be fine," she tells him. "He's been cooped up in the house long enough. And it's not like he won't be doing worse next . . . year."

We all look back at our plates. The decision's really been made for weeks, but I've been avoiding the discussion because starting a conversation about anything in this house requires some emotional preparation. Last time I tried, I asked if we were going to my grandparents' house for the holidays and we ended up debating whether or not to celebrate Christmas at all. Mom burst into tears just thinking about hanging Andrew's stocking, but the thought of not doing it made her cry too, and then Dad left the table so I was stuck there, handing her paper napkins to stanch the flow.

It has to happen, though. The longer I wait, the more I prove that's Mom's right about me being an asshole.

I work up the nerve at the end of dinner. Dad picks at a piece of pie, and when Mom goes to clean up, I clear my throat. "I made a decision about college."

Mom sits back down. "Since you look nervous, I'm guessing you've chosen to go early."

I nod, grateful she saved me from saying the words. "I know . . . I don't expect you to be happy or anything. But I feel like it's the best thing, for everybody."

Dad sighs. Mom takes a moment before replying. "I understand why you've made this decision," she says, choosing her words carefully. "And I want you to know that I don't think it's necessarily a *bad* decision. For you." She stacks her pie plate on her larger one, placing her folded napkin on top of the pile. "But don't fool yourself into thinking it's best for everyone."

I watch her get up and walk to the sink, unable to find words until she turns the water on. "I just . . . I thought it would let everyone move on faster."

She shuts the water off. "I wasn't ready to move on even before Andrew died," she says. Her tone is more teacher than parent, like she's practiced this lecture. "I don't want to move on. I want things to stay as normal as possible. But I know—" Her composure slips a tiny bit. "I know that isn't going to happen, regardless. So I will support you in this, because I'll just have to deal with it next fall if I don't deal with it now."

I didn't think that a few months made that much difference, but now I can see what Mom's really facing. She would have had Andrew here for a whole year more, easing her transition from mother of two to empty nester. But now all the Band-Aids are getting ripped off at once. While I'm in a new place, she'll still be ghosting through this haunted house, mourning all of us and what she thought we'd be, and the future she and Dad had planned.

I push my chair back and launch myself into her arms. She staggers but holds me there, like I'm half my size and half my age, and Dad comes over to pat us both disconsolately while I tell her over and over I'm sorry.

She doesn't tell me it'll be okay, and I'm glad. We've told enough lies already.

RAYCHEL

Asha wasn't kidding about dragging me out of the house. She shows up at five thirty on Saturday, way before I was supposed to meet her, and basically stages a kidnapping. Mom is her accomplice, now that she's talked to Eddie and forgiven me. We had a big awkward discussion about how we all need to respect one another enough to tell the truth if we're going to share a house.

Then they asked if it was okay with me for Eddie to really be in our house. He's moving in.

"You could stay up here," Asha says when I tell her. She hands me a beer I don't want. "It's sort of lonely with no roommate and no Spencer . . ." She trails off.

"Maybe next year," I lie, giving her the requisite sympathy

smile. It's nice to be giving instead of receiving one for a change. "I'm surprisingly okay with it."

"Eddie always was a nice guy," she says. "Remember that time we left school late after choir, and he turned all of the parking lot lights back on for us even though he'd just shut them down?"

"He's a good cook too." My beer bottle is sweating on my behalf. I pick at the label.

"You know . . ." she says, raising an eyebrow, and points at my drink. "That's supposed to mean you're sexually frustrated."

I snort. "Well, I *have* found sex to be very frustrating." I can't even begin to contemplate when I'll want to have a new relationship. I suspect my body will be ready before my mind, but they're going to have to work out some kind of deal. Right now they both still want Andrew. I expected to miss him, but I didn't know I'd still want him in all the ways I ever did. Maybe I could dull the pain against someone else's body, but I don't think it would work. The differences would just make it sharper.

"Maybe that's the problem," Asha says, pointing at me with her bottle. "You just need to get laid."

"You're one to talk." I snap my bottle cap at her, then lie back on her bed and cover my eyes with one arm. It's not like she's jumped back on the playing field either. "That's absolutely the last thing I need."

She lies down next to me. There are new posters on her ceiling. I should decorate mine, with as much as I stare at it. She points to the long-haired lead singer of some indie band. "Don't you think a good make-out session with someone like that would be—"

"Awful?" I say. "Traumatizing? Emotionally stunting? Yes. Yes, I do."

She sits up. I can tell she's staring at me. "You are way grumpier than normal, which is kind of impressive." I roll my eyes. "What's your deal?"

When I told her about Andrew weeks ago, I left out the stuff about Carson. But like Mom and Eddie suggested, I'm trying to eliminate as many secrets from my life as possible. So I try to gather strength from the picture of a cat in a tree with *HANG IN THERE!* scrawled above it. Or use it to stall, anyway. "What the hell is that poster?"

"It's ironic," she says. "Now spill."

I sigh. "Remember when you were bugging me about Carson Tipton?"

She pauses. "I'm scared to say yes." Haltingly, I tell her what happened, and when I get done, she shakes her head. "Jesus, Raychel, you take the cake for Shittiest Senior Year Ever."

"I should get a trophy."

"Or a tiara."

"I'd rather have an actual cake."

"I would help you eat that cake."

"You're a true friend."

"I do what I can." She stands up and returns from her desk with a handful of mail. "You know, there's clubs and stuff on campus you could come to."

She hands me a flyer. "Rape clubs?" I say, trying to be funny. It's not, but she's nice enough to ignore me. "Where'd you get that?"

"They're in our mailboxes all the time."

SURVIVOR SUPPORT GROUP, MEETING WEEKLY AT DENTON HALL. *NO MEANS NO* IS NOT ENOUGH! *YES MEANS YES*—NO CONSENT, NO CONTACT! I stare at the words, remembering what Mrs. R. said. What Andrew said. Asha's not worried that saying yes to him will have messed me up forever. She's worried that I said no to someone who didn't listen. "Why don't they teach us this shit in school?" I ask. Carson is right—there was a misunderstanding, but it wasn't little. He still thinks he's the mistreated nice guy and has no idea what he did wrong. And he'll probably never know. "Why don't they teach the *boys* this in school?"

Asha pretends to be shocked. "You can't talk about sex in school! It makes those horny teens want to . . . 'do it,'" she says, pretending to whisper.

I hold the flyer out. "Do you have more of these?"

"There's a bunch in the lobby, why?"

My face flushes a little, and I'm annoyed at myself for being embarrassed. "I thought maybe I'd hang some up at school." I can't make the boys understand shit, but maybe I can give some girls a fighting chance.

"I like that idea." The rest of Asha's beer goes down in one gulp, and then she grins. "But I also have a better one."

MATT

The problem with going to see Trenton Alexander Montgomery the Third's band is that he's *in* the band, which gives me no one to hang out with.

I thought nothing could suck more than another night in my parents' sad house, but it sucks enough to be solo at a party that I call Spencer and guilt-trip him into coming down for a while. I don't mention that TAM3 sound even worse than their name does. He's still acting weird around me, so I try to drink away the awkwardness, which gets me a lot drunker than I should be. It works, though. Once he realizes it's okay to joke and give me crap, he loosens up, and if I try really hard, I can pretend it's just like old times. Except I'm the one getting trashed for once.

I understand now why Raychel got so shit-faced falling down drunk all the time. It pisses me off that I understand, and it pisses me off that I feel bad for her, and it really, really pisses me off that she and Andrew did the "being a screwup" thing so thoroughly that I don't even get the option.

Still, I glance around the room with new, somewhat blurry eyes. "You gonna take any of these girls home tonight?" It sounds bizarre, coming from my mouth.

Spencer's forehead wrinkles. "I don't know, man. Feels like it's not worth it."

I laugh and drink more beer, pretending I was kidding. But there's some pretty girls in the corner, and they're definitely checking us out. I'm leaving in a few weeks. What could it hurt to pick up a girl?

Then I remember the party that feels like forever ago, when I wished I was more like Carson. I think of Mindy, and remember what it can hurt. I'm just not a one-night-stand kind of guy. At least I'm figuring that out before college.

So I stand around with Spencer and wait for Trent's band to get done. He does look like a Muppet when he plays, down to the Animal-style inarticulate screaming at random moments. I'm ready to split when he steps off the stage, but he claps me on the back and takes the extra beer I offer. "Whoo! Gotta take a break between sets."

"You're not done yet?"

"Just getting warmed up!" He slaps Spencer on the back. "How's life? Campus man!"

Spencer laughs, glancing nervously between us. He always let Asha do all the talking, and now I'm wondering if she did it out of kindness. "You want to grab the next round?" I ask him.

"Yeah, man. Be right back." He makes his escape, looking relieved.

"You havin' the time of your life yet?" Trent asks.

"Best night ever," I say. "You?"

"Nah." He pretends to get dreamy. "Best night of my life was kissing Rosa Gallegos in the ninth grade."

"Bullshit," I say, spilling some beer. "Rosa?"

"The one and only." He sighs. "Nobody's really compared since."

I look at the rim of my cup. I am just drunk enough to ask him this. "Let's say you found out Rosa was dating your brother on the sly." I meant for my phrasing to be a little more subtle, but alcohol has other ideas. "Would you still want her back?"

"Well, my friend, I do not know. Trenton Alexander Montgomery the Third is an only child."

"I can't imagine why."

He claps me on the shoulder. "And that, my friend, is why she picked your brother."

"Asshole."

"And that," he says, giving me a shake, "would be *you*." I stare at him, trying not to let on how much that word stings these days, until he laughs and lets go. "Seriously, was she your girl?"

Yes. "Not exactly." I take another gulp of beer.

"Did she know how you feel?"

I wipe my mouth. "He did." There's no way Andrew didn't know.

"I said 'she.'"

"No," I admit. "I didn't tell her in time."

Trent has the balls to laugh. "So you're mad she ended up with the man who expressed an interest?"

"No, I . . ." I take another big drink, and it's hard to swallow. "Yeah, I guess. But she slept with him! How do I overlook that?"

He shrugs. "Details, man. If she's not yours, she can screw whoever she wants. You're just mad it wasn't you." His guitarist bangs on the cymbals a few times. "If Rosa came to me tomorrow and said, 'Trent, I messed around with every guy on earth, but it made me realize I only want you—'" He drains his cup and hands it to me. "Well, I'd want her to get tested first, but I'd thank my lucky stars to be the one taking her to the clinic." He gets back onstage and pauses. "You can repay me for my wisdom by bringing me beer during our next set."

"I'd rather piss in it," I say, and he laughs. But I don't let him get more than half empty for the rest of the night.

RAYCHEL

Asha's plan is easy, but we have to buy a lot of tape. We also invest in Pringles, Dr Pepper, and a bag of Hershey's miniatures. Just the essentials.

Since Asha's had a beer or three, I drive her car to a residential subdivision on the west side of town. The houses are smaller than I expected. We jump out, motor running, but my phone rings when we're only halfway through plastering the Blazer in flyers. "Shit!" I whisper, and get back in the car. "Hello?"

"Raychel?" A girl's voice warbles through the speaker. "Hey, what are you doing tonight?"

It's a very drunk Keri. "Not having as much fun as you, apparently."

"Not *that* fun," she says. "This guy I met brought me to a party on campus, but he *ditched* me." She manages to lisp the word "ditched," which is impressive. "Can you, like, borrow your mom's car or something? My parents will *kill* me . . ." She pauses.

"Where are you?"

"At the . . ." She makes a frustrated noise. "Oh, I can't keep them all straight. The one at the very end of Greek row? That party we got handouts about. That Trenton Montgomery was begging everyone to come to."

"I can't believe you ended up going."

"Me neither," she says.

The door slams and Asha jumps in, cracking up beside me. "Go!" she yells, pointing at the porch. The light has come on.

"We'll be right there." I toss Asha the phone and hit the gas, squealing away in a gale of laughter.

．　．　．　．　．

The frat house is less crowded than last time I was here, but it's a lot colder outside and I'm glad I'm wearing more clothes. "Where did she say she'd be?" Asha asks.

"Out back." Keri called twice while we drove over, once to give better directions and once because she needed to pretend like she was too busy to talk to a creeper. "She said the band's so bad that everyone's outside." I step off the red-brick sidewalk, trying to see if there's a way we can walk around instead of through the house. But the backyard is enclosed with an eight-foot privacy fence. "No way out but through," I say, quoting my therapist. I suspect she didn't mean braving a kegger when she said it.

I was worried we'd look out of place, but no one pays us much attention since everyone else appears to have gotten dressed at the mall circa 1987. "Does that girl have crimped hair?" Asha asks, indicating with her eyes.

"Pretty sure." I sound like Matt. Annoyed, I stretch up on tiptoe, but I can't spot Keri. She's even shorter than me—she'll be impossible to find in this crowd.

But I do see one familiar face. And suddenly the room feels way too small.

MATT

By the time Trent's band goes on for their unrequested encore, I'm so drunk they almost sound good. Of course I'm also so drunk that I think I see Raychel and Asha. Worse, Asha appears to be walking toward me.

"What are you doing here?" she asks.

Oh. Crap. "Same as you, probably." I tip my drink back so I don't have to look at her.

"You're also here to pick up Keri?" she asks, putting a hand on her hip.

Raychel walks up with a staggering Keri in tow. I feel slightly chagrined. "No," I slur. "I'm just here for the music."

"Wow." Raychel looks at the band and bites her lip. "I didn't realize that was Trent. That is . . . wow."

"Yeah," I say. "Wow."

Spencer returns with two more beers, saving me from conversation, but he completely misses Asha's presence until he's right in front of us. "Shit. I mean, hey," he says, bobbling the cups. I take one to be helpful, and also to drink as quickly as possible. He tries not to stare at Asha, who's staring at him.

"Where're your glasses?" she blurts.

Spencer feels for his shirt pocket, pausing halfway. "I got contacts."

It's silent, or as silent as it can be with the blaring off-rhythm chaos behind us. Then Keri yawns theatrically. "I'm ready to go home."

I'm going to have to leave my car here, because there's no way I can drive. "Could you take me home too?" I ask.

"Keri's not driving anywhere," Raychel argues. But Asha looks at her pleadingly, and she sighs. "I'll take you both in Asha's car and then come back to get her."

· · · · ·

Keri and I decide to sing in the car. We turn up the worst of the worst Top 40, and I pretend it's to be chivalrous to Keri, but it's mostly because I know it'll set Raychel's teeth on edge. Payback for years of her doing the same.

Keri's so drunk she gives herself a Pringles duck beak, which means I have to do it too, and then we try to sing through those and end up laughing so hard that Raychel has to pull over to let Keri puke. Keri's not as much fun afterward, but luckily her house is near campus, in the historic district. I sit in the car as Raychel walks her to the front door, where Mrs. Sturgis meets them with her arms crossed. I can tell from the way Raychel bows her head that she's apologizing, but Mrs. Sturgis pats her shoulder as she leaves.

"Well, Keri's grounded for the rest of her life," Raychel says, getting back in the car.

"Bummer." Being so close to her makes my body react in embarrassing ways. Luckily it's too dark for her to notice, but it sours my buzz. *Just get home,* I tell myself. *Go to bed and don't make a fool of yourself.* I turn off the music and sit quietly. "How have you been?" I dare to ask.

She glances at me. "Fine. You?"

"Great. Dandy." I make a nonchalant gesture and whack my hand on the window.

She shakes her head. "You seem dandy."

"I'm drunk." I realize how stupid it sounds, but oh well. "Mom's gonna be pissed."

Raychel swallows a laugh. "Your parents are chill," she says, her tone changing. "You'll be fine."

"My brother fell off a cliff, Raychel. My parents are anything but chill these days." She flinches, hard enough that I reach for her out of habit and pull back at the last minute, staring out the windshield instead. The oncoming headlights make my head hurt. "They're already pissed, because I'm going to Rhodes next semester."

She glances at me. "For real?"

"Yeah. Headed to Memphis after New Year's."

"Wow."

A minute passes. "I'm too drunk," I say, closing my eyes.

She snorts. "Good thing you got a ride."

"Good thing Dad taught you to drive."

"My mom taught me," she says, cutting off my argument. "Your dad just took me to the test. That's why I did so much better than y'all."

It's true. Even when Andrew and I tried to distract her, she was always the best. I still can't drive a standard without stalling out. And my brother—

I open my eyes before I can finish the thought. Raychel parks a few houses away from mine and cuts the lights, but opening my door turns out to be harder than I expected. She sighs loudly and gets out, walking around to help.

"Thanks for the ride," I say, trying to sound sincere, but it's hard to sound anything but stupid when your mouth won't work right.

"Sure. Can you make it?"

"Pfft." I turn around and crash into a mailbox. "Crap."

"Oh for Christ's sake," she mutters, and hesitates. "Okay.

Come on." She puts an arm around my waist, making me drape one of mine over her shoulders.

My body relaxes, even as hers tenses. My mouth relaxes too. "I've missed you, Raych."

She doesn't answer. "Which door?" she asks.

"Back. But Raych . . ."

"No," she says. "How'd you get so drunk?"

"It was surprisingly easy."

That elicits a tiny smile. She drags me through the back door and up the stairs. I pretend to need more help than I do as a pathetic excuse to touch her, and insist that I have to brush my teeth so I can stare at us together in the mirror. *My girl,* I keep thinking, hating it. But it won't stop. *Mine,* I'm thinking as she turns off the bathroom light. *Mine.* I'm reduced to nothing but this basic, demanding need, and when she makes me sit on the bed, I tug her by the hand until she's standing between my knees. "Raych," I say quietly.

"Matthew."

I hug her, pressing my head to her stomach. Her fingers run cautiously through my hair. It sends tingles down my neck and arms, and I shiver. I can feel her abs through her shirt. But she pulls away. "Raych," I say again, and it sounds a lot closer to a sob. This is not quite what I had in mind with *Don't embarrass yourself.*

She lowers herself to one knee. "Hey," she says, making me look at her. "Hey. It's going to be okay."

"No, it's not." I sound like a five-year-old. "I lost you both."

She blinks, like she's trying not to cry. "Yeah. I lost you both too."

I tip her chin up. "You're still my girl, Raych."

"No, I'm not." She pulls away, lowering my hand from her face to my own leg.

"We never even talked . . ." I start, but she closes her eyes and stands up.

"Not tonight," she says. "If you still want to talk in the morning, you know where I am." She stops at the door. "It's not like I'm going anywhere."

RAYCHEL

It is so, so hard to be in this house again.

The familiar smell when we walked in was like falling into a sad dream. I navigated Matt up the stairs without turning on a single light. I got him ready for bed like he did for me a thousand times. It felt like home.

But it's not.

He said a lot of things—the beer said a lot of things, anyway—but I'm setting them aside. Taking it as a stolen moment, one of the last I'll ever get.

I pause at the top of the stairs, trying to soak up the end of my time here. I listen to the grandfather clock downstairs and the branch that taps the guest room window. My window. Tiptoeing, I sneak back down the hall and stare into that dark room.

There's no stab or tear or ache—just a twinge, like a phantom limb. It's my room, same as it ever was, and never really mine. Andrew and I were only one of many things that happened here. But as much as I regret so many things this year, I'll never be sorry for that.

Andrew. I might never get the chance to see his room again. His door creaks when I open it, and moonlight shines through the windows. No one's closed the curtains or the blinds. No one's moved anything, except for a pile of items on his bed. I don't dare sit or touch anything. I wish I could steal one of his shirts or something—a Dead tee to replace the one ruined with his blood—but I've taken enough from this family.

I just walk around, looking at all the things left behind. What would I leave? Some clothes, a half-dead plant, a decent music collection. Andrew had some basketball trophies. Some concert tickets. Some talents. Some gifts. He took those with him. He should have shared them more.

Andrew's room is no phantom limb—it's like hacking off pieces of myself that were barely hanging on to begin with.

I swallow any sound the pain wants me to make. I can't get caught here. I'm trespassing in all meanings of the word. Taking a last glance around, I force myself to close the door.

It's so hard. I don't understand how this is still so hard.

I take the stairs two at a time, less concerned about being quiet in my haste to escape, but halfway to the patio door, a throat clears. I freeze. "Hello?"

Someone exhales loudly. "Raychel."

I turn around. Mrs. R. is illuminated by the refrigerator light, a carton of juice in her hand. "I . . . I brought Matt home," I say. The fact that I did nothing wrong tonight helps to level my voice. "He needed a ride home and I had Asha's car, so I offered to take him and Keri."

Mrs. R. lets the fridge click closed. I can barely see her now. "He's drunk," she says.

"Yeah." No point in lying.

"You're not."

"No."

She's silent for a moment. "What do you want from him?"

"From Matt?" I assume she nods, because she doesn't say anything. "I . . . nothing." A real apology, maybe, but that's not what she's asking about.

She comes forward, and the microwave clock shines a blinking blue on her face. "Do you really think you can be friends again? Do you think you can be something more? He's not—"

"I never wanted to be something more," I interrupt. Even Mrs. R. can't believe I would voluntarily pick Andrew over his brother. It makes me too angry to keep a conciliatory tone. "Matt was drunk at a party and he needed a ride home. That's all."

She exhales. "Then thank you. I . . . I wish—" Her voice cracks. "You have to understand. He's my son. I can't pick you over him."

"I don't want you to."

"Then why did you make me choose?"

I haven't felt this helpless since I watched Andrew fall. "I didn't end up with Andrew as some kind of rebellion," I say.

"But you should have told us."

"We were going to. We just . . . ran out of time."

"I always thought . . ." She sighs and pauses for a moment. "I wanted you and Matt to be together. I thought that, in the long run, you would be. And then you'd be . . . family."

Her admission pushes me to say what I should have all along. "I thought I *was* family." She doesn't reply, which feels like a knife in the chest, but I make myself go on. "And it still could have worked out, you know? Maybe I picked the wrong one, but I loved Andrew. And I'm sorry you can't deal with that."

"I could have dealt with that," she says. "If I'd gotten the chance."

I'm not sure how to reply. "I love this whole family," I say finally. "Even Matt. Even though he hates me."

"He doesn't hate you," she says. "But you don't love him. You want to *be* him."

She's right, as always. Why wouldn't I have wanted to be Matt? His family, his finances, his future—of course I covet those. But she's also wrong, and I'm not leaving without saying it. "That may be true, but why would I want to be someone I don't love?"

She doesn't have a response for that. I slip out the door and go home.

MATT

In the morning, I have a text.

> I hope you're not too hungover. I meant what I said—if you ever want to talk, you know where I am. If not, good luck at Rhodes.

• • • • •

I don't answer it, but I don't delete it either.

Mom spends the day in bed, and doesn't say a word about me coming in late. I think I'm off the hook until right before bed. "Matt," my dad calls as I'm headed upstairs.

I pause at the top.

"If you wanted to go to a party with Raychel, you could have just told us."

My mouth opens and closes. "I didn't even know she'd be there," I finally manage.

He shakes his head. "You're not the only one that misses her, you know." He tilts his head toward the master bedroom, then walks away. It's the last I hear of it.

RAYCHEL

Matt doesn't answer my message, but I'm not surprised. Alcohol always makes promises it can't keep.

It's the conversation with Mrs. R. that won't leave me alone. I'm angry and hurt and frustrated, but also comforted. She wanted me as a daughter-in-law. The fact that she had such extensive plans for our future is a little alarming, but at least it makes clear that there's no way I could have salvaged this situation once Andrew died. Except maybe one. "You know what's bizarre?" I ask my mom.

She pats her head, glancing in the rearview mirror. "This haircut?"

"No," I say, reaching over to put a piece back in place. I talked her into going with me to Keri's hairdresser. I just got a trim, but Mom got a brand-new 'do that makes her look way younger. I keep doing double takes when I look over. "Your hair looks amazing."

She smiles. "Then what?"

"Oh. What's bizarre is that if I'd had a baby, the Richard-sons would totally have forgiven me."

Her eyebrow rises. "You think?"

"Yeah. I mean, they would have been super pissed, but then there would have been a baby to coo over. You can't stay mad at a baby." Especially not one that was Andrew's. A little piece of him for all of us to keep. "Of course it would have ruined *my* life," I go on, trying to push the sudden sorrow away.

Mom shrugs. "You didn't ruin my life. You just changed it."

I'm almost speechless. "Really?"

"Of course." She reaches across the console to squeeze my knee.

"But you always said . . ."

"Well, I'm not saying it's how I would have chosen, if I'd had my druthers." She pats her hair again. "Your dad and I moved up here because we wanted our kids to have it easier, but we fouled that up pretty quick."

"But I do have it easier." We're poor, but Mom grew up in a rusted-out trailer in Dumas, down in the southeast part of the state. We've visited a few times, and it's totally different from here—swamps instead of mountains, cypress and pine instead of oak and hickory, and the blues instead of bluegrass. The former plantations still grow cotton and rice, while farms here are mostly small homesteads wedged into valleys. They even have a different accent. But their economy is terrible, and the jobs available in Big Springs were the answer to my parents' prayers. "I know I complain a lot, but I don't want you to think that I . . . you know. I do appreciate it."

She smiles. "And see, that's what I mean. I didn't do it right, but look how you turned out anyway."

"A hot mess?"

She huffs. "That's my hot mess you're talking about," she says, and I laugh. "Besides, I'm not ready to be a grandma yet."

"Oh god, I didn't even think about that." But once the idea is out, I can't put it away—Mom and Eddie as Meemaw and Pawpaw or something similarly awful. Dr. and Mrs. R. would be ridiculous in a different way—she'd probably refuse any kind of nickname and he'd demand to be Grandpa Deadhead or something. They'd be amazing grandparents.

Will be amazing grandparents. To Matt's kids. Not mine.

Somehow I'd always pictured them in that role, even when I wasn't interested in either son. It just seemed like they'd always be there.

It's weird to miss a family you never really had, but I guess I always will.

MATT

Monday after school, I call the number I took off my Favorites weeks ago. Raychel answers, sounding hesitant. "You want to go for a walk?" I ask.

She comes to the house but doesn't come in. "Tell her . . . thanks," she says, handing me a stack of Mom's books.

I nod, though I'll probably just slip them back on the shelf.

We wander the neighborhood toward the back of the subdivision, where new homes stand in various stages of construction. Mud surrounds most but one has a sidewalk already poured, and Raychel follows me up the path into the frame of the house. She moves from room to room, stepping into each space. "Is this a closet?" She holds her arms out. "It's bigger than my bedroom."

I don't answer. Large window holes look out over the sloped backyard, and the recent rain has cut a gully at the base of the hill. Leaves and sticks float down the ditch and away into a stand of trees left by the subdivision planners, who are required by law to preserve a certain percentage of the trees. I wonder how they decide which ones get to survive.

"Ow." Behind me, Raychel inspects her hand.

"What'd you do?" I cross the house, stepping through the framed walls instead of going around them to the doors.

"Scraped my hand on a nail." She puts it to her mouth. "No biggie."

"Are you bleeding?"

The blood on her lip answers my question. "Not really."

The lie pisses me off more than it should and I turn my back, only to hear thumping. "What are you doing?"

"Going upstairs."

"It's not finished." I tilt my head back. The second story's floors are just rows of boards, not yet covered with plywood. She walks out on a beam and I gauge the distance to the concrete floor. She'll crack her skull like a . . . like . . . I climb the steps too, trying to hurry without appearing to.

She glances at me. "It's fine. See?" One hand pretends to shake the wall brace beside her. "There's plenty to hold on to." I start across the beam toward her. "Just don't look down," she adds. Of course I do, but it doesn't scare me. What scares me is that I can't hang on to her, and I shouldn't. But I still want to.

RAYCHEL

I pick my way through the house's skeleton, balancing on its bones to stand in its open eyes at the back. Thunder grumbles. "It's going to rain."

Matt makes a sound that could be agreement. Or not.

I can't believe he actually called. I almost didn't answer, but if I'm giving up the Richardsons, I might as well do it completely—including closure with Matt. Still, I'm not going to lead this conversation.

So I wait, letting my eyes wander the property. Everything has turned from brown to gray now. Dead leaves float, then swirl as the wind picks them up, teasing them past empty tree branches.

Matt sniffs, not looking at me. "Do you miss him?"

I swallow hard. "Of course."

He stays silent for a few minutes. "It's just . . ." He trails off, and though I want to follow, I can't pick it up because I don't know where it goes. So I wait, and wait, but he doesn't speak.

The rain begins, a light drizzle the roof mostly keeps off. It combines with wet sawdust to make a new smell, something like moss or decaying firewood. It brings back afternoons in Dr. R.'s workshop, the summer we "helped" him build a fort and Andrew broke his arm on his first trip down the slide. I bite my lip, chapped and stinging from the cold. If Matt's not going to talk, there's no reason to stand here. I turn to leave.

He clears his throat. "Where are you going?"

"Home."

"No, my dad said . . ." He coughs. "I heard him say you asked for a letter of recommendation, for your applications."

I lean against the window frame. The only thing more uncomfortable than asking for the letter is the mental image of the Richardsons still discussing me around the kitchen table. "Yeah, I, um . . . I'm applying to a few other schools besides here, for next fall. Just in case." With Eddie in the house, my mom has help with the bills, which means I might even be able to refill my savings some.

"That's good," Matt says. "Where at?"

"One in Missouri," I start, stalling. "One in Texas, one in Oklahoma, one in Colorado . . . and one in Tennessee." He doesn't react, but I rush on anyway. "Don't worry, it's really far from Memphis. Tennessee is super long, like—"

"I'm not worried." He shifts his weight, reaching with both

hands for the board above our heads. "I'm happy for you. I hope you get in somewhere good."

And then it's quiet again, because we both know what the opposite of good is—the place I'm most likely to be. But it's not worth arguing about. I'm not sure anything is. "Matt," I say, forcing him to look up. "I don't know what you want." I wish we'd had this conversation a long time ago.

He picks at the wood. "I don't either." The rain falls heavier, blowing through the windows, and he wipes his face. "I want . . . to forgive you," he says, staring out. "But I don't know how."

"Then don't." I straighten my spine in the space between the wall braces. "What good would it do?"

"You're my best friend, Raych—"

"Am I?" I snort. "Because last time I checked, you were ignoring me and I was banned from your house."

"I'm sorry," he says, stepping closer. "It's just . . . it's so . . ." He meets my eyes. "I'm embarrassed, okay? I'm embarrassed that I was *right there* when it happened. I thought you and I—"

"I didn't know!" I argue. "You didn't tell me!"

"I was going to!"

"When? Before or after you got me in bed?" I pretend to laugh. "Oh wait, I was there all the goddamn time!"

He lets out a roar and turns away, his hands balled. Suddenly he draws back and punches the window frame, leaving bloody knuckle prints on the wood. It obviously hurts a lot more than he expected. I wonder if he ever actually punched anything before. He let Andrew do all the real fighting. "Just talk, for Christ's sake!"

He stomps down the stairs. Good. This is a conversation we should have on the ground. But he keeps going when we reach the floor and the sight of him walking away makes me lose control. "Why couldn't you just be my best friend?"

Matt whirls around. "I wanted . . . more, all—I don't know!" he yells. "The whole thing, not a hookup!" He grabs his hair with his uninjured hand. "I just wanted you."

I don't want to hurt him more, but I'm not willing to be the only bad guy anymore. "You let me sleep in your bed believing you didn't." I step so close I could poke him in the chest. "And I was glad! I thought you liked me for who I was, not . . ." I gesture at my body.

His forehead wrinkles. "I did! I do. So much that I wanted us to be more. I just kept . . . waiting for the right time."

"That's messed up."

"No, what's messed up is that I loved you, Raych." He takes a deep breath. "I *loved* you."

Our faces are inches apart. And for one long moment, two futures stretch out before us again. His head tilts almost imperceptibly, but I know what it means: Matt still wants me. Or thinks he does.

There is one more way to salvage this situation, and it would be so easy. If only I wanted him too.

But I don't. Mrs. R. is right: I wanted Matt's family. I wanted his life.

But I don't want to *be* his life.

His mouth approaches and mine responds. "No."

He exhales and steps away, looking lost. I close my eyes so I don't have to see. When I open them, he's inside the house again, leaning out a window in the back. "I hate him!" He grabs the top of the frame and leans into the open air, tiptoes on the wet sill, like we're still on the second story. But there's nowhere to go from here. "Do you hear that, Andrew?" he yells. "I hate you!"

I'm past all tears. They're burning. Vapor. "And you hate me too," I say, standing in the front doorframe. "You wish I had died instead."

He doesn't turn around. And he doesn't deny it.

"What if it was me?" I demand. "Would you still be mad if I was dead?"

"Shut up."

I'm right. In ways I never wanted to be. "If I had died, your life would be fine," I say, "and so would his." My words are weapons, and each one strikes with precision, driving straight into his back. "You'd be mad, but you'd forgive him eventually and you'd both remember me sadly in twenty years as your shared long-lost first love."

"Shut *up*."

"I didn't die, Matt!" My throat hurts. "I'm still here, and you still have to deal with me!"

"Shut up!" he screams, and I'm horrifyingly happy to see him cry, so happy that I turn around to escape myself. I have to get out of here.

"I don't wish that!" he yells, following me. I pause at the curb but don't turn back. "If I had to choose . . ."

He leaves it unspoken as I walk away. It's the worst thing I've never heard.

MATT

She walks away.

After everything, Raychel's the one who leaves.

I stay in the unfinished house for hours after she's gone, flexing my hand to keep the pain fresh. I meant to have a very different conversation. I meant to tell her that she's right: it's messed up that I never asked her what she wanted, and that I assumed I knew what was best for everyone when it was really just what was best for me. What I *thought* was best for me.

I meant to tell her that I forgive her. But it's not even true. Getting to the point where I want her again isn't forgiveness. It's just more messed-up bullshit she didn't ask for.

As much as I hate to admit it, she and Andrew could have been something.

But I underestimated him so much that even after she told me point-blank that she liked him, I didn't believe her, or even ask why. Just like I didn't ask whether she liked Carson. Or if she wanted to be my girl.

Even today. She told me no when I went to kiss her, and I listened.

But I didn't ask first.

And the fact that I thought the answer could still be yes is the most messed up of all.

RAYCHEL

Tuesday morning, Keri catches me in the hall after second period. "So did you hear?" she asks.

"What about?"

"Carson Tipton," she says. "Somebody taped NO MEANS NO flyers all over his car this weekend."

"Yeah," I say slowly, and a grin spreads over my face. Dealing with Matt made me forget the good part of my weekend. "I did, actually. How did you hear it?"

"Rosa Gallegos lives next door to him." She leans in conspiratorially. "His mom was so pissed, she's making him take a women's studies class at the university next semester."

My eyes widen. "They're going to eat him alive."

She smiles sweetly. "We can only hope."

• • • • •

I keep waiting for my final fight with Matt to come crashing down on me, but I'm more relieved than crushed. We've said our respective pieces and he can leave. If Andrew and I burned a bridge when our lips touched, then Matt and I napalmed one when ours didn't.

So the last thing I expect to get is a package with his return address. But the handwriting is Mrs. R.'s. I tear it open, not sure what I'm hoping to find, and I'm slightly disappointed when it's just a few paperbacks I'd loaned her and some sealed envelopes—letters of recommendation from her, each labeled with the schools Dr. R. knows I'm applying to.

Nothing else. No notes. No explanation. Just one last boost on my ladder out of here.

For a petty moment, I consider burning them. I don't want to accept her help. I don't want to *need* her help. But then I realize that this is the only apology I'll ever get from Mrs. R. And it's the only one I've gotten that's worth accepting.

MATT

My Senior Seminar project was finished a month ago, but a week before finals, I finally finish reading *The Handmaid's Tale*. Raychel, however, ends up presenting Virginia Woolf's *A Room of One's Own*, and does a good job. I give her almost-perfect scores on my peer evaluation, and hope she'll recognize which one's mine.

So many girls chose *Handmaid*, though, that it takes two

days to finish them all. The first presenter is super nervous, reading a long quote about control and forgiveness and how they are and aren't the same thing. I try not to look at Raychel, and she tries not to look at me, but I know she's hoping I heard it.

I hear it loud and clear. A lot of things have gotten clearer, like the fact that I never really knew her as well as I thought. Dr. Shin says I'm pissed that Raychel isn't the person I thought she was, but that she's glad I'm realizing my expectations were unfair. "You don't accumulate kindness points with women," she said. "They're not games that move you on to the next level when you've beaten their initial defenses." When I told her what Trenton said, she nodded and suggested he had a future as a psychologist. I told her that was good, because he sure doesn't have one as a musician.

The second presenter does well, contrasting the handmaids' uniforms with nuns' habits or Muslim head coverings. I'd thought of the latter as I was reading, but the presenter points out that habits and the hijab are both supposed to be choices. "Ideally, Christians and Muslims are allowed to choose their dress as a way to express piety," she explains. "Handmaids have no say at all."

I keep thinking about it during the next two presentations, in part because I don't know enough about Islam to know if she's right, but also because before class, I saw Carson watching Raychel as she walked down the hall. She could wear a burka and he'd still stare at whatever body he imagined underneath it.

I'm not sure imagining what was in her mind makes me much better.

The last *Handmaid* presenter focuses on a scene where the women are forced to tear apart a condemned man. The girl wants to argue that the main character is irredeemable for taking part, but Ms. Moses asks how much blame an individual really deserves in that situation. "She's forced into a corner," Ms. Moses says. "These authorities have put her in a position where every choice is wrong."

"She doesn't have any other power," another girl says. "Except for having babies, but that's not something she can control."

"And he's the only target she's allowed to hit," a guy near me adds. "I mean, she's trapped twenty-four/seven and barely allowed to talk. Showing the leaders she's still strong is her only chance to be a threat."

Raychel clears her throat. "But even that's a punishment," she says from across the room. "If they can't force her to carry babies, they can force her to carry that blame. Her only chance to show strength makes her weaker in the long run."

"I don't know about weaker," Ms. Moses says. "It certainly shows that on some level, she's flawed just like the leaders, but also that she has the same potential for power."

"But does she?" I ask. "Even in their position, she couldn't force them to carry a baby. It's the baby part that makes this book, like . . . uniquely horrifying." It sounds like a prepared answer, because it is, in a way. I still don't like the book, but I've been thinking about this a lot. "They can't carry equal guilt," I say, "because they can't inflict equal punishments." I look at Raychel as I add, "Because they're inherently different."

Ms. Moses nods and moves on, but Raychel stares at me until I shrug. I don't have to like it to learn from it.

RAYCHEL

The holidays go by slowly. I don't have work or school to distract me, though the past few months have paid off in straight As, including my Senior Seminar project. I had wondered if Matt would present on *The Handmaid's Tale* in some big gesture to make things up to me. I'm glad he didn't. And that he liked my project enough to give me an A.

My current project is making our duplex look like Christmas threw up all over it. My mom thinks I'm getting in the spirit. But secretly, it's a way to feel close to Andrew, who was like a little kid about the holidays. There's not an inch of space that isn't glittered, tinseled, snowflaked, or otherwise Kris Kringled. Eddie helps me reach the high spots. Mom reminds me I'm cleaning all this up.

Good. It'll give me something else to do.

MATT

Christmas is predictably awful. Dad brings home a Charlie Brown tree because he can't stand the bare room and Mom tries to decorate it, but she keeps finding ornaments Andrew and I made out of handprints in clay or painted macaroni, and she ends up in bed for two days.

I unpack things just so I can repack them.

Our friends come home from college and aren't willing to leave me or Raychel out of get-togethers. We make some small talk when we're in a group, but never one on one. I used to like how affectionate our friends are, but it's a pain in the ass now. She and I manage to avoid any hugs until Christmas Eve, when she accidentally ends up in front of my open arms as everyone's leaving. I'm not sure I can handle it, and obviously neither is she, but we try.

It hurts, but we survive.

. . . . .

On Christmas Day, I cry before I even get out of bed because Andrew didn't jump on me at 5 a.m. But I drag myself downstairs and give my parents some lame presents: a cookbook for Dad and a journal for Mom. They give me things for my dorm room I already knew I was getting, like a mini fridge and some sheets for my dorm bed. Mom makes Andrew's favorite cinnamon rolls and we eat them around the breakfast bar, trying to recount past Christmases without getting upset. Over the weekend, we visit my grandparents' house in Illinois, where my aunts try to make things cheerful and my grandmother keeps glaring at them for it. By the end of the trip, things are so bad that we actually laugh about it on the drive home.

Then it's New Year's Eve. Nathan and Eliza come over to hang out with me. They toast to my college career with white grape juice and leave before midnight to go to a real party. I go to bed.

New Year's Day, my dad and I watch twelve straight hours of football.

Then it's January, and I'm not sure I still want to leave, but it's time.

· · · · ·

One last get-together, and I'm free.

As free as I'll ever be, anyway.

On my way over, I stop at Trenton Alexander Montgomery the Third's house, parking behind a black Jeep in his driveway. He looks surprised to see me. "Ali!" he says, raising my arm. "How's it hanging?"

"Just wanted to say goodbye," I say, embarrassed now that I'm here. "Thanks for . . . stuff."

" 'Stuff' is my specialty," he says, stepping out onto the porch. "Good luck, man."

I give him a one-armed bro hug. "You too. Let me know if Rosa ever comes around."

He grins. "Whose car do you think that is?" he asks, pointing to the driveway.

I whistle appreciatively, recognizing her fancy silver hubs. "Maybe *you* are the greatest."

"Undoubtedly." We do another bro hug and I get in the car.

RAYCHEL

It's harder to hang out with the crew when Matt's around. Asha and, by extension, Spencer know the whole truth, so they stay close to me, and Bree follows their lead. But Eliza is barely tolerating my presence, and everyone else is just awkward. I know Matt sees it and does what he can to alleviate the weirdness. He even toughed it out for a Christmas Eve hug, which I suspect was as terrible for him as it was for me. But we're not rebuilding a friendship. We're just providing scaffolding to hold up the others.

Christmas morning was almost fun, though. My household declared it a "DIY holiday" and made each other hideous handmade gifts. I knitted Eddie a lumpy hat that he insists on wearing in public, much to Mom's horror. "Do you want me to take it off?" he asks as he drops me at Spencer's parents' house for one last party. "Someone might see."

"Definitely not. You should come in and model it."

He laughs. "Call us if you need a ride home."

I won't call—he's taking my mom to a fancy-ish hotel to-night for their one-year anniversary—but I thank him and go inside. Spencer's folks are letting us use their basement. They look the other way, literally, when Nathan and Fischer walk by with two cases of beer. They're probably just glad their son's back together with Asha—and glad it was just a promise ring he gave her for Christmas.

Matt nods at me and I nod back. We move around one an-other like repelled magnets. It's some kind of force. I want to punch him. I want to hug him. I want him to understand.

But mostly I just want the holidays to be over so we can all move on. And I don't feel that guilty about it. I'll never, ever use the phrase "Andrew would have wanted it that way," but he definitely would have kicked our asses by now.

MATT

I have to get up at the crack of dawn to leave for Memphis, and I use that as an excuse to leave Spencer's early. They're all used to saying goodbye and it doesn't make them sad anymore, hav-ing started practicing at the end of last summer, but I'm saying goodbye to a lot more. When I get to Raychel, she doesn't even pretend to smile. I intend to hug her quickly and move on, but instead I hear myself saying, "Walk me to my car?"

It comes out too much like a demand, which I can tell makes her balk. But she comes with me, fidgeting while I try to figure out what to say. "So . . . this is it."

"Yeah." The streetlight reflects in her eyes. "Are you nervous?"

I shrug, but I know she can tell. "A little."

"You'll do great." She hides her hands under her arms for warmth.

"Thanks." We stand for another moment. "It's freezing," I say. "You should go in."

She doesn't move. "Well . . ."

The hug starts awkward, like the last one, all limbs and pats on the back, but then we remember how to do it right. We cling to each other and I remember that hug after the hike where she hurt her ankle. I can't even contemplate how different things might be now if I had just told her then how I felt. She would have been mad, I know now. But maybe we could have still been friends after.

Finally, she pulls herself out of my grasp. "Good luck."

"Thanks," I say again. She turns. "Raych," I say, my voice cracking. She turns back. "I really am sorry."

"For what?" she asks. I stand there, frozen, and she nods. "That's what I thought." She runs into the house before I can reply.

RAYCHEL

Inside, I pretend like nothing's wrong. That's all I ever do these days anyway. I destroy Bree at Ping-Pong and she kills me at air hockey, so we call it a draw. "This summer," she says, when everyone else is playing darts. "We'll hang out lots. Maybe you can come to Chicago for spring break? Check out the school? The dorms will be closed, but we can stay at my aunt's or my grandma's."

"That'd be great." I didn't apply to Northwestern, but I appreciate the offer more than anything, and when Bree gets ready to leave the party, I decide to go too. We get our coats and give a round of goodbyes. Eliza makes a big show of avoiding a hug from me and I don't press it.

It gives the ride home an awkward tone, and Bree tries to chatter it away, complaining that she has to sit through another twelve-hour car ride with The Nuge and the awful metal bands he likes. "At least his boyfriend's not with him this time," she says. "He sings along. Loudly."

She tells me some funny stories about their last trip home, but halfway through she realizes they were coming for Andrew's funeral, and the story ends on yet another uncomfortable note. Then the only sounds are her fingers tapping nervously on the steering wheel and the hum of road under the tires.

"Can I tell you a secret?" I ask out of nowhere.

She looks genuinely terrified at the prospect.

"I've never liked Eliza."

She bursts out laughing. "Me neither."

"But Nathan does," I say, leaning back against the seat. "So we put up with her."

Bree doesn't answer, and I wonder if we're thinking the same thing. Spencer likes Asha, so the boys put up with her. Matt liked me, so they put up with me. But why do we have to put up with them? I try to remember if Bree and I ever hung out, just the two of us, and wonder why not. "We should definitely try for spring break," I say.

"And I'll be home all summer. If nothing else, maybe we can, like, go on a road trip or something. Bring Asha, maybe? And your friend Keri?"

"That would be awesome." And I mean it. I need to make some new friends. Starting with the ones I already have.

MATT

I have no idea what I'm doing here.

I sit in the car so long that the windows steam over. I don't like the trapped feeling they give me, so I climb out to sit on the hood. The cold air feels good, like it's hardening my resolve to do this, whatever it is. My breath clouds as a wind chime dings lonely nearby.

I don't know what I'm going to say, but Raychel needs to know all the things I'm really sorry for, and this feels like my last chance to tell her.

When Bree's car rolls up, she and Raychel both pile out, laughing. Bree comes over to slap me on the chest. "You left without hugging me!"

"I'm sorry," I say, ducking my head. "I didn't want to make a scene." They both snort. "What?"

"Eliza," Bree says. "She . . . never mind, who cares."

"I care," I want to say. But I don't. And then I realize that's the mistake I always make. "I care," I say, and she gives me a huge hug. Then she squeezes Raychel and gets in the car, hollering something about spring break and how maybe they should go somewhere warmer. Her headlights cut us in half and slice down the street, disappearing as she turns.

Raychel watches, hugging herself and shivering. "Hey," I say lamely.

"Hi." She waits a moment, then breathes on her hands. "I know it'll probably be super weird, but if this is going to take a while, can you come in? I'm freezing my ass off."

This is exactly what I shouldn't do, because I want this conversation to be short, but I don't want to get frostbite . . . and if I give her my coat, it'll smell like her for days. "Okay," I say, following her through the screen door, which closes silently. "Hey, it's fixed."

She gives me a weird look. "Eddie moved in."

"Huh." Just one more thing we never got to discuss. The

inside of their duplex looks like Santa's workshop if the elves were tripping on way too much acid. "This is . . ."

"I was bored," she says shortly, and takes off her sweater-jacket thing. "You want me to take that? Or are you leaving right away?"

"Um . . ." I can't tell from her face what she wants me to do. I decide to err on the side of not being an asshole and hand her my coat. "I'll stay for a bit, if it's okay."

She gets us some water. "So," she says, when we're sitting an entire couch cushion away from each other.

"So."

She waits, fiddling with a button on her shirt. Finally she looks up, and now I can tell how she feels: pissed off. This is a Raychel I know. "So?"

"I leave tomorrow," I mumble stupidly.

"I know." She stares at the coffee table. "I'll miss you."

It's the last thing I expected her to say, and it makes me blurt the truth. "I'll miss you too."

"I wish . . ." She shakes her head and gives a fake laugh. "I wish lots of things."

"Me too." We stare at each other. It's now or never. This summer will be too late. "I'm sorry I never gave you a chance to explain," I say in a rush. "I never even asked. But if you're willing to tell me now, I want to listen." It's still a selfish request. I want to understand and I want her to help me. But I hope it will help her too.

She waits to see if I mean it, and I don't know how else to convince her. So I scoot over, meeting her halfway. She exhales

315

and slides over too, breathing quietly as I hesitate, then wrap an arm around her shoulders. This is okay. This is what we did as friends, with all our friends. She still fits just right, and I don't know why I'm surprised. She's a different shape and size in my mind now, I guess.

"Please," I say, so close her hair flutters. "Tell me what happened."

So she tells me. Everything.

RAYCHEL

When I'm done talking, we sit for a long time. Matt gets up to refill his water and sits back down close to me, our shoulders touching. I don't say anything. I'm afraid it will give him an excuse to leave, and I just want to hang on to this last unexpected moment where we feel like friends again.

"I'm sorry," he says finally. "That I just . . . assumed . . . you and me . . . you know . . ." He looks down at his hands in his lap. "And that I couldn't protect you. That I made it worse."

"The Carson stuff wasn't your fault." I mock punch his leg. "And I forgive you for the rest."

"But—"

"I get to decide who I forgive," I tell him. "I'm not saying it because I have to, or because I want you to say it back." I've had an awful lot of time to think through what the word really means. "We've both lost too much for me to just . . . ignore that you're trying." I shake my head. "But I don't forgive Carson. And nothing he did was your fault."

"I want it to be," he says, letting his head rest on top of mine. "It's easier to pretend I missed the chance than admit I couldn't do anything at all."

"I know," I say. "But you'll make yourself crazy."

"I make myself crazy anyway."

His heart speeds up against my arm, and I'm worried he'll say something stupid and ruin the moment, so I stand and grab his hand. "Come here. I want to show you something."

MATT

She leads me down the hall to her bedroom. I slow at the door and she rolls her eyes. "You're tall," she says, pointing in her closet. "Get that down."

I retrieve a shoe box and hand it to her. Inside, there's a jumble of small things, but she pulls out Andrew's pipe, the one he lost right before. "Where'd you get it?"

"Eddie. He saved it from the memorial."

I turn it over in my hand. It glows slightly in the lamplight. I'm not sure what she wants me to say, or what I *can* say with this giant lump in my throat.

"You should take it."

I shake my head and hand it back. "He wouldn't let me use it, even if I wanted to. No way would he want me to keep it."

She hesitates, then laughs. "Okay."

Once I've put it back, there's not much else to say, but I'm not ready to leave. "Oh hey," I say, grasping at straws. "I should get your stuff out of my glove box."

"You don't have to—"

"No, hang on." I don't want it to be a reminder in Memphis. "I'll grab it."

She sits on the bed to wait. I jog outside and open the glove box slowly to prevent the avalanche. Hair ties, ChapStick, tampons . . .

I sit in the passenger seat and rest my forehead on my hands. The condom is gone, and I sure as hell didn't use it. I remember Andrew almost knocking me down the stairs that night, and it's not anger or even jealousy that I feel.

I'm still embarrassed. My pride is slowest to heal, and I hate myself for it. I want to let this go.

I fill my coat pockets with everything that might belong to her. "You can put it on the dresser," she says when I return.

For a moment, I still want to bring the condom up, and see her squirm when I mention that my brother stole it from my car, probably because his were all gone.

My forgiveness just doesn't seem to work the same as hers. Mine's more like a slow trickle of sand than her dumping of a bucket. Or a glove box.

Unless forgiveness doesn't mean putting it all in a pile and moving on. Maybe it just means carrying it, but wanting the best for the person who gave it to you anyway.

In which case maybe I'm closer than I think.

She's staring at the ceiling and I follow her gaze. She's covered it in posters since the last time I was here. "What is *that*?"

"Asha gave it to me."

"Kitten torture?"

She laughs and clears a spot on her bed. "Here, you can see better this way." I watch apprehensively as she pats the space beside her and sighs. "Come on, Matt. I'm not going to jump your bones."

I bristle, but she's not being cruel. She still trusts me, after everything.

I settle in beside her and we gradually relax enough to get comfortable, adjusting ourselves back into old habits. We really talk, without fighting, for the first time in months. "Have you met your new roommate?" she asks.

"I got a single, actually."

"Nice."

I don't tell her it's due to my "special circumstances," or that it costs a lot extra. But I do admit I'm nervous about making new friends. "If I don't have a roommate, how am I going to meet people?"

"Join a team or something. You'll play soccer, right?"

"Yeah," I say, though it hadn't even occurred to me. We talk about which schools she's applied to, and how if she does have to stay here next year, she might room with Asha. She sounds kind of excited about it. It doesn't make me feel better about leaving, but it does make it a little easier.

As it gets later, she starts to nod off. I'm tired too, but I don't want to miss these last minutes. I breathe her in. I let her put her cold feet against my legs. Around four, she can't keep her eyes open, but I can't close mine. They trace her arms, neck, collarbone, hips. My hands stay still. The moon casts shadow branches over the wall and her body and I memorize how she looks, right now, in her own bed.

When the light turns from silver to gold, I know it's time to go.

She stays asleep when I slide my arm out from underneath her, so I decide not to wake her. I don't know if it's harder to be the one leaving or the one staying behind, but I lean down to kiss her forehead, and it hurts so much I almost can't stand up.

But I do. And I leave her on her own.

RAYCHEL

I wake up crying.

I go back to sleep.

I wake up a few hours later, more lonely than I've ever, ever felt before. I hurt so much. I can't believe how much I still hurt.

I should make myself get up. Eat. Shower. At least change clothes.

But I don't want to. I don't want to do anything. Ever.

I stretch my legs and something falls off the bed. Cussing, I roll over. There's a photo album that's not mine on the floor.

Except it is mine. It has my name on the cover.

Inside there's page after page of us, smiling, laughing, arms around Andrew, holding hands, kissing cheeks. Our friends, his family—our family—laughing, laughing, laughing. I flip through quickly, hoping there's a note, and I'm disappointed— the last page is just a strip of pictures, the three of us in the photo booth at the beginning of the end.

I start over, going slower, laughing and crying my way through. I *knew* Matt could see my underwear in those climbing pictures. When I reach the end, I'm positive I haven't missed anything. All I have left are blank pages.

Andrew will never be in them, and maybe Matt won't either.

But they gave them to me to fill. And the only way to repay them is to fill the pages well.

So I get dressed. I eat breakfast. I face the day.

I say yes.

RESOURCES

After the Fall is not a depiction of my high school years, but it's informed by my own experiences as an assault survivor, as well as the unrelated loss of a friend during the aftermath of my own attack. I know how important the support of friends and family can be —and that it's not always available. So if you or a friend needs help, or if you want to help create safe communities, please consult the list below. Take care of yourself, and each other.

HOTLINES

Rape, Abuse & Incest National Network (RAINN)
www.rainn.org
24/7 telephone hotline: 1-800-656-HOPE
Bilingual online hotline: online.rainn.org or rainn.org/es
Live chat also available

Suicide Prevention Lifeline
www.suicidepreventionlifeline.org
24/7 hotline: 1-800-273-TALK
Spanish: 1-888-628-9454
TTY: 800-799-4889

Love Is Respect
www.loveisrespect.org
bilingual 24/7/365 hotline: 1-866-331-9474
TTY: 1.866.331.8453
Text: loveis to 22522
24/7 online chat

The Trevor Project
www.thetrevorproject.org
24/7 hotline: 866-488-7386
Chat and text support available during limited hours
Serving LGBTQ young people ages 13–24

OTHER RESOURCES

The Dougy Center: The National Center for Grieving Children and Families
www.dougy.org
"The mission of The Dougy Center is to provide support in a safe place where children, teens, young adults and their families grieving a death can share their experiences."

Know Your IX
knowyourix.org
"Founded in 2013, Know Your IX is a survivor- and youth-led organization that aims to empower students to end sexual and dating violence in their schools."

Men Can Stop Rape
www.mencanstoprape.org
"[S]eeks to mobilize men to use their strength for creating cultures free from violence, especially men's violence against women."

National Online Resource Center on Violence Against Women

www.vawnet.org

"[A] comprehensive and easily accessible online collection of full-text, searchable materials and resources on domestic violence, sexual violence and related issues."

National Sexual Violence Resource Center

www.nsvrc.org

"The NSVRC's mission is to provide leadership in preventing and responding to sexual violence through collaboration, sharing and creating resources, and promoting research."

Not Alone: Together Against Sexual Assault

www.notalone.gov

"Information for students, schools, and anyone interested in finding resources on how to respond to and prevent sexual assault." Resource page includes information for survivors who are people of color, Native, LGBTQ, disabled, immigrant, male, and more.

Take Back The Night

takebackthenight.org

"Our mission . . . is to create safe communities and respectful relationships through awareness events and initiatives. We seek to end sexual assault, domestic violence, dating violence, sexual abuse, and all other forms of sexual violence."

ACKNOWLEDGMENTS

All my love and gratitude go . . .

To everyone at Regal Hoffman and Associates, Wolf Literary, and Foundry Literary + Media, especially Michelle Andelman, who never gave up on me or this story, and to Adriann Ranta, who saw me through the final stretch and into the next chapter of my career.

To Margaret Ferguson, who saw this book's potential even in its earliest draft; to Susan Dobinick, who helped me shape it into the story I wanted to tell; and to Joy Peskin, who ushered it into the world as painlessly as possible.

To Elizabeth Clark for a beautiful cover, Rachel Fershleiser for her help with its reveal, and to everyone at FSG, especially Nicholas Henderson, Ashley Woodfolk, John Nora, and Brittany Pearlman.

To my fantastic beta readers—Tanaz Bhathena, Preeti Chhibber, Kristin Halbrook, Amanda Hannah, Cory Jackson, Kelly

Jensen, Kody Keplinger, Kaye M., Samantha Mabry, Myra McEntire, Phoebe North, Kristin Otts, Kathleen Peacock, Emilia Plater, and Shveta Thakrar—and to the brave souls who read multiple drafts over the years: Sarah Enni, Joshua Hart, Kirsten Hubbard, Stephanie Kuehn, Catherine Ozment, Michelle Schusterman, and Kaitlin Ward.

To the cheerleaders whose support made more of a difference than they knew: Raychel Ackley (who let me steal her name), Leila Austin, Lindsey Culli, Somaiya Daud, Laurie Devore, Debra Driza, Alice Fang, Maurene Goo, Susanne Hopkins, Michelle Krys, Amy Lukavics, Sarah McCarry, Veronica Roth, Heather Stout, Courtney Summers, and Kara Taylor, plus everyone at the Sweet Sixteens, the Swanky Seventeens, and Madcap Retreats, and especially to YA Highway, the yawning sloths, and my fellow bog hags.

To my high school crew, none of whom are in this story. Thanks for all the hikes and fun and ridiculousness, and for the bits of real life I borrowed—I'll try to work the apple juice into a future book. I love you all, almost as much as you love Zach's mom.

To my college crew, pretty sure.

To my entire family. Special thanks to my parents and my in-laws, whose help in sending me to retreats and conferences was a much-needed vote of confidence, and to my nieces Madelyn and Sydney, who patiently answered my questions about "the youths."

To Flynn, who was proud of me for getting the beer (for which I paid in cash). I couldn't have written this flawed friendship without yours as counterpoint.

To Catherine, who's been reading it all since we were twelve. Best best friend ever.

To Thomas and William, who are extremely patient, not to mention excellent hikers and great at puns.

And to Joshua, for everything and always. You're my favorite.